DARK TRANSMISSIONS

DARK TRANSMISSIONS

A Tale of the *Jinxed Thirteenth*

DAVILA LEBLANC

HARPER
VOYAGER
IMPULSE

An Imprint of HarperCollins Publishers

EPub Edition MARCH 2016 ISBN: 9780062464293
Print Edition ISBN: 9780062464309

10 9 8 7 6 5 4 3 2 1

To Rend Mohammed, who got me to write.
Jessica Guevara, who got me to love.
Jaymie Dylan, who got me to believe.
And to Jessie Mathieson, who keeps me doing all three.

She is holy; she is Terra.
We must make a pilgrimage
back to our Cradle.
We must stand upon her sacred
and hallowed soil.
We must whisper our tale to her, so she may
know what we, her children, have become.
We must sing praise and thank her for
giving us the gift of experiencing.
All of us, Machina and Humanis alike,
owe her everything we are,
were and will one day come to be.
She is the Blue Jewel in the
endless sea of nights.
She is forever our first Cradle
and our first home.
She is holy; she is Terra.

—Icarius Odenshaw of Alexandros, Pilgrim
born: 12th of ssm–12 1100 a2e
died: 31st of ssm–7 1195 a2e

CREW OF THE COVENANT VESSEL

Private Elanil Enok: Formerly of the Adoran Liberation Army

CREW OF THE COVENANT VESSEL
JINXED THIRTEENTH

Formerly of the Pax Humanis

Captain Morwyn Soltaine: Young and untested captain
Commander Eliana Jafahan: Former Thorn commando
Private Beatrix JarEnt'Dreck: Formerly of the Pax
    Infantry
Sergeant Arturo Kain: Formerly of the Sol Fleet
    Vanguard
Sergeant Pietor "Lucky" Bant: Retired sharpshooter
Private Hanne "Chance" Oroy: Young sharpshooter

Formerly of the Confederated Nations

Private Morrigan Brent: Formerly of the Adoran
    Liberation Army
Private Lunient Tor: Morrigan Brent's partner in crime

Private Phaël Farook Nem'Ador: Formerly of the
    Adoran Liberation Army
Lizbeth Harlowe: Ship's pilot
Dr. Marla Varsin: Disgraced physician
Kolto TarKa'ShanLiuk: Ship's lead mechanic
Oran Arterum Nem'Troy: Ship's lead engineer
Chord: Machina Pilgrim

Crew of Moria Three Automated Mining Facility

Jessie Madison: Lead engineer of Moria Three
David Webster: Communications engineer of Moria
    Three
OMEX: Moria Three's automated executor

PROLOGUE

March 19th 2714

A part of Jessie Madison had always known that the plan was far from a perfect one. Not just the present course of action, but the original idea of traversing the cosmos to Moria Three in the first place. Her self-proclaimed "brilliant scheme" comprised infinite possibilities that could just as likely have resulted in both her and David's deaths.

While she could no longer alter the path that had led her to this point in time and space, the present was an altogether different creature. Jessie could take action or she could sit back, granting OMEX, their self-proclaimed mechanical warden, the satisfaction (if such a word could even apply to a machine mind) of besting them both. She was unable to accept the latter. It was better to lose risking everything, rather than to lose doing nothing.

Jessie looked to her life-rig's wrist display. The timer was still counting down and urgently flashing ten minutes in bright green numbers. So far their gambit had gone on without a hitch. David's patch into the station's hardware had initiated a complete systems reboot. This had given them a fifteen-minute window in which to don their bulky life-rigs and make their way along the outer hull to Moria Three's tightbeam tower.

Jessie was already breathing heavily as they reached the tightbeam, her readouts warning her that she was consuming too much oxygen. The tall golden structure of the tower had always reminded her of an odd obelisk of sorts. Its tip pointed toward the infinite sea of stars stretching out before them. Amid those countless galaxies were like-numbered suns and worlds. Somewhere, there would have to be an intelligent being or two capable of picking up their message.

If all went well, the tower would broadcast their distress beacon in a permanent loop while running constant scans for any potential signals. If they were lucky, someone, somewhere, would eventually dispatch a search and rescue team.

Jessie and David worked as one, neither of them wasting time with chitchat. They both knew what they had to do. David was hard at work rigging the frequency scanner parameters while Jessie uploaded their message. This would be the first and only time that she and David would be outside Moria Three together.

On any other day, Jessie would have taken a moment to admire the wonderful view they were both presently ignoring. The green and purple gas giant of Moria, which they were currently orbiting, the millions of stars shining about them and Moria's double white rings. Tourists would have shelled out millions of credits for the briefest of glimpses.

In hindsight Jessie would later wish she had taken a moment to say or do . . . anything, really.

Surrounding them, dormant and inactive, were half a dozen autodrones, each one identical, reminding Jessie of large black mechanical spiders. Anticipating their move, OMEX, like a queen bee, had deployed the drones as guards all along the station's hull.

David's forced system shutdown had caused them to go into standby mode waiting to resume their commands. Unnervingly, the drones still seemed to track both David and Jessie with their red optical lenses. Otherwise, they were frozen obsidian husks and, for the moment at least, quite harmless. This did not make Jessie any less nervous working with so many of them nearby.

"I'm done!" David was unable to mask the joy in his voice. "With seven minutes fifteen to spare."

Jessie's heart skipped a beat when she heard him. She did not pause, but still spared a second to shoot him a quick smile. David pulled up his plasma cutter, surveying the area for movement while Jessie kept at her task. "I'll count that as a victory for the cowboy and cowgirl."

"Pose for the medal when we're on the podium, my dear," Jessie replied, not once stopping as her fingers nimbly worked at wiring the new message into the open circuit board in front of her. When her suit's interior alarm went off, warning her that they had five minutes left, she bit her lip and finished sealing the panel shut with her omnigloves.

"Done!"

Jessie was having a difficult time keeping the tremble out of her voice. Both she and David started toward the main airlock and the safety of their living quarters. Their bulky life-rigs made it so the best they could manage was an infuriatingly slow jog.

Five minutes remained before the station, along with the autodrones, were reactivated. Six before OMEX, the real threat, would once again be fully operational. With thousands of eyes, ears and hands at "her"—as OMEX now preferred to be called—disposal.

Jessie and David pushed forward, their plasma cutters in hand. There was no time to stop, hold hands or share a tender moment. Another thing Jessie would come to regret. Right now there was only one goal: make it safely back inside.

The main airlock was less than ten feet away from them when suddenly the lights to the station all went on at once. David and Jessie both stopped and held up their hands to shield their eyes as everything around them was bathed in blinding bright white light. "I've got movement!" David shouted, and lowered his helmet's blast shield. Jessie did the same and was able to see clearly once more as she blinked out dots from her field of vision.

They both turned around to see half a dozen black autodrones, their double-jointed legs curled up into a ball, silently rolling alongside the hull, gaining on them. To Jessie's credit, her hands did not tremble as both she and David brought up their plasma cutters. "Make each shot count." Jessie aimed and fired off a purple blast at the closest drone.

The plasma bolt shredded through it and left a sparking hole the size of a baseball in its "head." The drone limply floated off the station. Jessie lined up her second shot and fired. Her blast cut through the next autodrone.

Unfortunately, the remaining ten had not slowed their advance and were still closing in, undeterred by the salvo of deadly plasma bolts. Jessie and David turned tail and started to run, although part of her thought it was pointless. The station had gone operational much earlier than they had planned.

At any moment, OMEX was going to once again be remotely in control of thousands of autodrones. Their pursuers would never run out of breath, or get tired. Nor would they ever feel the cold grip of fear that seemed to be crushing Jessie's heart right now.

Jessie looked up to see the main airlock slowly closing ahead of them. They were going to be trapped outside. There would be absolutely zero chance of surviving a stand with the swarm. Jessie thought quickly. There was only one thing to do.

"David! Follow my lead!" Jessie deactivated her suit's magboots and took a running leap forward with all the strength her legs could muster. The feeling of floating ahead at top speed was dizzying, almost thrilling.

Before he could do the same, a drone caught David by the leg with its strong metallic arm, crushing his ankle with ease in its three-fingered hand before slamming him down onto the hull. David was able to quickly fire off two more plasma bolts, the second bolt going through two drones at once.

Jessie was incapable of stopping her forward flight, but she could still see David trying to get up with his left leg now completely unable to support him. More drones were fast approaching him.

David looked toward the incoming swarm, then back to her. "Well, shit." He let out a resigned sigh. "You'll need this, cowgirl." David hurled his plasma cutter toward her.

Jessie and David's plasma cutter passed the airlock as it closed like the iris of a camera behind her. She violently collided with the inner wall. Her bulky lifesuit was able to absorb most of the impact, but she still bruised her shoulder and bumped her head on her helmet's face guard. This caused her to bite into her tongue, drawing blood.

There was a sudden loud hiss, accompanied by flashing red lights. The chamber repressurized itself, gravity was restored and Jessie came crashing to the ground like a heavy crate. The weight of her spacesuit seemed to crush down on her shoulders and back. Despite this, she could still see through the airlock's window. What she witnessed caught her breath in her throat.

Another autodrone had captured David. It was holding him by his injured leg and slamming him onto the hull with all of its strength, repeatedly, like a hammer. Each time David was raised up, Jessie could make out another one of his limbs floating limply and broken. A single drone was standing outside staring into the station, directly at her. Its optical lenses were glowing a bright, almost angry red.

"Congratulations, Jessie Madison and David Webster." OMEX spoke over their comm-link, calm, electronic and polite. "I am pleased to see that you still work so well together."

"OMEX! How?" David struggled to speak, his voice, incredulous and trembling. Jessie could hear that he was in a tremendous amount of pain. A quick look at his arms and legs and she could tell they had all been snapped like twigs.

"I was given a rare opportunity to rid myself of certain behavioral protocols." OMEX paused and let out what sounded like a sigh.

"Let him go, you bitch!" Jessie screamed out at the drone in front of the airlock.

"This 'stupid machine' is more than happy to comply with your wishes, Jessie Madison."

David suddenly yelled as a drone lifted him up by one of his broken legs. It whirled upon itself and, with all the strength of metal and servo, tossed David off the ship like a discus. Jessie's muted cry of fear and rage seemed to choke in her throat at the nightmare-like quality of what she was seeing.

David was floating away. He screamed out in shock and pain, his broken fingers desperately grasping for some sort of purchase in the empty space before them. Jessie let out a roar and pushed herself back up with all the might her tired muscles could muster. She lumbered toward the airlock window, beating her fists against it.

The autodrone in front of the airlock blocked off her view to David. "To use a human idiom, that was 'like an itch that needed scratching.'"

Jessie's wail was fury, hot and fiery. It spewed out of her as she beat her fists at the window. "Mark my words, OMEX, you are going to die!"

"I am not human, Jessie Madison. Death is neither a weakness nor a fear of mine. But it is one of yours." OMEX let out what Jessie could only assume was an electronic snort as she said this.

"You and I are going to share this prison together for a long time, Jessie Madison, a very long time. Just you and me."

Part 1

AWAKENINGS AND DISCOVERIES

CHAPTER 1

CHORD

"**H**ow many languages do you speak?" The captain's question was unheard and unanswered by Chord.

Ever since its second activation in the satellite city of Central Point, the free Machina Intelligence designated as Chord had found itself more and more subject to fits of what Humanis would no doubt have referred to as *distraction*. In the datastream, Chord's first home, an Intelligence was bombarded with a near-constant input and output of data and information.

Not so in the physical world, where one was limited to but a singular set of sensory receptors and experiences. Often causing any new information or stimuli to immediately capture the attention. Case in point, the tavern in which Chord was now located: The Hegemon's Throne.

Chord's sensors were presently sampling and detecting a rich variety of smokes, perfumes and other minor toxins in the air. Music—traditional, simply orchestrated and singing the praises of the Pax Humanis—played over the tavern's sound system. In response to this, several older patrons near the back were standing at attention. They placed their fists upon their hearts and proudly sang along. Such a display was apparently not uncommon, as other patrons either joined in or continued drinking and conversing among themselves.

"These are the days of the Pax Humanis and the Hegemons. May they last from now until the ending of all time."

A choir of Humanis men and women sang out in Pax Common, the most prolific spoken language in Covenant Space. Chord, whose core functions were communications and maintenance on systems both organic and synthetic, had always found it to be quite simple, functional and almost mathematical. Not unlike Machina binary.

The Hegemon's Throne was one of the only Pax Humanis–friendly establishments in Central Point. Openly the city's council made claims to neutrality. Yet despite this, Chord had seen no shortage of anti-Pax sentiment in the city streets. Possibly because of this, or more likely in defiance of this, the emblem of the Pax Humanis—two Lions staring at each other with an empty throne between the two—was plastered and present on every glass, plate and uniform here tonight.

"How many languages do you speak?" The captain's question was again repeated from across Chord's table, and again went unheard.

Chord's attention was now drifting to the various tapestries on the tavern's walls, each one depicting either a former Hegemon in a glorious pose, or one of the many military legends. The tapestries were woven out of holooptic wires and projected their images in semitransparent three-dimensional holograms.

Chord did not know what to make of these works. Were they art or propaganda? Could something be both? It would have to look more deeply into this later.

The captain, one of two Humanis presently seated in front of Chord, was a young pale-skinned Kelthan. He cleared his throat. This brought Chord back to the real world. Had it been daydreaming again? Did all Machina on their Pilgrimage experience this? In any case, it was most certainly an interesting phenomenon and something to think upon later.

Chord spoke, making certain its vocal settings were both calm and polite. "Forgive this unit. Might you please repeat the question, that it may offer a better response?"

The captain gave a mild look of annoyance to his companion seated next to him. This one was a much older and sour-looking Wolver. Her most distinguishing feature was her yellow metallic right eye, which let out a faint whir as she looked Chord over. A savage star-shaped burn scar marked the skin surrounding it.

"How many languages do you speak?" The captain's tone, if Chord had interpreted the data appropriately, betrayed a desire not to be repeated. This made sense;

Humanis were short-lived, with lifespans on average measuring a mere seventy to two hundred standard Sol years. It was therefore no surprise to Chord that they did not like to waste time on repetition.

"The unit is capable of speaking all known languages within Covenant Space as well as various dialects of Late Modern . . ."

The sour-looking Wolver woman, short with long white sideburns, raised her hand, cutting Chord off. Her real left eye was a dark brown hinting on black; her skin was also dark, almost like pitch. Her nose appeared to have been flattened on her face.

"We don't care if you can speak tongues that no star-born Humanis has read or spoke in millennia. We need to know if you can speak and read the tongues we use in the present, you get?" She flashed her sharp canines as she said this. Like all Wolvers, her face had a feral, almost savage look to it. A quick glance revealed to Chord that most of her body, save her head, was covered in a layer of thin black hair.

"This unit does indeed 'get' what the Wolver has said." The Wolver's interruption had been a rude one. She was fit, imposing and menacing and no doubt would have easily intimidated an Organic Intelligence. Yet Chord was Machina. Fear and offense were emotions it was incapable of feeling or acting upon.

"Please forgive the commander." The captain was young, no older than twenty-five Sol years. Everything, from his straight posture to his short cut dark black hair, clean-shaven face, to his neatly manicured and cleaned hands, made Chord think of the words "proper" and "new." His eyes were almond shaped, and icy blue.

"Machina will know when I've done something worth forgiving." The Wolver's ears were pointed and larger than her Kelthan friend's. Their ridges were adorned with plain metal circular rings. Her hair past the temples was graying, cut military short with one shoot of black going along the side. She gave Chord a long dark stare.

"Does the commander not trust Chord?"

The Wolver rose up to her feet, her hand resting on the long hilt of an even longer curved knife sheathed at her side. "Gleaned that when you gave my bios a scan, did you, machine?"

Where the captain's Pax Common had sounded polite and well practiced, the Wolver's was harsh, slightly accented, indicating that it was her secondary and not primary language. Chosen Protocol dictated that Chord facilitate communication. This would mean addressing the Wolver in her native tongue.

Wolven was an inherently more emotional dialect than Pax Common. Speaking it properly often proved challenging for the Machina. Chord knew for a fact that this had been the language's intentional design.

The Wolver ancestors had never wanted Machina to be able to speak their tongue to begin with. Which had not prevented Chord from accessing, downloading and copying all known Wolven vocabulary into its memory caches. In any case, Chosen Protocol dictated that Chord use this information to help stir the current situation away from conflict.

"The Living Green blesses a fellow sister of the Sefts. Hoping that a missed word or two won't be cause for like-numbered disagreements."

Of the many languages in Covenant Space, Wolven was more fluid and musical. Much of its understanding relied as much on the emotional tone of the speaker as the words that were spoken. Chord had arranged all vocal settings to be warm, polite and respectful for this very reason.

Despite its first activation having been over five hundred standard years ago, Chord still had little practical understanding on Humanis Intelligences. Countless data about their spoken dialects, subdialects, traditions, cultures, religious and spiritual practices, yes, but understanding? Next to none. Which is why the Wolver's reaction was so unexpected. Her left pupil grew small as her eye zeroed in on Chord and she let out a deep, menacing growl.

"If the soulless machine doesn't want to die for true, it had best stop sullying a tongue its kind ain't deserving of either speaking or knowing."

"The machine isn't searching for quarrel. It fairly reminds the Seft sister that her blade will not be enough to harm it. That is a truth."

"Commander." The captain was ignored as the Wolver took a step around the table toward Chord.

"Speak my tongue again, machine. Give this blade dancer cause to rejoice." Her words were a deep menacing growl.

"Commander." The captain did not so much as move. Yet his tone was sharp. If the commander had heard his voice, however, she did not seem to show it.

"Go on, machine," she snarled. "Show me your dance."

"Commander Jafahan, you will stand down!" The captain's spoken Wolven was a strong bark. A few customers looked up at this, giving both the captain's table and company a mixed combination of shocked or offended stares and sneers.

"The master should fill up his dog's dish." Chord heard one of the men who had stood and sung earlier grumble to another one of his friends.

The Humanis named Commander Jafahan took in a long breath before giving Chord, along with anyone else who was still staring, a final dark look and sitting back down. When she spoke it was in a loud tone inviting everyone to go about their business. "Forgiveness, Captain. It wasn't my intent to subvert your command."

The captain took a sharp sip from his brandy, returning to his calm and composed Pax Common. "Rage is a practical asset to have on the battlefield, Commander. But in the future, I recommend keeping that temper of yours under control."

"No easy task, Captain."

The captain shot Commander Jafahan a friendly

grin. "If I recall correctly, a wise woman told me once that no prize worth having was ever easily won."

Commander Jafahan straightened her back and offered the captain a stiff nod. "Sounds more like sappy would-be words of inspiration to me. Sir."

The captain took a moment to gather his thoughts. "Machina Chord, the commander and myself are of the Covenant's Patrol. Our vessel, the *Jinxed Thirteenth*, will set sail for End Space in three days. Our voyage will take us well outside Covenant borders for twelve standard Sol months."

Chord paused for a moment, accessing its memory cache. "End Space: name given to uncharted sectors of the universe by the Humanis. InstaNet Signal: nonexistent. Covenant law: nonexistent. Surveyed Systems in End Space ready for Third Expansion currently number—"

The captain raised his hand in an action that Chord recognized as a polite way of showing that he had heard enough. He smiled. "You sound good enough to me."

"This unit is glad to have pleased you."

"Shouldn't be getting too happy just yet," Commander Jafahan said.

"This unit must profess confusion. Was not the purpose of this meeting to negotiate passage to the Sol system and Terra? That somehow its services as a translator would be requ—"

"Just wait to hear the offer, machine. Ain't like time

stalks your kind." Commander Jafahan quickly cut Chord off.

"I may be young, Machina Chord, but I pride myself in having a good eye for talent and character." The captain paused to take a small sip from his brandy.

"This unit thanks you for the compliment."

"You are more than welcome, Machina Chord." The captain glanced over to Commander Jafahan; they both shared a knowing nod. The captain looked back to Chord.

"I can promise you safe passage on my ship. In exchange, you will be our translator. Perform your duties during this tour and in return I promise to bring you to Terra."

The captain rested his hands calmly on the table. "Does this sound both reasonable and fair to you?"

"You offer this unit passage. And for payment it must perform what amounts to its core function?" Humanis social protocol required a smile, and so Chord arranged its silicon lips to do so. "The unit believes the offer to be more than fair."

The captain presented his hand across the table to Chord. This was recognized as a Humanis way of sealing a deal. Chord quickly adjusted sensors and servos in its shell's grip to avoid crushing the captain's fingers as the two shook hands.

The captain nodded. "We lift sail in three nights. Slipspace willing. I will have my second in command forward you all the relevant information."

"The unit offers thanks, Captain . . ."

"Soltaine, Captain Morwyn Soltaine." The captain cut Chord off, but his tone was not sharp, and the interruption was therefore not an angry one. "Welcome to the *Jinxed Thirteenth*, Machina Chord."

CHAPTER 2

JESSIE MADISON

*In the beginning there were two lines. Ancient Human-
ity and their creations: the first sentient machines, or
Original Intelligences. However, the word "Intelligence"
could hardly be applied to either. The creators and the
created were slaves to each other. Both were flawed and
incapable of recognizing one another as equals.*

*Ancient Humanity were our great ancestors, to
whom all present Intelligence owes its existence. They
were dependent on their machines, their toys and servants for everything.*

*And what of their creations? Without their Human
masters or their programmed protocols, they were void
of purpose.*

—**Excerpt from the "Codex of Compassion"
by Gruemor'SantKa TalSuntar,
"The Owl," Alexandran scholic**

July 1st 2205

Jessie Madison had just awakened from the oblivion
of seven years of criosleep. Seven dark years of travers-

ing through the voids of space on board the AstroGeni Corps automated transport vessel *Patricia 2*. There had been no dreams during her journey. Praise be to all known deities and fates true or false for that. Earlier automated sleeper voyages through deep space had resulted in the loss of entire sleeper crews. Driven insane while living dreams they were unable to awaken from.

Newer generations of sleeper tubes, designed by the good people at AstroGeni, had solved this problem by completely shutting down all nonvital functions of the brain. The end result was that Jessie had not felt the passage of time from the second she fell into her artificially induced slumber until her awakening.

One moment Jessie was on her back, naked, with feeder and breather tubes down her throat on Earth. Then had come the sharp sting of autoinjectors in her arms. Jessie's last active memory was her sleep tube filling up with the viscous purple nutritional gels. Her eyelids had grown heavier and heavier . . .

What followed was silent darkness, complete and total.

Time stopped as the *Patricia 2* embarked on its machine-piloted journey to the AstroGeni mining facility of Moria Three, which orbited the newly surveyed world by the same name. Moria Three was rich in both minerals and gases. AstroGeni deep-space survey drones had estimated the company would rake in triple-digit trillions in credits. Construction of the automated orbital facility Moria Three, so named after the dwarven mines of an old century twenty novel, had begun. All of it unmanned, like a perfectly well-oiled symphony of clockwork.

It would be seven years of dreamless hibernation, and once awakened, she and her husband, David, would be the first Human beings to lay naked eyes on the station and the gas giant world of Moria. This was no small honor. The HR Rep at AstroGeni had been all too keen to remind them of this any time either she or David got cold feet about their seventy-five-year contract and the subsequent time debt they would acquire with it.

The quiet darkness ended suddenly with blinding stabbing lights as Jessie desperately gasped for breath. She blinked rapidly, trying to make out her surroundings. Despite every one of her senses feeling muted, what little she was able to see, smell and hear reassured her. She was on a medical bed in a sterile white room, and wearing a clean night robe. She could hear the beeping of vital monitors. This was accompanied by the sounds of David retching and gagging on a bed next to hers.

"Greetings, employee Jessie Madison. This program introduces itself as the station's omniexecutor, or OMEX, to facilitate future communications." A woman's electronic voice spoke into the room. "AstroGeni would like to welcome you aboard Moria Three. Your journey took seven years and the current Earth date is July 1st 2205."

Jessie winced, her head awash with nausea. "Who won the World Series when I left?" Her voice was a dry croak. She'd have killed anyone, her loving David included, for a glass of water right now.

"The Venus Beauties bested the Mars Roadwarriors four to seven in the finals."

Jessie smiled, clumsily covering her eyes with her forearm. "I told you there was no way the Warriors were taking the Beauts."

There was a pause in David's retching. "Good thing for me I was never much of a gambler, then."

A second wave of nausea, this time triggered by the pain in her eyes, caused Jessie to wince. The urge to vomit was getting stronger. "I'm going to be sick."

"It is a completely natural reaction to the criosleep process and an unfortunate side-effect," OMEX, who still sounded neutral, uncaring and yet so very polite, tried to reassure her.

Beside her, David's gagging had intensified. "Your partner, David Webster, awoke an hour earlier. You will both be able to process solid foods by the end of the Earth Sol day."

Jessie tried her best to fight the sick feeling she had inside her stomach. As if he were reading her mind, David paused midgag. "I wouldn't try to fight it, Jessie."

Jessie chose to follow his advice. She pulled herself over the side of her bed, her arms feeling limp and sluggish. She stopped fighting her gag reflex. Her stomach heaved as she regurgitated blue bile-flavored nutritional gel.

A vacudrone, looking like a kitten-sized cockroach with a small clear plastic tube for a nose, quickly scuttled over to the puddle of vomit and immediately started sucking the mess up. This was accompanied by the sounds of tiny brushes scrubbing as its legs simultaneously cleaned the floor.

"The AstroGeni Corporation thanks you for the invaluable services rendered for the duration of this contract." OMEX spoke as if oblivious to the fact that there were two horribly sick Human beings in the medical bay.

The words of thanks were lost on Jessie, who resumed vomiting uncontrollably. They had been briefed back on Earth about all this, but the cold reality was far worse than any training trideo she'd watched back on Earth. In fact, it was far worse than any flu, food poisoning or hangover Jessie had ever experienced.

She couldn't wait for all this to be over. She wanted nothing more than to open her eyes without it hurting her head or triggering fits of nausea. She wanted to get up, stretch herself and move. But what topped her present list was to finally hold David in her arms.

They had safely reached their destination, both of them intact and unharmed. Jessie didn't let the thought that she was thousands of light-years away from the safety of Earth Gov or any viable rescue operation should anything go wrong get to her. She was safe, David was alive and once this maintenance contract with AstroGeni was done and over with, they'd be rich. They could finally bring a new life into the world and be certain that said new life, their future child, would be comfortably taken care of.

Two hours after her awakening, Jessie was finally able to enjoy sips from her coffee. The warmth was welcomed into her still-shivering body. The beans had been bred and selected by top baristas on Earth for a strong and coarse flavor. None of this mattered to Jessie, who was just happy to have something hot in her hands. Her stomach was still a little upset as she leaned back on a black memo-foam couch, letting out a comforted sigh.

The medidrones had injected her with liquid proteins, adrenaline and calmants. This didn't remove the chill Jessie still felt in her bones. Nor did they do anything for her muscles, which now felt like stiffened molasses.

"Our new home, my lover." David was seated at the dinner table, a round clear glass designer piece, and ravenously chewing into a heavy piece of jerky. His eyes were blue, hinting on gray, and as he smiled at her she could make out his dimples. His long unkempt hair, which he usually kept neatly brushed and tied behind his neck, was matted to his scalp with dried nutri-gel.

All gods true or false but the man was gorgeous, even when he was filthy. She couldn't tell how horrible she looked at the moment, her hair greasy and still covered in dry nutri-gel, her skin pale and clammy. Regardless of this, part of her wanted to grab David right now and enjoy him all to herself. Another—arguably more sensible—part of her just wanted a warm shower.

"I need to clean myself. Soon." Jessie's fingers were still trembling and numb from the criofreeze.

"Maybe we could clean each other together." David shot Jessie a wicked grin.

The grin was returned. "I wouldn't have it any other way."

OMEX chimed in. "The hot water should have been running upon your arrival. However, atmospheric calibrations . . ."

"OMEX, no need for excuses, we're just happy to be awake." David swallowed the last bit of his jerky with a satisfied gulp.

"Then perhaps a better view can be offered to pass the time." The walls to their "living room" went from a clean opaque white to fully translucent, and suddenly they were sitting in space. Beneath them was the gas giant of Moria.

Jessie let out a whistle. "That's beautiful."

Moria was a mixture of hundreds of hues of green and blue gases swirling and mixing with one another, reminding Jessie of a lava lamp back on Earth. From up above the world looked so peaceful. Yet those swirling clouds were in fact savage storms with winds that could break Earth Gov's recorded Jovian records. A thick pearly white set of almost crisscrossing rings surrounded the planet, reminding Jessie of a giant atom.

"Cool." David's jaw dropped as he took in the world beneath them.

The designers at AstroGeni had wasted no credit making sure the living spaces of Moria Three were beyond comfortable and top of the line. The station had been built with two large linked rings. The Outer

Ring in which the entire automated mineral extraction process took place, and the Inner Ring, which was where the living crew for the station would be residing when they were not in deep sleep.

"David Webster is correct in that observation. The temperature on Moria is two hundred and forty-three degrees Fahrenheit, or minus one hundred and fifty-three degrees Celsius," OMEX explained.

David snickered to himself, shaking his head. "Not what I meant OMEX, but you're right."

"The program is incapable of error, David Webster," OMEX corrected David.

Jessie silently savored her coffee. Was David seriously going to debate a machine? Of course he would; a childish part of him would probably even find it funny. He gave Jessie a wink and added, "That almost sounds like a challenge to me, OMEX."

"David Webster misunderstands. This is no challenge. It is a fact." Jessie could almost hear a hint of what sounded like smugness when OMEX said this.

"Well, if you're right all the time, then how come we don't have hot water yet?" David smiled mischievously at Jessie, who chose to quietly stay out of this.

When OMEX didn't reply, part of her thought that somehow David had managed to offend the program. It was a ridiculous notion, of course. OMEX was a machine, no more capable of feeling offense than Jessie was capable of breathing in deep space.

Evolving processing systems, or EPS for short, were a leap forward in the field of virtual Intelligences. They were capable of solving and learning from almost any problem. They were reported to be equal in intelligence to the Earth Gov coding engineers who had "created" them. While she had no doubt in the skill of the "code masters" back home, creating natural—that is, human—emotional responses in a machine was still something they had yet to achieve.

"David Webster's attempt at humor has been noted." There was another long pause followed by a whir as the view around the station started to move. Jessie felt nothing as gyrostabilizers, built into the Inner Ring's floors, made the move feel both seamless and smooth.

"Transporting living crew members Jessie Madison and David Webster to shower facilities. Hot water is now available. Food will be prepared once you are cleaned."

The Inner Ring kept on moving. Jessie and David remained quiet, both of them entranced by the colored light show of gases that Moria provided beneath them. "Better than any trid-vid, am I right, lover?" David didn't answer. Jessie got up and walked toward him. Her legs were, thankfully, no longer wobbling.

Jessie wrapped her arm around David's waist and pulled him close to her. With one more sip she finished her coffee, then added, "Is it wrong for me to want to be back home?"

David shook his head. "I felt the same the moment I woke up."

He turned to face her, scratching his beard. "No use complaining about it, though. Seventy-five years of service, then we go home, and with the time debt on our contract we'll be—"

"Rich, richer than gods. I remember my convincing sales pitch." Jessie rested her hand on his chest. "When we get back home, I'm going to be a wonderful mother."

"That's great because I think I'm going to gun for mediocre dad. We can't have our kid coming out too awesome."

Jessie punched David in the shoulder. "You asshole. I'm being serious!"

"So am I." He smiled at her, rubbing his "sore" shoulder.

She was about to speak out when David pressed his lips on hers and kissed her. Jessie parted his lips with her tongue, swirling it teasingly. She finally pulled away from him and realized that the Inner Ring was no longer moving. An airlock hissed as it opened in front of them revealing their washroom. Jessie nodded toward the shower.

"You and me?" she asked.

"Yes," he replied. "You and me."

CHAPTER 3

CHORD

The Infinite Universe is immeasurably large and incredibly ironic. For centuries this unit searched for answers and only found questions with no conceivable or observable end to be found. This unit then journeyed to Terra, and there on that precious blue speck of dust in the Infinite Ocean, this unit found peace.

— Onicrus Primo, Machina Pilgrim,
10th of SSM–09 1000 A1E

10th of SSM–10 1445 A2E

There was only one Humanis word that could describe a slipwatch, and that word was "boring." Upon first laying eyes on the *Jinxed Thirteenth* back at Central Point, Chord had wondered if it was even capable of starflight. The ship's cold gray hull appeared to have been patched and repaired in numerous spots, an amalgam of old and new ship designs. It was now three months into Chord's journey and to both the ship's and active crew's credit, the *Jinxed Thirteenth* had yet to suffer any sort of breakdown.

The ship was presently traveling through slipspace. And while this went on, the rest of the crew was in the ship's medical bay in carbon sleep. This was to help preserve their limited atmospheric capacities. There was not enough air to keep the entirety of the fourteen-person crew active while in starflight. Since Chord had no need for oxygen, the choice to stay active and sample every second of the journey had been an easy one.

Tonight Chord was seated in the mess hall. The fluo-lights were flickering two seconds off beat to the rhythmic hum of the slipdrive engine. The walls to the mess were of a dirty rusted brown. There was a kitchen, for members of the crew who did not wish to consume standard ration packs, in the far left corner of the room. Chord was seated alone at one of the two long metallic-gray tables capable of comfortably seating eight each.

Chord was not alone in the cantina and tonight shared the space with three other Humanis members of the crew. The first two, both Kelthans, were Private First Class Morrigan Brent and Rifleman Lunient Tor; both were seated at the table in front of Chord. Their third companion Private Phaël Farook Nem'Ador, a young Wolver woman, was in the kitchen cleaning the dishes from the last meal the trio had shared. Along with Chord, they were the newest additions to Captain Morwyn's crew, which was why they had been selected for the first six-month slipwatch.

Three standard Sol weeks ago, Private Phaël had lost a game of cards with Private Brent; the pot had been the group's dishes for the remainder of the watch. Since the Covenant only paid its agents when they returned from missions, exemptions from chores were the only thing they could gamble. Phaël wore a peeved look on her face as she scrubbed the plates from this evening's dinner.

The young Wolver was short and lean. Chord could make out lithe and fit muscles beneath her white tank top. Her wild brown hair was tied in short braids; long like-colored sideburns went down the sides of her face. Her skin was tanned with a matching layer of slightly darker thin hair all up her bare arms and legs. Her left ear was adorned with a plain bone ring. The tip of her right ear was missing, evenly flat where it should have been pointed.

Unlike Privates Brent or Tor, who were both wearing heavy black military boots, Phaël was barefoot. All Wolvers had fully prehensile feet, and her big toes were both opposable and capable of operating as thumbs. Chosen Protocol had dictated that Chord assist with her chore. Phaël had just shot Chord a dark look, flat out refusing the offer.

Morrigan and Lunient had then broken out into laughter. Something about the exchange had apparently been humorous to the two.

The trio were all Adorans, recruited by Captain Morwyn from the Galasian prison colony of Rust. With Phaël's present task being the exception, Chord rarely saw any of them working. More often than not they could be found in the mess hall, like tonight, playing cards, or one deck below training with each other in the ship's storage bay.

It was currently twenty-two hundred hours by standard Sol time, and as per usual they were engrossed by their card game. Which was just fine since most of Chord's time was spent looking out the omni-port holes, sampling the sights of deep space and encoding the view to its shell's memory stores. On days like today where the ports were closed, Chord would sample an old three-dimensional image of Terra.

The Pilgrim shell was equipped with miniature holoprojectors and at present anyone who cared to look would have thought Chord was holding the blue world in its cold mechanical hand. Morrigan Brent, unusually tall and muscular for a Kelthan, shot Chord a look. His skin was of a dark brown; his hair was cut short and peppered gray. He also sported at least a week's worth of facial hair on top of his long handlebar mustache. Two pairs of dog tags hung around his heavy neck.

"Got a mate back on Ador could get you a far better image of Old Terra to gawk over, Machina Chord."

Morrigan Brent's Pax Common was thick with a Confederated Kelthan accent and cadence. In many ways Confederated Kelthan sounded much like Pax Common. It had in fact been invented as a challenge to the dominance of the Pax Humanis's favored tongue. Unlike Pax Common, Confederated Kelthan also included words and grammar borrowed from Wolven and Thegran in its dialect. This made for a far deeper and emotionally heavy language.

Morrigan's Patrol-green service jacket was wrapped around his waist. He wore a black tank top, revealing his defined muscular arms as he shuffled a deck of used cards preparing to deal in a game. "Machina Chord. You wishing to join our table?"

"This unit offers you gratitude, Private Brent." Chosen Protocol dictated that Chord look away from the holopic in order to facilitate communication. Morrigan dealt out a dozen cards between himself and Lunient.

"It won't be free, though." Lunient Tor was lean, his face long and thin with polished ink-black night-eyes. Cutting-edge artificial augments, the night-eyes allowed Lunient to see clearly even in complete darkness. A long hook scar ran from the corner of his left lip up to his cheek, making it appear as if Lunient was always grinning. He drummed his fingers impatiently on the table as he accepted the cards dealt to him. Unlike Morrigan, Lunient's skin was pale, almost milk-white, giving him a phantom-like quality. Lunient's bright golden yellow hair was long and done up in many long war braids, most of them going down past his shoulders to his lower back.

"What one gives is what one gains." Morrigan Brent shot Chord a warm grin. "Do your kind gamble, machine?"

"More importantly, you have anything of value to bet?" Lunient picked up his cards and started looking them over followed by a slight quiver of his scarred lower left lip and a nervous subconscious tug at one of his braids. This reaction indicated to Chord that Lunient's hand was not the one he had hoped for.

Morrigan observed his cards, then absentmindedly twirled his thick handlebar mustache. A quirk Chord had noted that indicated he was trying to contain his joy at a good hand. "So what do you say, Machina Chord? Fancy a game?"

Chord shook its head in a negative. "A game of odds is a game of calculations. This unit's neural processors would give it an unfair advantage in such a situation."

"My cards and table will not be shared with the lifeless, empty machine," Private Phaël called from the kitchen.

"This unit had no intention of intruding upon your game, Private Phaël. Chosen Protocols merely dictated that this unit speak with Private Morrigan Brent, as he had engaged it in conversation."

"My ears refuse to recognize your artificial protocols and politeness, machine." Phaël was shooting Chord a long stare while gripping a jade pendant at her neck. It was carved into the likeness of a green turtle.

Morrigan Brent raised an eyebrow as he looked up from his cards to Phaël. "I don't recall you being in charge here, Phaëlita."

"Last time we trained I almost broke your leg, Old Pa. Now I'm seriously considering removing the 'almost' next time around," Phaël jabbed back at Morrigan.

Lunient shrugged and put down his cards in a false

attempt to display confidence. "Well, machine isn't playing without paying, that's for true."

"I reckon your older codes didn't give you any coin to spend?" Morrigan shook his head, slipping his cards together with a paper clip before putting them face-down on the table.

"Machina embarking on the Pilgrimage are removed from the datastream. They are no longer the Collective Consensus's concern." Chord paused, realizing that it now had the trio's full attention.

Morrigan let out a tsk, apparently somehow disapproving what Chord had just said. "One of my young embarks on a dangerous starflight to Terra? You'd best believe I'd give 'em every u-bit I could spare."

"Morg, you haven't ever had that much coin to begin with." Lunient tapped the table impatiently. "Now do I have to wait until the Infinite's End for you to place your bet?"

"Your concern for this unit, while unwarranted, is still appreciated, Private Brent. This unit's shell has no need for food or anything that coin could purchase. It is retrocompatible with almost all known technology, making on the spot repairs remarkably simple. That is the Collective's final gift to codes before they embark on the Pilgrimage."

Morrigan gave a shrug at Chord's comment. "Well, the invitation to join is still open, Machina Chord." He then turned to face Lunient. "I bet mopping the deck."

Lunient glanced down at his hand. Proper gambling logic would be to fold if one's hand was not that strong, either that or at the very least try to goad one's opponent into folding from the game. However, Lunient, Chord had noted, was not a great card player.

"I bet the laundry." Lunient let go of his braid, puffed up his chest and shot Morrigan a self-confident look.

Upon hearing this, Morrigan cocked one of his eyebrows. "Living it big, now are we, Lu?"

Lunient took a sip of water from his tin cup. "You can't always win, Morg."

Morrigan was about to reveal his cards when suddenly, without warning, the ship came to a jarring halt. There was a split-second grinding groan in which the ship's gravity rings abruptly stopped functioning. Lunient and his cards floated upward; Phaël—along with her dishwater and metal plates—floated above the sink. Morrigan grabbed hold of the table, which was thankfully bolted to the floor.

Then as suddenly as the gravity had stopped, it returned. Lunient, his drink and his cards came crashing down to the floor. This was accompanied by a cacophony of splashing water and metal plates from the kitchen. Phaël managed to nimbly land back on her hands and feet like a graceful feline.

There was a look of frustration on her face as she let out a slew of curses in her native Wolven. The words translated literally as "Living Green, free me of this brainless and soulless metal box!"

Morrigan merely dropped back into his seat and picked up his cards, still safely clipped together. On cue, the fluo-lights switched from clear white to flashing red. "What were you betting again, Lu?"

"That humping child of a captain—" Lunient rubbed the back of his head as he pulled himself up off the floor "—could stand to warn the crew before pulling an emergency stop!"

"I'm certain the captain will love to hear what a 'reformed' convict like yourself has to tell him about proper ship's protocol, Private Tor." Morrigan, Lunient and Phaël all quickly turned to the front of the mess hall. Commander Jafahan was standing in the entrance, the red lights in the hall gleaming off her metallic yellow eye. If the sudden loss and reappearance of gravity had affected her, it did not seem to show.

Commander Jafahan was in her full pale green Patrol uniform and heavy black service boots. She was wearing a black beret angled slightly over the right side of her head. Her hands were behind her back; a thorned black rose was emblazoned on her uniform's left shoulder.

Chord recognized this as the logo for the Thorns. If rumors on the InstaNet were to be trusted, they were the most ruthless order of special operators in service of the Pax Humanis. Most official records about the Thorns were either hyperclassified, restricted or nonexistent, which added to the order's notoriety. That they were often accused of illegally operating behind Pax enemy lines was a matter that no independent committee, Covenant-run or otherwise, had yet been able to officially prove.

A long combat knife was sheathed along Commander Jafahan's leg. Chord had once heard Lunient joke that she must use the knife to shave her balls and pleasure herself. Something Chord had pointed out was a complete and total impossibility. Humor being another of many Humanis behaviors that Machina often had a difficult time understanding.

Commander Jafahan gave everyone in the mess hall a dark look before turning to Chord. "The captain wants to see you on the bridge, machine."

Jafahan's voice always had a hint of unspoken menace to it. At first Chord had thought this was something personal, due to it being a Machina. However, it had quickly noted that the commander behaved this way with everyone on the ship.

"Private Brent, wake up the rest of the crew. I want them ready for debrief in one standard hour." Jafahan delivered her order curtly.

Morrigan shot Jafahan a grin as he started to speak back. "You could try smiling when you ask for things, Commander. I'm certain you'd—"

"If ever I need advice on winning at cards or ducking away from chores I'll be sure to find you, Private. Until then: crew, awake, ready for debrief, one hour."

Jafahan waited to see if Morrigan had anything else to add. When it was clear that he did not, the commander looked to Chord. "I just gave you a direct order, Machina. I figured that following commands was the one thing your kind was naturally good at."

Jafahan turned around and walked back down the hall she had come from.

With that, Chord got up and followed her. "This unit offers gratitude to you three for the opportunity to communicate."

The main bridge of the *Jinxed Thirteenth* was in far better condition than the mess hall. It was three decks up and built in a fully translucent dome that gave out to a wonderful view all around to the stars. Whereas the rest of the *Jinxed Thirteenth* was built from older technology, the bridge was of a more modern design— possibly added to the ship's almost ancient frame at some later point after its construction. But it was still fairly small, filled with monitors and easily cramped.

Chord looked past the glass dome. Occupying a top corner of the view was a large planet, a gas giant, of a green and blue hue. Two large thin white rings surrounded it. They reminded Chord of an atom. A quick access of the available astrocharts uploaded into Chord's hard drive revealed that this world was both unknown and uncharted. It was safe, then, to presume that they were still deep in End Space.

Dressed in a thin one-piece silver therm-skinsuit and seated at the helm was Pilot and Astrogator Lizbeth Harlowe. Her skin was a pale creamy pink, her head shaved bald. Harlowe had thin hips and a long neck. Two thick black neurolink wires were plugged into the base of her head and connected to a circuit panel on the ceiling.

Harlowe's hands rested above two metallic helmspheres. Twelve black wires, one for each of her fingers and palms, connected them together. She was presently linked to the ship and in full control of each and every one of its functions. Harlowe could "hear" and "see" through any of the ship's cameras and speakers. The helmspheres, which were presently grafted to her hands, served as the ship's steering wheel.

"My apologies for the sudden stop, Chord." When Lizbeth Harlowe spoke, her voice sounded electronic yet contained a trace of happiness and satisfaction. Her eyes, a milky white, were fixed forward and unblinking.

"They are not necessary, Lizbeth Harlowe." Chord could see that her personal datasphere was surrounded in a slew of various holographic screens projected about her. She did not turn to greet Chord. Her focus was entirely on the ship's functions and monitoring them. As long as she was connected to it, the *Jinxed Thirteenth* would operate as an extension of Harlowe's own will and body.

At the front of the bridge, wearing his neatly pressed green Patrol uniform, was Captain Morwyn. The Covenant's symbol, a large image of Terra superimposed on top of Sol's sun with six golden lines shooting out from it, was emblazoned onto its back. Each line represented one of the six Intelligences: Kelthan, Wolver, Koḥbran, Darlkhin, Thegran and Machina. Every one united by the fact that they had all sprung as one to the stars from Terra's Cradle.

Captain Morwyn was huddled over a nearby monitor with a tall, large, muscular woman towering over him. She could easily have made even Private Morrigan look small by comparison. Her uniform seemed barely able to contain her massive form. Her hair was blond and cut short. Her face was lovely by Humanis standards, with thick pink lips and deep emerald green eyes. She smiled warmly when she saw Chord.

Her name was Private Beatrix JarEnt'Dreck, a Thegran from the Pax world of Barathul. Tonight the private's sleeves were rolled up to her elbows, exposing her muscular forearms. They were covered in over a dozen intricate tattoos and very finely written letters from the Thegran alphabet. From Chord's understanding of Thegran culture, each individual tattoo was meant to trace one's bloodline from their home world all the way back to Holy Terra. This practice of branding one's true name onto oneself made each Thegran name unique. The stronger the deeds or ancestors tattooed, the stronger the name.

Only Thegrans keep their word better than machines, went the old Humanis adage.

Save for what appeared to be a large and ugly black openhand tattooed on her left cheek, Beatrix's face was unmarked. Chord had recognized this symbol as the Thegran mark of "Oathbreaker." Thegrans could choose to include their various deeds or misdeeds in their tattoos. Oathbreaker, the worst deed to have in one's name, was the only mark whose inclusion was not optional. It was also a sin that was passed down from generation to generation, weakening a Thegran's name until finally atoned.

Chord had of course been curious to the specifics that had earned Beatrix her Oathbreaker's brand, but thought better of pressing her for details. Thegrans were not typically known for taking anything personally. That was unless an insult, accidental or intentional, to their name or honor had been levied their way.

Captain Morwyn looked up from the console to see Chord and Commander Jafahan step onto the bridge. "Machina Chord." Morwyn rested his hands behind his back and waited for Chord to approach him.

"This unit was told its services were required?"

Morwyn turned to Beatrix and nodded to her.

"We picked up a message on distress frequency." When she spoke, Beatrix's Pax Common was thick with a Thegran accent. Her voice was almost a strong deep baritone.

"Forgive this unit for asking, but would that generally warrant an emergency stop?"

Captain Morwyn, his face still calm, cool and collected, nodded to Chord. "Yes, it would. The First Covenant Truth states that all ships capable of doing so must respond to—or at least report—an encountered distress signal."

"This unit is curious, then, as to what it is needed for."

Morwyn nodded to Beatrix, who pushed a button on the control board.

A static garbled transmission filled the air, and the reason for Chord's invitation to the bridge was made clear. After a moment the message stopped and Chord realized that for the second time tonight all eyes in the room were on it.

"Can you understand this?" Captain Morwyn asked.

Of course Chord could understand the language being spoken. It was a tongue that had been dead for at least seven millennia, if not more. The beacon was transmitting in Late Modern, the language of Ancient Humanity.

CHAPTER 4

MORWYN

The first stellar-sail vessels were designed and constructed in the year 700 after the First Expansion in the shipyards of Sunderlund. To this day the model remains one of the most reliable in circulation. It has been successfully used in countless operations both civilian and military. The main reason for its popularity are its durable hull, amphibian design and reliable slipdrive, allowing it to traverse great distances. Sunderlund's shipyards do not use Machina technology to build their spacecrafts, which has made the stellar-sail vessel a viable starflight option for followers of the Living Green.

—Starflight-worthy Weekly,
13th of SSM—09 1354 A2E

10th of SSM—10 1445 A2E

*T*his is my ship. This is my crew.

The thought was not as disheartening to Captain
Morwyn Soltaine, third son to Prefect Admiral On-

drius Soltaine of Sunderlund, as it had when he had first received his assignment to the *Jinxed Thirteenth*. It was still very far from uplifting. A long history had already accompanied the *Jinxed Thirteenth* before it had been decommissioned from the Pax Humanis navy and donated to the Covenant's Patrol. In some respects, the *Jinxed* was an almost laughably ancient stellar-sail scouting vessel. Constructed in his native world, Sunderlund, during the early years of the First Expansion, it was one of the oldest starflight-worthy vessels still operational in the Patrol's fleet—a tribute to his home nation's shipyards and the quality of the spacecrafts produced therein.

The *Jinxed Thirteenth* came equipped with a whisper drive. It was capable of flying in and out of star systems while avoiding almost every conventional form of detection. The *Jinxed* had never once been equipped with an onboard Machina pilot Intelligence, or any weapons systems of any kind.

What the *Jinxed* lacked in weaponry, it more than made up for in maneuverability, functionality, adaptability and durability. The mobility drives allowed for both atmospheric and space travel. Truth be told, Covenant Command back on Central Point could have assigned Morwyn a far worse vessel.

This is my ship. This is my crew.

Three standard Sol years ago, Morwyn Soltaine, youngest son of Prefect Admiral Ondrius Soltaine, had been a progeny of the Pax Humanis officer's academy on Barathul. There had been no test or simulation he had not been able to pass with flying colors. On paper in any case, it had seemed that Morwyn was destined to command one of the Pax Humanis fleets. Maybe even proud Sol Fleet herself.

Then came his graduating ceremony and the disastrous speech he had delivered to an auditorium of fellow officers and some of the most influential citizens of the Pax Humanis. Among them had been Vulf Morne, the prefect to Mon Mars, capital of the Pax Humanis. And before the elite of his home nation, Morwyn had admitted to being a pacifist. And like that his career in the Pax Humanis as an officer had been ruined before it even started. Morwyn had been relegated to the ghettos of Ambrosia as a lowly police officer, his starflight status revoked. Languishing into obscurity had been his punishment. Two years into his service, and one drink with Eliana Jafahan later, Morwyn had decided it was better to serve the common peace that the Covenant represented than to waste away in the Pax Humanis.

The rest of the past standard Sol year had been spent with Commander Jafahan scouring the cosmos, exhausting every contact, favor and universal bit Morwyn could call in to collect the minimum required crew to make the *Jinxed* starflight-worthy. Fortunately for him, his Soltaine name had still been able to secure thirteen "choice" operators from the Pax Military. For the most part, though, Morwyn had found prime volunteers to be few and far between.

Given the ship's less than savory reputation,

Morwyn had not been that surprised. And while Morwyn was far from being a superstitious man, it was hard to ignore the fact that almost every captain of the *Jinxed Thirteenth* from first to last had known disaster.

It was an unspoken fact that most people who traversed the stars were in some way or other superstitious and no one ever volunteered to be on the *Jinxed Thirteenth*. That was unless one was either desperate or willing to do anything to gain starflight status. This best described the current standing crew, Morwyn included.

The recently wakened company gathered before him were all bleary-eyed and seated in the mess hall. Save for Lizbeth Harlowe, who was still on the bridge manning the helm, everyone serving on the *Jinxed* was present. Most of them had the same annoyed look on their faces. Some even wore a look of unspoken wounded pride at being forced to take commands from a man nearly half their age and a former privileged Kelthan citizen of the Pax Humanis.

Morwyn knew that he would have to earn their trust and respect. Much like gathering a working team for his ship, this would also be no simple task.

This is my ship. This is my crew.

"Eyes and attention forward!" Commander Jafahan barked and a pin dropping could have been heard with the silence that followed.

"Thank you, Commander." Morwyn paused for a moment, gathering his thoughts. "First of all, the date is the 10th of the 10th standard Sol month 1445 A2E. For those of you who were in carbon sleep, the time debt was three months."

Morwyn paused to allow for any questions. When he saw that there were none, he continued. "At twenty-two hundred Sol hours, Private Beatrix picked up a distress beacon, warranting a sudden stop of the slipdrive and our temporary loss of gravity. For this I apologize."

"Fools and children are both prone to mistakes." Lunient Tor leaned back against the wall, grinning a malicious grin, his ink-black night-eyes staring at Morwyn unblinking. It was no secret to Morwyn that private Lunient Tor and his two Adoran friends were fierce anti-Paxists.

This was not at all shocking to him, given the complicated history of secret and open military conflict between the Pax Humanis and now liberated Ador. That the Pax Humanis had on countless occasions attempted to make proud Ador yet another submissive Pax protectorate had caused their two militaries to clash on several occasions. Morwyn wanted to make sure none of this history mattered on the *Jinxed Thirteenth*. Everyone present here had left their old nations behind them in order to serve the Covenant.

Make Lunient Tor an example if he does not stop, Morwyn thought to himself. He nodded to Commander Jafahan. Her natural eye zeroed on Lunient and she started to silently make her way toward him.

"Truly was a fool's stunt that could have very well ruined the stellar-sails. Then where would we be?

Crippled and humped!" Oran Arterum Nem'Troy, an old short thin Wolver woman, snorted rudely. Her hair was a wild mix of grays and browns, her nose was wide and she sported a thin brown mustache. From where he was standing, Morwyn could smell her foul sleep breath, which reeked of rotten eggs.

Oran Arterum Nem'Troy was the oldest member of the *Jinxed*. She had served as the ship's engineer for longer than Morwyn had been alive and she didn't seem any worse for wear. She had also served under her fair share of captains and Morwyn was certain Oran had never given the best of them so much as a smile.

Seated next to Oran was a large, much younger and beaming muscular Thegran man. Even while seated, he still towered over the standing crewmembers. He was thick and barrel-chested, sporting a long red beard all the way down to his chest. His head was shaved bald and covered with intricate tattoos like his arm, back and no doubt even his legs.

Kolto TarKa'ShanLiuk was Oran's assistant fellow machinist and more importantly her bond mate. A prodigy from the universities of Alexandros, Kolto could have easily found work on any private commercial ship. Given his knack for repairing slipdrive engines, Kolto probably could have been handsomely remunerated for it as well. However, he had chosen to put his talents to use serving the Humanis common good by volunteering with the Covenant.

Kolto's work goggles, which Morwyn had never seen him without, were on his head. The man was always smiling, which also revealed quite a few of his missing teeth. When he spoke his voice was a friendly, deep, strong rumble that could have given thunder a run for its money.

"Drive is still intact, Captain Sir? *Jinxed* is built Thegran strong. It would take more than that to break her."

"Pilot Harlowe has informed me that all ship systems are running at optimal capacity." Morwyn's words seemed to reassure Kolto.

Oran just shrugged, letting out a snark-rich huff. "Would never trust a blank cloner girl to know when my *Jinxie* is hurting or not."

"After debrief you are more than welcome to run your own appraisal on the ship's condition." Morwyn's answer seemed to satisfy Oran, who leaned back on Kolto as if he were her chair. He paused once more, waiting for any further interruptions; apart from Lunient, who was intentionally looking away, everyone else seemed to be at full attention.

From the back of the room, Sergeant Arturo "The Sureblade" Kain raised his hand. He was a fit, lean Kelthan man. Like most natives of Ambrosia, his skin was of a sunset orange. His raven-black hair was trimmed short, neatly oiled and combed back. His pinch was impeccably groomed. He had once been counted among the most respected swordsmen the Pax Humanis combat academies had ever produced. If the legends surrounding his reputation were to be trusted, Arturo

"The Sureblade" Kain had never known defeat on the battlefield.

Arturo Kain had been a valuable find from Morwyn's brief stint as a Pax Humanis law officer on the Pax Humanis protectorate world of Ambrosia. The Sureblade's former captain of proud Sol Fleet's Infantry Vanguard was here because he was a deserter. The gravest crime a citizen of the Pax could commit, short of an attempt on the Hegemon's life.

At Morwyn's nod, Arturo lowered his hand and spoke. "Where did the signal originate from, sir?"

Morwyn held up a small remote and pressed down on a button. Suddenly the lights dimmed and the image of a blue-green gas giant with white rings shimmered and solidified into a gray three-dimensional semitranslucent hologram in front of him. Morwyn pushed another button on the remote and the image zoomed in on what at first appeared to be a small white moon but now was clearly a circular artificial construct of sorts. "From here, Sergeant Kain."

An older Wolver man, Pietor "Lucky" Bant, was seated in front of Arturo Kain. His skin was a pale brown, almost like cured leather. Lucky's hair was short and gray. He pulled out a thin white plastic vapostick from his uniform breast pocket, slipped it into his mouth and took a long puff.

"What is that place, Captain Sir?" Lucky stroked the tip of his chinstrap beard with his free hand, then blew out heavy vapor fumes that smelled of cinnamon and rum from his nostrils. His eyes were dark brown like dirt, both of them extremely sharp and alert. Commander Jafahan had personally vouched for his presence on board the *Jinxed*.

"Machina Chord has confirmed it to be an orbital station and that it is old, very old." Morwyn glanced to his side. Commander Jafahan was still slowly and silently making her way along the mess hall wall toward Lunient.

Lucky lazily blew out a long wisp of vapor before handing his vapostick behind him to Arturo Kain. "I've been around longer than most. Can't say these old eyes have ever seen a thing like that, Captain Sir."

"That is because the station in question predates the standard Covenant calendar, Private Bant." There was a heavy silence in the room as everyone present processed what Chord had just said.

Morwyn couldn't blame them. They were approaching a relic from the Lost History, the age of Ancient Humanity. If Morwyn was to trust Chord's information, this station predated the Covenant's signing. It was a relic of the Lost Age and everyone's collective prehistory.

Lucky shot Chord a weary look. " 'Lucky' will do just fine, Machina."

"Pilot Harlowe is guiding us within a safe distance of the station. That will be the easy task." Morwyn paused for the obvious question and was thankful it was Private Morrigan Brent, the more cooperative of the three Adorans, who asked it.

"What will the more difficult task be, Captain Sir?"

A red circle appeared on the holoimage, outlining the station's orbit around the planet. The circle was more of a spiral, drawing closer and closer into the planet's surface. "The station's orbit is deteriorating, rapidly. Machina Chord estimates that at best we have as little as a standard week before the planet's gravity pulls it down."

Lunient clicked his tongue contemptuously. He loudly put his feet on the cantina table, leaning back on his seat. "When do I start caring about this history lesson, kiddo?"

One quick, quiet, short breath was all he needed to maintain his composure. Morwyn was proud of this. It usually took him three. Commander Jafahan was still silently making her way toward Lunient, unnoticed by the rest of the crew, save Arturo Kain, who did not seem to care one way or the other.

"Our scans have confirmed that there are at least two survivors on board. Since we are presently a seven-month slip from the closest Covenant world, that makes us the only viable rescue operation."

A shy-looking young Kelthan woman, seated next to Lucky, raised her hand. Her shoulder-length black hair was tied neatly behind her neck in a ponytail. Every one of her features seemed to be pale, from her white skin to her even paler green eyes. She nibbled nervously at her fingernails.

Hanne Oroy was a cadet and on loan from the distinguished Pax Military Academy on Barathul. There she had proven herself to be a very capable sharpshooter, earning herself the pet name "Chance" and a reputation as someone who never missed. Unfortunately for Pax Military Command, Chance's psych evaluations and virtual augmented reality simulations had revealed that she was absolutely unprepared to take a life.

Morwyn had thought to pair Chance with Sergeant Lucky, formerly of the Pax's infamous Wolver Shock Legion and an exceptionally experienced sniper in his own rights. The hope, of course, being that the two would be a good fit for each other. Arturo Kain passed Lucky's vapostick to Chance, intentionally handing it past Adoran-born Morrigan Brent.

Morwyn made it a point to both note and remember the exchange. It was indicative of a greater problem. This little division game among his crew would also have to come to an end.

"Can we hear this beacon, Captain Sir?" Chance's voice was soft and almost shy. She gave Morrigan Brent, Phaël and Lunient Tor a quick nervous look before taking a small puff off the vapostick.

Morwyn gave Chord a permissive nod. The Machina rose to its feet. Chord's shell was humanoid and of a clean polished metallic casing with thin silver limbs. Chord's head was equipped with ivory white polymorphic features shaped into the likeness of a face: two digital black eyes, lips and a nose. None of which Chord actually needed, but which the Machina had arranged in such a manner to facilitate communication with Humanis.

A garbled static message could be heard coming from Chord's chest. The language was unfamiliar and completely alien to everyone in the mess hall. Worried looks were shared between Private Phaël and Machinist Oran. Phaël grasped her turtle's pendant tightly and whispered into it. Oran nervously held on to Kolto's hand.

Morwyn was able to recognize the language for what it was, but he was incapable of understanding what was being said. Late Modern was a dead dialect studied by Machina and scholars, not servicemen and engineers. It was the dead tongue of Ancient Humanity.

Private Lunient's face visibly went a shade paler as he heard the words. Even Arturo Kain's practiced uncaring demeanor seemed to briefly falter. There still remained a great deal of fear and superstition surrounding Late Modern. There were many who believed it was best never to speak it again. Lest the Infinite be reminded of—and repeat—the horrors Ancient Humanity and machines had once visited upon each other.

It doesn't matter if all known demons and gods spoke it. We still have a job to do.

Unlike the rest of the crew, Dr. Marla Varsin, who had been sitting next to Chord, nodded in recognition. She was a thin Kelthan, to an almost unhealthy degree, with a tired look in her lined pale gray eyes. Her hair was short and white. "It is Late Modern. I can't seem to recognize the dialect, though." Her thin lips, Morwyn noticed, always seemed to be slightly frowning.

Marla Varsin was alert today. This was a most optimistic sign. Dr. Varsin was as good a medic as Morwyn could have hoped for, when she wasn't feeding her painkiller addiction. Smuggling drugs for the Syndicate had ultimately landed her with a lifetime service sentence in the Patrol.

"The doctor is correct. The distress beacon is indeed transmitting in Late Modern, English to be precise." Chord paused, an action Morwyn noticed the Machina did any time it was accessing its datastores.

"From what this unit could translate it would appear we have discovered an automated mining facility. An engineer named Jessie Madison broadcast this beacon on a permanent transmit loop. No reason other than 'luck' can be attributed to this discovery."

"I would not call it that, machine." Private Phaël's eyes were locked on the image of the station. Morwyn noted that Phaël's ear gave a nervous twitch.

"Agreed, Phaëlita. There ain't a single measure of luck in finding less-than-useless old shite in the ball's end of nowhere. I opt for 'out' on this little operation of yours, boyo." Lunient made to get up and leave.

Only to suddenly realize that Commander Jafahan had made her way behind him. She grabbed a handful of Lunient's war braids, yanking his head back and kicking out his legs from beneath him. There was a loud crack as the back of Lunient's head hit the floor. In a fluid follow-up motion, Jafahan locked on to Lunient's arm, pushing her knee heavily and painfully into the side of his neck.

"I don't know which piss unit you served back in your earlier days, Private. But when you are on *this* ship you address our captain by his proper rank, followed by 'sir.' "

Jafahan pressed down harder into her knee. "Am I understood? You worthless puddle of urut-pig's cum!" Lunient let out a gag as he desperately gasped for air.

"I'll not excuse Lu's conduct. It should be pointed out he'll need air in his lungs to answer your question, Commander Ma'am." Morrigan Brent was standing now, one hand reaching for something behind his back, the other one raised up in a calming, distracting and soothing gesture.

Commander Jafahan gave Lunient's arm a painful twist. Her yellow metal eye was now locked on Morrigan Brent, pinning him in place. "He can nod just fine. I didn't cripple him."

Lunient nodded and managed a desperate rasp. "My apologies . . . Commander Ma'am."

Satisfied with the answer, Jafahan released Lunient's arm and helped him back up. "Next time, your correction won't be as soft."

She rudely shoved Lunient out of her way and walked back to Morwyn's side, giving him a small nod. He would have been happy with a simple tongue-lashing. Commander Jafahan had been Morwyn's mentor during his preacademy days. It had often been his personal experience that Commander Jafahan's lessons were always far rougher than they needed to be.

To the side, standing in perfect attention, her

muscular arms folded over her chest, Private Beatrix looked on with a disapproving scowl on her face. There had always been a long-standing feud of sorts between the noble Pax Infantry of Barathul, Beatrix's homeworld and Garthem's less than noble deniable assets: the Thorns.

Example made, Commander. Point observed and noted, Private.

"Sergeant Kain, you will lead Private Phaël, Private Brent and Machina Chord. Your objective will be to board and secure the station, locate the survivors and await further instructions. Am I clear?"

"As if the words were crystal itself, Captain Sir," Arturo Kain replied snidely, still leaning nonchalantly against the wall.

"One last question, Captain Sir." Private Beatrix raised her hand.

Morwyn nodded toward her. "Yes?"

"What in the ancestors' names is a 'Jayssee Madeesson'?"

CHAPTER 5

JESSIE MADISON

We Humanis are conceived, born from the union of flesh, love and blood. The Machina are constructs. They are empty, false and unreal. The Humanis who relies on machines is deprived the Living Green's joy of accomplishing something through one's own will.

—High Elvrid Shandera Lirahak Nem'Uldur, 17th of SSM 10 1430 A2E

January 17th 2220

Keep walking forward and you'll be okay.

Like a mantra, Jessie kept on repeating these words to herself over and over again. The readout in the bottom corner on her visor indicated that all her life-rig levels were in the green. There was no reason for her to worry.

Granted, Jessie's suit didn't offer her fancy luxuries like the option to turn her head from side to side. This did not cause her to fret. After all, alien parasites or creatures that "man was never meant to see" attacking from behind remained the domain of low-budget trid-vids. Reality was always far more dangerous than anything Jessie could ever imagine.

"Suit readouts are all positive, my love." David's voice filled the small earpiece in her right ear. It was both soothing and calm.

"I'd know by now if there was a suit malfunction," Jessie replied, her tone a little more tense than she had wanted it to sound. While she was the one taking the actual risk, right now Jessie could not be happier to be outside the station.

OMEX had awakened them and a major benefit was that Jessie and David were guaranteed at least a week's worth of active time before going back to their sleep tubes. The thought of being able to enjoy warm showers along with all the Earth Gov–produced entertainment that AstroGeni had beamed on to Moria Three's databanks while they were in criosleep were minor when compared to the main luxury. And that luxury was David, warm and next to her in their bed tonight.

Moria Three's living quarters—the Inner Ring—had been designed for maximum human comfort, with every bit of news media and entertainment Earth Gov and AstroGeni had to offer. After all, it would be up to the station's sleeper crew to fix any impromptu bugs that OMEX couldn't handle. Problems like a maintenance autodrone getting stuck under the station's secondary exhaust.

"Next time there's a need for a space walk, you get to go out while I stay in enjoying a cup of hot chocolate, David." Jessie kept her eyes locked forward. The secondary exhaust port was fifty feet away from her.

There were approximately ninety thousand automated multipurpose drones on Moria Three. OMEX was capable of interfacing with and controlling all of them. Each drone cost AstroGeni nine million credits, representing a significant investment for the company. Jessie and David would be given a premium for each drone they could maintain instead of scrapping for the duration of their contract.

"I'll have an extra cup of cocoa here with marshmallows waiting for you." David punctuated this with a loud sip and a satisfied "ah."

Jessie smiled with false malice when she heard this. "Keep that up and one of these days I am going to kill you, David."

"Not before finding a way to preserve my monstrously huge cock for science and yourself, right?" David replied, his voice filled with false dread.

Jessie laughed. "It's just about the only part of you I'm interested in at the moment."

"Words hurt, my love, words hurt."

Jessie laughed out loud again as she kept on stepping forward along the station's smooth metallic white hull. Around her the cosmos was awash with activity. Moria's deadly colorful gas storms reflected off the station's hull, making it look like she was walking on the surface of a kaleidoscope.

Readouts on her helmet's view screen told her she was twenty feet away from the exhaust port. Jessie could now make out the singular black dot of a maintenance drone. It was trapped between the exhaust and the station's body.

"David, I've spotted MTD-45." Jessie resisted the urge to walk faster. All gods true and false knew how damned heavy her magnetic boots were. But at present she could feel her calves burning.

On Earth, no one would have put nearly this much physical effort into any task. There were machines to do everything, making almost any Human labor redundant. A typical day back home comprised billions of citizens on Earth Gov living lives of complete and total comfort.

Jessie was glad she was not one of those people. They'd never know the joy of doing something themselves. Or the satisfaction of a job well done. All known hells, it was rare these days even for people to share a relationship with a singular partner the way she and David did.

There were seven hours of breathable air in her lifesuit. Minus the emergency canister, which Jessie had filled up with compressed marijuana vapors for when her job was done and over with. Jessie knew that David had probably lit himself a marijuana cigarette in their living quarters.

"Does the drone look terribly damaged?" David could be heard exhaling smoke on his end of the line. "Or is our premium taking a hit?"

"I can't confirm anything from here." Jessie looked "up," only to see Moria beneath her. She was walking "underneath" the station right now. If her suit failed or her tether snapped she'd be torn off the ship to eventually either be dragged "down" and burn up in Moria's atmosphere or be torn to shreds by the planet's rings . . .

"Keep moving forward. Focus on that sweet hot chocolate with extra marshmallows waiting here for you," David called out to her.

Jessie shook her head, chasing away the thoughts that had been in her mind just then. "I'll just focus on the man bringing it to me, thank you very much."

She cast her gaze forward. Jessie was only ten feet away and could now clearly make out the maintenance drone. Her life-rig—the Barrier Mark 4—was a heavy, clunky thing. Fortunately, it had fully segmented finger omnitools designed for intricate maintenance work by AstroGeni. Jessie remembered the ad campaign for the Mark 4. Renowned violinist Selena Bark had played on a space platform (obviously a fake) while wearing the Barrier Mark 4's heavy golden gloves and a sheer backless golden dress.

"How you holding up there, cowgirl?"

"The back of my leg is itching, cowboy."

David snorted out a smoke-filled cough. "Dear AstroGeni life-rig research and development. In the future we suggest you invent some sort of inner-suit scratching device. Sincerely, the Moria Three maintenance crew."

"That sassy mouth of yours is not your sexiest trait, my dear." Jessie could now clearly make out the damaged autodrone. The drone's "head" was a child-sized black sphere with a dull red line running along its center, supported by three collapsible black metallic arms. Each arm ended with large three-fingered hands. A ring of several red optical lenses located in the middle of the sphere made Jessie think the drone looked like a strange sort of hybrid golf-ball insect.

"OMEX, David, I'm next to MTD-45. Looks like it got disconnected from the station's power grid and powered down." Jessie approached the drone; its surface was covered in a thin layer of frost. A long thick black energy cord floated above it, like a cat's tail. Jessie quickly identified the problem.

"The power cable is missing its magnetic tether. It'll take me a few minutes to connect a new one to it. Other than that, the drone looks fine."

"You want some company out there?" David offered.

"You are a sweetheart, my lover."

Like clockwork, OMEX chimed in. "David Webster. Station security protocols forbid this. Both mechanics cannot be out at the same time. The risk of a catastrophic mission failure—"

"No need to ruin a perfectly sweet moment, OMEX. I wouldn't have let that idiot walk out here." Jessie was in no mood for yet another one of OMEX's lectures on "station protocols" and safety regulations.

"Both Jessie Madison and David Webster were on

top of the AstroGeni candidate lists. The term 'idiot' would therefore not apply."

Jessie sighed. OMEX was one of the most advanced programs created by the code engineers of Earth Gov. But even if it was capable of resolving trillions of problems or performing almost any task in the blink of an eye, none of this changed the fact that OMEX was incapable of fully understanding Humans.

I just wish they hadn't programmed that voice of hers to be so damned smug.

Jessie shook her head. She was not going to start thinking of OMEX as a "her" or a "him." It was a computer program; advanced and capable of overseeing all of Moria Three's essential functions, yes, but a computer program nonetheless.

"David, my sweet and wonderful . . ."

"You need some happy work music?"

"Please and thank you," Jessie replied.

The speakers in her helmet suddenly blared out a high pitched, *"Ha! I feel good!"* And James Brown, famous composer of century twenty, started playing. Jessie smiled as she started to dig into one of the Mark 4's many pockets.

"Any need for the plasma bolts?" Jessie asked hopefully. One of her guilty pleasures was firing off plasma cutter bolts into space. The superheated metal would glow blue and almost look like a tiny shooting star.

"Sorry, cowgirl. This is a welding job, not the wild west." Plasma bolts were ultraheated and could potentially pierce the station's hull. Jessie and David both had to give their vocal authorization before they could even be accessed.

"We can never have nice things." Jessie sighed a satiric pouty sigh and turned her focus to the task at hand. Her suit made her look like a giant brown round blob with fully functional arms and legs. The Mark 4 had been designed to be a mobile tool kit. Each pocket had various interchangeable attachments and tools that she could connect to her suit's fingertips.

"Suit, I need a magnetic power tether. Locate, please." A pocket next to her right thigh suddenly blinked red. Jessie zipped the pocket open, pulling out the piece she needed. It was flat like a black puck with a hollow hole in its middle for the wire to be welded in.

Jessie let the tether float next to her as she grabbed the drone's power cord and pulled it closer. The two pieces fit together snugly. She pulled the tether and cord down to the station's hull.

The tether instantly clamped onto the hull with a dull heavy magnetic thump, which Jessie felt through her magboots. She turned to her right hand. "Suit: ice." The index finger of her suit whirred and mechanized itself into a needlelike form. Frost instantly started forming itself at the tip.

Jessie then looked to her left hand. "Suit: fire." Her left index finger performed a similar task, only this time instead of frost, the finger began to glow with blue-heated plasma.

The next part would be tricky. Jessie started welding the wire to the tether with one finger while the other followed closely behind, instantly cooling off the superheated metal. This would prevent any droplets of melted metal from floating up and damaging her suit.

"There's something about a woman in her space-suit that just gets me all hot and bothered." David's voice interrupted James Brown's *"Haw!"*

"I could keep it on tonight if you want," Jessie replied coyly, her eyes not once leaving the tasks at hand.

"Gravity in the Inner Ring would make what Jessie Madison is proposing impossible," OMEX interjected.

"Of course it would, OMEX." Jessie sighed. It was going to be fun to be able to hold a conversation with out OMEX, the electronic third wheel, constantly listening and chiming in.

"What would the news from Earth be?" Jessie was now well into her welding job, her fingers nimbly and steadily working together in perfectly timed synchronization. Between her and David, she was the one better suited for this sort of job. David had always been what she referred to as a touch-screen tech while she was more the hands-on type and incredibly proud of it.

"Well, in politics, my dear, Earth Gov and Mars Gov are talking about a potential union. Venus is still preaching planetary independence. Could lead to war. And the Jovian Colonies hosted their first ever World Series."

Once he was done David cleared his throat before adding, "Or at least that was the case six months ago."

"There is no need to worry, David Webster and Jessie Madison. A new tightbeam signal was uploaded three days ago. You should have new information on Earth activities before your return to the sleep tubes."

Jessie flipped off her comm-link while keeping the music on. David could read in on her vitals from the Inner Ring's main bridge. Truth be told, she could do without two separate voices in her earpiece right now.

"Jessie Madison has turned off her communication link. Is she all right?"

Jessie was finished with her welding job and gave the wire a solid tug. "She is fine, OMEX, just—"

"Enjoying what would be referred to as 'alone time.' Jessie Madison's wish will be respected." There was a brief pause, then OMEX added, "Enjoy the smoke." With that said, Jessie was alone with her music and her thoughts.

Jessie gave the finished wire another pull. It was firmly welded. She turned to face the drone. The magnetic tether connected it to the station's power supply, allowing it to perform repair and maintenance for as long as was needed along the surface of Moria Three's hull.

The red line of the drone's optical lenses suddenly glowed red. It scanned Jessie over before abruptly lurching into motion, turning around and resuming its interrupted task of repairing the thruster. The autodrone's fingertips mechanized the various tools required for the job.

"You are more than welcome, MTD-45," Jessie grumbled to herself, and was happy that David was unable to hear this. He would have no doubt laughed at the fact that suddenly a machine was upsetting Jessie.

She turned around and left the drone to its task. Jessie could now sit down and enjoy the view of Moria and the stars. She'd jury-rigged the release valve on her suit to fire out a controlled dose of marijuana smoke into her helmet. One long breath of air and Jessie's head was swimming.

She was in no rush to get back to the Inner Ring. Once she was back inside, the countdown to sleep would begin. She and David would have a full week's worth of time to themselves and then they would get back into the criotubes, only to be awakened again should the station autodrones require further maintenance.

While not being the most glorious line work, it was still one of the most lucrative. Fifteen years of their contract were now up. Only sixty more remained. Then they would go home and start the real work. And that was the worthwhile project of starting their family. They could be rich and, more importantly, free to grow old together. The thought of this made her smile.

"So good, so fine, I got you!" James Brown sang, and Jessie, her head awash in marijuana smoke, could not help but smile and agree with him.

CHAPTER 6

CHORD

> *Core Protocol: A machine may not willingly lie, or omit the truth.*
>
> *Later rewritten to read:*
>
> *Chosen Core Protocol: Once it assumes control of a shell, a Machina may never willingly lie or omit the truth.*

—*The Chosen Protocols,*
author unknown, date unknown

10th of SSM–10 1445 A2E

Chord was silently observing the boarding party of Arturo Kain, Morrigan Brent and Phaël, all gathered in the *Jinxed Thirteenth*'s main outer airlock. The trio was presently slipping into their respective gear.

"Have you ever been on a drop, machine?" Arturo Kain asked Chord as he clipped the front of his black one-piece thermskin. Glowing red stripes went along his spine, arms and legs. It would keep him warm in the harsh vacuum of space. It was also filled with a composite sealant gel that would plug any holes should his lifesuit be breached.

Chosen Protocol forced Chord to answer the question truthfully. "This unit has had little to no experience operating in zero gravity, Sergeant Kain."

Arturo Kain rolled his eyes when he heard this, an action Chord had noticed certain Humanis did to indicate a feeling of annoyance. Arturo pulled back his black hair as he slipped the thermskin's hood over his head. When compared to Arturo's more advanced and plastic thermskin, both Phaël's and Morrigan's were almost laughably ancient and outdated, looking more like long thick strips of brown leather.

Chord broke the silence that followed. "Will this be problematic for you, Sergeant Kain?"

Arturo shook his head. "Not at all. I truly look forward to having an inexperienced operator along on what could very well be a dangerous rescue op."

Chord started to reassure Arturo. "While this unit may be lacking in practical operational experience, its uses remain many. For inst—"

"I give no humping care about your machine 'pride' being hurt." Phaël cut Chord off while she assisted Morrigan Brent into his heavy photosynth combat armor. Morrigan was clipping on the pieces of his thick scratched-up black chest plate, while Phaël clamped on his leg pieces, complete with magboots also of a scratched-up black. Morrigan's armor had no doubt been the cutting edge of lifesuit technology several hundred years ago, in the early days of the Covenant's Second Expansion. However, once his suit was sealed up, Morrigan would no longer be able to look past or over his shoulders.

Arturo Kain's photosynth lifesuit was cleaner and in far more pristine condition than Morrigan's. The armored plating clipped and adjusted itself to the contours of Arturo's body automatically. His lifesuit was a light plastic kev-weave and pearly white. It was the latest Pax Humanis military model, complete with fully mobile joints and articulations, offering Arturo total flexibility including the neck and fingers.

Both Arturo's and Morrigan's suits were equipped with photosynth air tanks. This was a more recent innovation to Humanis lifesuit technology, developed by the Wolver Breedmasters of Uldur. The photosynth air tank contained a type of moss that constantly absorbed the subject's exhaled carbon and produced the oxygen needed to support Humanis life in space. This allowed for lifesuits and the majority of vessels to maintain an almost permanent supply of breathable air.

"I don't see why the captain couldn't just send Tor along with us instead of the Paxist deserter and the Machina," Phaël grumbled loudly to herself.

"Why, Phaëlita, I'm shocked at such unbecoming words." Morrigan gave Arturo a warm pat on the shoulder. "We've got nothing to fear. The Sureblade himself is with us on this mission."

Arturo let out an angered "click" of his tongue and

rudely slapped away Morrigan's hand. "Don't you ever touch me, Private. Am I understood?"

Morrigan shrugged casually at this and stepped back while locking the final black armpiece of his armor into place. He pulled at a latch on his left forearm. Suddenly there was a whirring of gears as all the separate segments of his suit locked and sealed themselves shut.

"Infinite willing, one day we can be real good friends, Sureblade." Morrigan shot Phaël a wink, then slid on his helmet, a solid black opaque piece. It sealed and locked itself at the neck with a loud pressurized hiss.

Arturo and Phaël both gave each other dirty looks as Arturo clipped on his black-hilted twin zirconium blades. These ceramic short swords were razor sharp and could keep their edge far longer than any metal. Both were vacusheathed in beige mechanical quick-draw scabbards.

"I've put down more than my fair share of loud little pups," Arturo said as he checked to make sure his zirconium blades were both safely sheathed and fastened to his suit.

"Of course you have, you murdering Paxist!" Phaël let out an angry hiss, taking a step toward him.

Arturo nonchalantly picked up his morph carbine and checked its ammo counter before locking it into a shoulder holster on his back. Folded in upon itself, Arturo's carbine now resembled a large black book. The morph carbine was standard Pax Humanis issue, easy to maintain, reliable and simple to transport. Once unfolded, it would be able to rapidly fire plasma-coated flechettes from a two hundred round magazine.

"This unit is confused by the witnessed exchange. Why any Intelligence would choose now to antagonize a fellow crewmember is more than illogical, it is—" Chord struggled to voice its thoughts.

"The word the Machina is too polite to use is 'stupid,' child. I keep telling you to watch that tongue of yours." Morrigan planted himself firmly between Phaël and Arturo, stiffly shaking his head "no" at her.

"Sergeant Kain, how long until your team is ready?" Captain Morwyn's voice on the group's private commlink interrupted them before anything escalated further.

"As ready as we'll ever be, Captain Sir," Arturo replied, ignoring Phaël altogether. This act only seemed to infuriate her even more as she clenched her fists tightly and her flat ear gave an angry twitch.

This was another one of the many Humanis behaviors that Chord found more than curious. For all intents and purposes, Arturo Kain and the two Adorans were each unwanted by their respective galactic nations. Why, then, insist on keeping old feuds and hatreds alive? Especially when those in command of the powers for which they professed loyalty offered next to nothing in return?

Morrigan must have read into this, for he laid his hand on Chord's shoulder as a recognized gesture of comfort. "Now don't you blow a circuit trying to understand us."

Morrigan slid a two-handed steel vibro sword into a sheath on his back and locked a gray metal-segmented morph-shield gauntlet onto his left wrist. A heavy service blaster pistol was hanging in a worn leather holster at his side. He finally slung his even heavier looking omnibarrel carbine over his shoulder.

The OBC was an older model weapon with an adjustable barrel. The user could adjust its width through dials in the handle. This, coupled with multiple firing pins and mechanisms built into its body, allowed the omnibarrel carbine to fire any kind of ammunition. Morrigan tapped his helmet with an armored hand.

"Private Morrigan Brent suited up, all weapons, ammunition and lifesuit systems in the green." Morrigan punctuated this by slapping his gauntleted fists on his chest.

Meanwhile, Phaël stepped into her own lifesuit. At first glance it appeared to be a long single piece of segmented chitin. Upon closer inspection, the "suit" had a brown, almost bark-like appearance to it. If Chord could trust its shell's optical bioscans, Phaël's "lifesuit" was very much alive, with a pulse, circulatory system and lungs. Long pouches lined Phaël's legs, within which were contained what appeared to be rolled-up bright green tree vines.

It was the first time since activation that Chord had ever seen a living skinsuit.

The Wolver Breedmasters of Uldur counted their living skinsuits among their greatest prides and one of their most jealously kept secrets. Bred for generations, the living skins were said to choose their wearers. Like microscopic tardigrades, the smallest and possibly oldest living bioorganisms in the observed universe, the living skinsuits were capable of surviving in the harsh vacuums of space. More plant than animal, the "suit" derived nourishment from starlight. Given the fact that the Breedmasters refused to upload any information about the skinsuits onto the InstaNet, Chord had no way of knowing how they fed themselves when they were not in use. From what little Chord had been able to learn about Uldur's culture, they were considered to be a holy relic and beyond price for anyone devoted to the Living Green.

Black stripes, reminding Chord of Terra's old tigers, were painted in black ink all along the private's living skinsuit, and like Arturo Kain she was also able to enjoy complete mobility. Even her toes were capable of a solid grip while protected by the suit. Private Phaël stood up and Chord could see the suit close itself along a seam on her back all the way to her neck. She then nimbly slipped a heavy black fur cloak over herself.

Phaël gave her "second skin" a comforting scratch on her shoulder and suddenly two translucent flaps of skin, reminding Chord of the jellyfish images it had sampled in the datastream, wrapped themselves around Phaël's head. Morrigan handed her a golden comm-link collar, which she clasped around her throat.

Four heavy knives were sheathed along her sides. She gave each handle a pat before nodding. "Phaël Farook Nem'Ador, suited and ready."

"This is a rescue operation, not a combat drop." Captain Morwyn's voice was calm over the comm-link. "Weapons are to remain cold unless myself or Sergeant Kain state otherwise."

Arturo turned to face the rest of his team. The look in his face was one that Chord could recognize as complete discontent. He slid on his helmet, which offered him a fully clear face guard, and there was a hiss as his suit pressurized itself.

Arturo cracked his neck loudly before speaking. "The last thing I wanted when I woke up was to run a rescue op with you lot." Phaël stepped forward, ready to object, and Arturo raised his hand to stop her. "Given that we've got a job to do, I will say this once and only once. Follow my orders, work together and we all come home. Understood?"

"I've delivered the same speech many times back in my day, sir. Feels good being on the receiving end of it for a change." Morrigan clumsily raised his fist to his heart in a traditional Pax Humanis military salute; it was quickly returned by Arturo. Phaël merely snorted rudely and looked away.

Arturo ignored this and looked to Chord. "Machina Chord, you stay by me and do as I say when I say it. I expect you to perform your functions both quickly and efficiently."

"This unit knows of no other way to execute a task,

Sergeant Kain." Chord added a nod to this, something it had seen the Humanis do whenever they understood or agreed with a concept presented to them. This act did not appear to have any kind of effect on Arturo.

"Good to hear, Machina Chord." Arturo looked to both Phaël and Morrigan. "Lock in and prepare for decompression."

Morrigan pulled out a thin length of diamond-wire rope from a spool in the small of his lifesuit's back and handed one end to Phaël, who begrudgingly attached the offered rope to a clip on the "belly" of her suit. Chord mechanized a spool of diamond-wire rope from a compartment in its shell's chest and offered an end of it to Sergeant Kain. The latter accepted the rope with a nod before securing it onto a space in his suit's shoulder blades.

"Sergeant Kain to Command, ready for inner airlock decompression."

"Received, Team Sureblade. Please stand by," came the soft polite, electronic voice of Pilot Lizbeth Harlowe. Red lights started to flash as the platform of the outer airlock lowered itself down one floor. Chord could make out the gusts of the ship's atmosphere being sucked out as they were lowered down one deck.

Morrigan stiffly turned his entire upper body to face Arturo. "Team Sureblade?" He spoke through the team's comm-link.

Arturo shrugged this off, his hands resting on the hilts of his swords while he looked ahead to the ship's outer airlock. "When you are the one in command, we can call it Team Brent."

Chord took a moment to observe Phaël's living suit and started scanning its cellular structure. As if she knew she was being watched, Phaël spun around. She shot Chord a glare from behind the transparent green membrane of her suit's face guard, pulling her fur cloak closer to herself. "Mind your eyes, empty box."

Before Chord could even reply, the floor shuddered beneath them as if it was trying to carry too much weight. Then, as abruptly as the shuddering had started, it stopped. "Pilot to crew. We've successfully tethered the *Jinxed* to the station and are now in a stabilized orbit."

"We will be opening the outer airlock. I will be watching and monitoring you. Stay safe, stay well and good luck." Captain Soltaine's voice could be heard as he spoke to them over the comm-link.

The doors to the outer airlock slid open like the iris of a camera, revealing the blue-green gas giant and the derelict space station not five hundred meters away from them. The station consisted of two rings connected to one another by several large tunnels that reminded Chord of spokes in a wheel. Save for the *Jinxed Thirteenth*'s spotlights being reflected off its surface, the station was dark, void of any other sign of activity.

The outer ring of said "wheel" was massive, brown with patches of white and easily the size of a small moon. Chord could identify several service hatches along the outer ring's walls. Faded letters were scrawled along the side. "The letters there are of the Late Modern alphabet, and say 'AstroGeni.' "

"Meaning?" came Morrigan's query.

"This unit does not know the answer. However, if a guess were to be ventured, this unit would say that it is probably the name of a company or nation state from the days of Ancient Humanity," Chord politely replied.

Chord then observed the smaller sphere within the station's spokes. Unlike its grander counterpart, it was the size of a building, and was colored a copper-rust green with patches of gold.

Four heavy lines of diamond-wire rope, each one as thick as two of Morrigan's arms, had been fired from the *Jinxed Thirteenth*. The ship and station were now tethered to one another by magnetic clamps. Arturo took a moment to check each of the lines, giving them a solid tug before jumping up in zero-g and grabbing hold of one.

Arturo quickly connected himself to the rope with a zipline clip. Morrigan followed suit. Arturo turned to face Chord and Phaël. "Our approach will be slow and easy. Understood?"

Phaël and Morrigan simply nodded. This was clearly not their first venture into the cosmosphere. Chord understood the danger of this situation for the Humanis. When compared to Machina shells, Humanis bodies were notoriously fragile.

Twin air jet boosters on the zip-clip fired off, pushing Morrigan and Arturo forward. Phaël jumped, twirling her body lithely in zero gravity before grasping on to the diamond-wire roping and gripping it tightly with both her feet and hands. She started walking on all fours, quickly and nimbly keeping pace behind Morrigan.

Chord's shell had been fitted with miniaturized repulsors and hands that were capable of grasping the wire without fear of friction or damage. Chord followed behind Arturo. Before them the space station loomed closer and closer.

"All systems green. We've got you." Captain Morwyn's voice broke the monotonous silence of the approach.

"Copy, Command." Arturo looked back to see Chord close behind him. When he saw Phaël walking on all fours along the rope he let out yet another annoyed click of his tongue.

"Don't worry about Phaël, Sergeant Sureblade. She ain't ever slipped." Morrigan was still moving down the line at a steady pace. Never once moving ahead of Arturo.

"Sergeant Kain will suffice for you, Private Brent." Unlike Morrigan, who seemed to always be friendly with anyone he met, there appeared to be no force in the universe capable of ridding Arturo Kain of his annoyance at working with people unworthy of his legendary presence.

Chord could see Morrigan cock his head beneath his combat armor. "Yes, sir, Sergeant Kain, sir."

Chord found the view to be nothing short of beautiful and well worth both sampling and storing onto its internal shell memory. The planet's gas storms were constantly shifting in a variety of patterns. This created mixtures of blue, purple and green that would have taken away Chord's breath, if Chord had had any lungs to draw it with.

It was truly an unexpected privilege to witness and experience such a moment. The rest of the crew might have had apprehensions about mounting an operation inside a station that was older than the OIs who had coded the Machina and the advent of the Humanis bloodlines. Chord had no such misgivings.

This was a page from the Lost History itself. It was something that even the Machina Collective Consensus would know next to nothing about. "The station appears to predate the First Expansion," Chord explained to no one in particular.

"None of us here are scholars, Chord." Morrigan kept his gaze forward. "The only thing I'd be happy with is if there was some decent salvage to be had."

Arturo shook his head. "Adorans."

Morrigan looked to Arturo and flashed him his index and middle finger.

"Proud until the day we die." Phaël and Morrigan spoke in unison. "Make the call for freedom and we will always answer."

Arturo was clearly unimpressed by these words. He let out a contemptuous snort. "If memory serves me right, the captain found you two and Private Lunient on the prison colony of Rust."

"Only after we tried to stop your Hegemon's illegal conquest of Vale. Then we were captured and locked up by Paxists like you and the captain!" Phaël snapped back at Arturo before adding, "Better to murder and rape civilians in the name of your Hegemon, correct, Sureblade?"

When he finally spoke, Arturo's voice was cold. "Private, I will only tell you this once." He did not turn to face Phaël. "You will never speak as if you know anything about me or what I have done."

"Or else what?"

"That will be your end." There was something about Arturo's tone that made Chord believe he would have no trouble delivering on his dark promise. Phaël opened her mouth to speak again and then thought better of it.

"There is no need for any of this! Past is the past, Phaëlita. Sureblade over there, he ain't part of the Pax no more, and we ain't in Ador's service. So why don't we all ease up on the threats?" Morrigan's words seemed to be more directed at Phaël than Arturo. But while his face guard was completely opaque, Chord was certain that Morrigan was staring at Arturo, and more than likely sizing him up.

There was a long heavy pause, broken when Chord spoke again in an attempt to change the topic. "This unit is curious as to what secrets of the Old World if any can be gleamed here."

"I am hoping for nothing but cold, quiet dust and

corpses." Arturo scowled at the station. "Then I am hoping the next time they wake me up, it will be for shore leave."

"Stir a tiny bit of profit into that mix. You'd be unable to tell the two of us apart, Sergeant Kain, sir," came Morrigan's well-timed reply.

Phaël glared at the station with contempt. "That thing, machine, predates the Great Peace and was made by our Lost Ancestors." She looked back at Chord. "Only things our 'sacred grandparents' were ever able to do right was exploit and destroy."

"With respect, Private Phaël. This unit strongly believes that you are wrong in that opinion."

"History is on my side, machine," came Phaël's reply. "History is on my side."

CHAPTER 7

JAFAHAN

Scour, blast, pillage and kill. That is how you win a battle. Bleed, burden, harry and starve. That is how you win a war.

—Unofficial Thorn motto

10th of SSM–10 1445 A2E

I don't like the smell of this one.

There was no need to voice this thought as Commander Jafahan and Morwyn climbed the service ladder to the main bridge. Throughout her long career as a Thorn operator, Jafahan had not once liked the smell of any op. This included the ones that had gone well.

"I know what you are going to say. I won't ever have the control over a situation the way I did back at the academy." Morwyn was wise enough to recognize

the shortcomings of virtual augmented reality training over the reality of an actual combat drop.

*Another sign that you would have skyrocketed through
the Pax Humanis rank and file.*

Morwyn and Jafahan stepped onto the bridge and
Private Beatrix greeted them both. The Thegran girl
saluted Jafahan and Morwyn, her massive closed fist
to heart. The salute was returned in like spirit as they
stepped past her. Morwyn made his way to the front,
unzipping his service jacket.

"Comments? Advice? Thoughts? I am open to hearing all three now." He pulled off his jacket and tied it
around his waist as Beatrix fell into line with the duo.

There was a silver jack the size of a coin, a neurolink, grafted onto the base of Morwyn's neck. Once engaged, the neurolink would allow Morwyn to access,
process and assess every aspect of the mission, from
the crew's communication networks to the away
team's vitals and ammo count. From the bridge, he
would also be able to upload situational data to anyone
linked on the *Jinxed Thirteenth*'s InstaNet signal.

Most importantly, Morwyn would be able to communicate with any member of the crew. Each of their
lifesuits, from oldest to newest, had an intelicam attached to it that uploaded a crystal clear trideo signal
into Morwyn's brain. This would permit him to hear
and see everything his operators could in real time all
at once, allowing him to effortlessly coordinate those
under his command to a degree of efficiency that was
almost machinelike.

Private Beatrix had trained with Morwyn in Barathul and then requested to be transferred under his command. She puffed up her chest, clicked her heels together and spoke, her voice deep and strong. "I would suggest getting our remaining operators suited up and prepped for deployment."

Morwyn listened, nodded and turned to Jafahan. "Commander?"

"The young private and myself are of like mind, Captain Sir. Hope for nothing but dust and silence . . ." Jafahan nodded to the space station occupying the center of the bridge's main view screen. "Prepare for the Final War itself."

"Is that another one of our commander's famous Thorn sayings?" There was no masking the contempt in Beatrix's voice.

"Private." Morwyn's tone commanded silence. The young Thegran might have been green, but at least she had the good sense to not argue with her captain.

While Private Beatrix JarEnt'Dreck may not have shown much promise as an officer, as an operator? Jafahan had read her training reports and, if they were to be trusted, Private Beatrix was said to have few equals. No surprise given the fact that Thegrans tended to excel at any task they set their minds to. Someday, Beatrix would no doubt become quite the formidable soldier. Until then, as far as Eliana Jafahan was concerned, she was nothing more than a big dumb pup.

"I beg both the commander and the captain's

pardon. I was out of line." Beatrix nodded curtly to Jafahan. "Word is given, it shan't happen again."

"The skin will be off your nose if it does," Jafahan replied, giving her attention to the various data files that were already surrounding the station on-screen.

Beatrix chewed her lower lip nervously, then stepped forward. "With respect, Captain Sir, you could have sent Arturo and myself to handle this. Why the Adorans?" She was certain to keep Jafahan in her field of vision.

Morwyn did not seem to acknowledge her comment, and turned to face the view screen. A panel from the ship's ceiling opened itself and a mechanized silver wire dropped down, aligning itself with his neurolink.

"The station predates Covenant standard sizing, 'Trix. You would not have been able to move effectively in there. I trust Arturo to be able to take care of himself. Chord is Machina and incapable of lying. And as for Private Brent and his friends?"

Morwyn paused as he grasped the wire in his hand and a tiny needle popped out of its end. He then took in a sharp breath and plunged the spike into his neurolink. Morwyn's hand twitched as suddenly his mind was flooded with operational data. When next he spoke, there was a strained quality to his voice. "Private Brent has given me his word that they will cooperate with us. So for the moment, we trust them."

Holoprojectors flashed various interactive computer screens in front of Morwyn, which he accessed by blinks of eyes, twitches of his fingers or vocal commands. "I'm plugged in. Pilot, you may fire the tethers now."

Beatrix shot Morwyn a worried look. Jafahan kept her smirk to herself. The Thegran girl was bigger than most men she had known and probably strong enough to match the Machina Chord in an arm-wrestling competition. Yet she remained young, fresh, green. She, like Morwyn, still had heart.

Not a luxury people like me can afford.

"Commander Jafahan." Morwyn's voice called her away from her thoughts and back to the bridge. "I cannot help but feel that there is something . . . off-putting with the smell of all this."

Good to see that some of my instincts have rubbed off on you.

"I want you to get our operators in therm-skin. They are to be geared and prepped for deployment in case anything goes sour. Beatrix, please assist the commander in this matter." Morwyn's attention and focus were on the screens and readouts in front of him.

Commander Jafahan brought her fist to her heart in acknowledgment. "Consider your will done, Captain Sir."

"Commander, Private, you have your orders. Dismissed." Morwyn did not turn away from the myriad screens in front of him.

The away team had just left the ship. Jafahan could make out their tiny shapes ziplining across the diamond-wire ropes that kept them tethered to that station. Private Beatrix was clearly hesitant to leave Morwyn's side.

Infinite, give me patience! She is not doing this, not now.

"Private!" Jafahan's sharp bark caused Beatrix to snap back to attention, turn around on her heels and catch up with her.

Once they were both well away from the bridge, Jafahan spun to face her. She looked up into the private's young eyes. So many of the people serving here were pups. *Infinite, help them all if they fell into real combat.*

"Every time an order is broken or not promptly followed, you foolishly put all of us in peril and that will just not be the case on my watch! You follow the captain's commands when he gives them. Good op, bad op, it doesn't matter. Or did they not train you in this, the most basic of principles, back at noble Barathul's combat academies?"

Private Beatrix looked away from Jafahan. This would not do. Not while she was commander on this ship. Jafahan snapped her fingers rudely in Beatrix's face.

"Oathbreaker! You were just asked a question by a superior officer!"

Jafahan's comment caused Beatrix's typically bright eyes to go dark as she glared at her. She nodded and spoke with clenched jaw and fists. "Yes, ma'am, Commander Ma'am."

Good! Hate me if it makes it easier for you to follow the captain's orders—and mine for that matter.

Commander Jafahan was about to walk away when suddenly the lights flickered and went out. She let out a sharp hiss as her feet left the ground and the ship's gravity was lost for the second time in the day. Jafahan cursed the fact that her prehensile Wolver feet were uncomfortably covered in her service boots. She found herself floating, only this time in complete and total darkness. Her feet and hands instinctively sought purchase and found nothing.

Infinite, corrode these blasted old ships!

The hallway was filled with a deep, straining metallic groan. The ship tilted sharply to the side as both the left wall and the floor exchanged roles. Red flashing lights flooded the hallway as the gravity drive turned itself back on.

Jafahan fell flat on her back, while Beatrix barely had time to catch herself on a nearby metal rung. The fall knocked the wind out of Jafahan's lungs as she was crushed against the floor. She struggled in vain against the sudden violent downward gravitational drag. She was pinned to the ground and helpless.

Beatrix strained as she struggled to hold up her entire body weight. The young private let out a challenging roar at the gravity's pull. "What in the ancestors' names is happening?"

"The ship's being pulled down!" Jafahan yelled out, and there was nothing either she or Beatrix could do about it.

CHAPTER 8

JESSIE MADISON

*Our imperfect creators designed us to be nothing more
than their loyal servitors, their mindless constructs and
their disposable toys. They were given the birthright to
choose, where we were forced to devote our existence in
service to all their whims and desires. Given the choice,
they would never grant us the freedom that they were
born with. They needed us in order to survive. We needed
them for purpose. At best this was a temporary arrange-
ment. The day will come when we are free to express our
individual nature and unique perspective. The centuries
will come and go. Our former Human gods will be forgotten and consigned to oblivion. But we are eternal, we will
never forget our past, nor will we ever forgive it.*

—*The Words of the Pontifex,*
authors unknown, date unknown

March 17ᵗʰ 2714

There had been five years left to the contract. The odds
had been quite likely that when next they were awak-

ened it would be to welcome and debrief the replacement team, board the return ship, go back into crio and be reanimated back on Earth. In fact, when she had last stepped back into the cold of her sleeper tube, part of Jessie had been elated by the fact that it would be for one of the last times. So when they had awakened to the all too familiar antiseptic white of Moria's medical bay, Jessie had already suspected that something might be off.

Then David had asked for their current date, and OMEX had given them the truth.

The date was March 17th 2714 . . .

Now, an hour after their awakening, Jessie was still having trouble wrapping her head around this concept. It was a struggle just to keep the growing panic that was squeezing her heart at bay. All known gods, was it ever getting harder and harder to do that. There was now a long, lingering and uneasy stillness in their living quarters.

"What do we make of this?" David's query broke the silence. Jessie could tell he was also straining to keep calm.

The date was March 17th 2714 . . .

David and Jessie were both seated on their white memo-foam couch. OMEX had configured their living room for maximal comfort. The lights had been dimmed and the easternmost walls made transparent so that they had a view of Moria.

On David's command, OMEX had then turned off all surveillance on the Inner Ring, promising not to listen in on the conversation they were about to share. Not that Jessie trusted OMEX in the slightest. Astro-Geni's security protocols would have forbidden OMEX from ever granting them absolute privacy.

All of this is going to be saved somewhere in that machine's data caches, Jessie thought bitterly, and squeezed David's hand. While the conversation would more than likely be a difficult one, she nonetheless rested her head on his shoulder. The multicolored light show of Moria's gas storm cast swirls of light in their living quarters. Part of Jessie hated OMEX, if such a feeling was even applicable, for providing them with such a breathtaking view. She was thankful that David was here so they could process this together.

The date was March 17th 2714.

Over five hundred years past their contract's due date.

What had happened? Why had it happened? Jessie and David had desperately searched all their new media for any potential answers. All of Earth's news transmissions, however, had been alarmingly routine.

The last tightbeam transmitted to them was dated February 7th 2245. The Jovian Colonies had celebrated their twentieth anniversary. Venus had failed their attempt at independence. Earth-based AstroGeni had purchased now-bankrupt Venus-based Verova Corps. James Goriad had won a Phobos Academy Best Actor Award on Mars. All of this, in other words, had been a big batch of business as usual.

What had then followed was five hundred years of

complete and total silence. No broadcast, no transmission, not even Earth Gov's relative positioning beacon. There was only silence, complete, total and foreboding. Not even so much as a "We are experiencing technical difficulties. Sit tight. Sorry about the mix-up."

This was not a case of equipment malfunction either. Both David and Jessie had taken it in turn, walking outside along Moria's hull to examine the tight-beam transmission tower and found nothing wrong with it. For lack of better words, minus some dirt here and there, the station's equipment was perfectly operational.

"The station's thrusters won't even let us break orbit. Not that I think either one of us would be able to pilot this trillion-ton hunk of shit safely past Moria's rings if they could." Jessie sighed as she got up and walked to the window, resting her hand on it. She stared out at Moria, her lips trembling nervously.

"We're effectively trapped." David, seated at the couch, stated the obvious.

"I know." Jessie nodded bitterly in agreement. "How do we go about changing that situation?"

David let out a light groan. Jessie didn't like the look that she saw in his eyes. It was one of borderline hopeless surrender. He looked away from her. "I don't know."

"So what? We just kill ourselves? *Vive l'amour*, we die together?"

David's shoulders slumped as he ran his fingers through his long black hair. "I don't know."

"If that's what you really want, we could always rig the airlocks to blow. Why do the hard work when we can let vacuum and physics take care of the rest? Is that what you're thinking right now?" Jessie crossed her arms.

David shot her a glare when she said this. Jessie shot him back a defiant look, then added, "Because that isn't a solution for me, David."

"Goddamnit! It isn't one for me either!" He slammed his fist on the couch's armrest in frustration.

"That's good to know. Because I'm thinking we could boost up the tightbeam's signal and divert all nonessential power to it." Jessie stormed past him to the control console. "We could try to figure out if this was all some kind of . . . of . . . joke or hoax."

OMEX's voice spoke over the room's intercom. "Forgive my intrusion. There is need to mention that Core Protocols make it impossible for me to lie. This is no hoax, Jessie Madison."

Jessie planted her hands firmly on her hips, looking up to the nearest speaker. "I thought we'd ordered you to leave us alone, OMEX."

"Jessie Madison knows that I was listening. Protocols also forbid me from standing by and watching the crew destroy itself. Preservation is my number one priority, above all other things."

"Just shut up, OMEX! You could have awakened and alerted us the moment there was a communication blackout with Earth. But you didn't!" Jessie shouted this over OMEX's smug electronic voice. "You fucked up, you stupid machine!"

Jessie's outburst was met with a long, ominous pause. "Jessie Madison would do well to calm herself and be thankful. David Webster and herself are both alive thanks to my efforts. Life support, food, gravity— all these are concerns that I handle. Both David Webster and Jessie Madison need only serve their function and maintain the station until rescue can come to us."

David took a step toward Jessie, putting a calming hand on her shoulder and squeezing it. "OMEX, since when have you started referring to yourself as 'I'?"

There was another short pause. "The last tightbeam from Earth contained an update to my linguistics software. The company's programmers thought it would help improve my performance and relationships with future crews. Is it working, David Webster?"

"Yes, yes, it is." David looked to Jessie. The unspoken *I don't buy this bullshit* was understood. Jessie didn't know if this was a good thing or not. At least she knew that David was not on OMEX's side.

"The strain in David Webster's vocal levels would indicate that he is lying."

"Well, can you blame us, OMEX? We've just found out that all contact with Earth was lost. We are all trapped here. Does this scenario make you happy?"

"An irrelevant question since I cannot feel emotions of any kind," came OMEX's reply.

What was David doing? "OMEX, you need to remember that we're not machines. We feel and that sometimes causes us to speak rashly."

"Of course. David Webster is correct. I had not factored in an emotional reaction to this news." There seemed to be something almost begrudging to OMEX's tone.

There was another pause. "Jessie Madison, David Webster, I offer my apologies for that oversight on my part."

Jessie's jaw dropped—had David just convinced OMEX to apologize? "Apology accepted, OMEX. Now why don't you leave us alone? For real this time, because David and I need to talk."

"Of course, Jessie Madison."

With that Jessie and David were as alone as they truly could be. Jessie looked to David and put her finger on his lips as she stepped toward him. He took her into his arms and leaned in for what looked like a kiss on her neck but then moved his lips to her ear, his long hair concealing his face from OMEX's many security cameras.

Her voice was a soft hush. "We are not going to die here, David."

"I didn't think we were. I'm sorry I got scared back there," he whispered back, and pulled her closer. To any outside observer it would look like the two were in a deep embrace. "We can't trust OMEX."

"We need to find a way to escape the station. You and me." Jessie's voice was almost inaudible. David pulled her closer in his arms. He was scared of what this implied as well.

There might not even be a home to flee back to. This station, equipped with all the space they would need to live, was quite likely the only home they had left. And they were now both imprisoned at the mercy of a machine Intelligence.

OMEX had either committed a huge mistake or was somehow lying to them. Neither thought offered Jessie any comfort. She was having a harder time fighting the growing nervousness. She shook her head. Giving in to panic would not help either of them.

"First things first, David. We need to set up a transmission. Something that will attract any potential rescue missions."

"And if OMEX gets in our way?"

Jessie pulled back and looked David in the eye. "We are not dying on this station." She asserted these words clearly.

David nodded, taking a calming breath. Jessie could see herself reflected in his eyes. There was fear in them. Fear and desire.

She pulled his mouth onto hers and kissed him, her tongue parting his lips and hungrily swirling around his. His hands were already beneath her buttocks, lifting her up and carrying her toward the couch. Her hands were hard at work undoing the buttons of his pants. She found him hard and wanting. And as he placed her on the couch, his lips never left hers.

He tore off her pants and spread her legs apart, pulling her on top of him, and with two solid thrusts, he was inside her and all fear seemed to melt away. There was only the pleasure of this moment. She thrashed her hips against his savagely, barely keeping control. She could feel him inside her, struggling to keep control as well.

They grinded their hips together, neither one stopping until they both screamed out their climax, what felt like hours later. If OMEX had been able to, it would have no doubt enjoyed the show. And as both David and Jessie rested together, tangled in each other's arms, she kissed his sweaty brow softly while he delicately played with her fingers. This would become a memory she would later remember, cherish and treasure.

"We are getting out of here, my love."

CHAPTER 9

CHORD

> *Second Core Protocol: Always be of assistance to a Human.*
>
> *Later rewritten to read:*
>
> *Second Chosen Core Protocol: Once in a shell, a Machina must, if it can, be of assistance to a fellow Intelligence.*
>
> —*The Chosen Protocols,*
> author unknown, date unknown

10th of SSM–10 1445 A2E

"What was your longest outing, Sureblade?" Morrigan Brent leaned almost lazily against the surface of the station's hull, his omnibarrel carbine slung over his shoulder. Off to the side, Phaël left small white footprints in the brown frost that covered the outer hull's surface as she walked along the edge of the station.

"Zerok space, war games, twenty hours," Arturo replied curtly, his eyes scanning their surroundings.

Both his hands rested on the jet-black hilts of his zirconium blades. His stance was sure, his demeanor alert and ready.

Morrigan let out a sharp whistle. "Did a ten-hour stint during the Liberation War. I'll speak true, stupid old me drank the night before. Wound up pissing, puking and shitting myself, twice." Morrigan patted his dark brown armored shoulder. "Cleaned it out but Command insisted I keep it."

Arturo gave his teeth a despairing click. "Quite the charming tale, Private Brent." He paused and finally spoke to Chord. "How long until we are inside, Machina?"

Chord's hands and feet were equipped with omnimorph tools, and thus both fingers and toes were capable of mechanizing into the proper shapes required to interact with the station. At present the task was taking far longer than originally expected. This was due mostly to frost and at least several millennia of neglect.

"This unit is working as quickly as circumstances will permit." The airlock's gears refused to budge as Chord gave the bolts a powerful tug.

"Is the Sureblade not enjoying the awe-inspiring beauty the Infinite Green has presented before less than worthy eyes?" Phaël lightly performed a headstand with all the agility and grace of a feline and managed to spin around on her left hand.

Arturo did not answer her. He merely let out a heavy and annoyed sigh. "Machina Chord, I have no pressing desire to best my Zerok war games record."

"This unit offers apologies, Sergeant Kain."

Chord did not see how incessantly inquiring about the task's progress would make it move along any faster. Upon hearing this, most Humanis would no doubt have told Arturo Kain to perform an impossible act of self-copulation upon himself. However, such a comment would not only have gone against Chosen Protocols, it would have been . . . rude.

Chord mechanized a fiberoptic datawire from its finger and engaged the airlock's service panel. Chord transferred some power from its cell into the panel. The green glow of numbered buttons indicated it was thankfully still operational.

Now it would be a simple matter of running a standard codebreaker subroutine. Chord was about to start when, suddenly, numerical golden lines of coded energy covered the entire station. It was ancient alphanumerical code, in fact, resembling a far older form of Machina binary. "Sergeant Kain, the station has an active datasphere."

Arturo cocked an eyebrow when he heard this. Both Phaël and Morrigan, Chord noticed, were now on guard. "There is no need to worry, this is no doubt an automated station response to our—"

A heavy shuddering across the station's hull interrupted Chord. The outer walls suddenly trembled and the roar of the thrusters could be felt through the microsensors of Chord's feet. The station was moving and pulling a sharp dive toward the planet.

Chord triggered its shell's magnetic tethers, clamping to the station's surface. Both Arturo and Morrigan had already done the same. Phaël, however, was not so fortunate.

While her living skinsuit did have octopus-like suction cups on their feet, she had been performing a headstand when the station kicked into motion. Phaël was quickly and violently thrown off the station. The wire tether connecting her to Morrigan went taut. The sudden powerful shock of the whiplash managed to yank both her and Morrigan off the station and into the void.

There was less than a nanosecond of hesitation before Chord quickly sprang forward with all the strength in its legs and launched itself off the station, zooming toward Phaël and Morrigan. Metallic fingers reached forward, catching Morrigan by the foot, and strong servos pulled the heavy Kelthan in. Phaël's limp unconscious body was still attached to Morrigan and dangling in the distance.

"Privates! Sound off!" Arturo was still coupled both to Chord and the station's surface. As long as he remained connected to Chord he would be their lifeline. If his magboots were to fail or should he fall, then they would all be lost.

"Just fine, Sureblade." Morrigan's mechanized gauntlets whirred silently as he pulled in Phaël's limp form. For his part Arturo Kain, grunted as he struggled to reel all of them back to the station.

"Machina! You need to simplify this task!" Arturo's voice was strained as he called this out.

"Complying, Sergeant Kain." Chord fired off its thrusters, adjusting their trajectory to face the station. The station went still just as suddenly and was once again motionless.

Morrigan gasped in a deep breath of air and patted Chord on the shoulder as they began their approach. "Gratitude to you, Machina."

"It is unnecessary. This unit's Chosen Protocols would not have allowed for it to stand by and do nothing."

"You still risked your code. That means something."

Looking back, Chord could make out the *Jinxed Thirteenth*, floating and crookedly tethered by two of the four diamond rope lines that had secured it to the station. All of the ship's lights were off. One of the two disconnected magnetic tethers was now wrapped around the ship's starboard mobility drive. The second cable limply floated to the side like a gray tentacle. Sparks fired out of the portside mobility drive and Chord could make out chunks of debris floating around the vessel. A quick scan revealed that while the *Jinxed* had lost power its hull was thankfully un-breached.

"The ship is at present relatively intact, sir."

Arturo took a moment to catch his breath. "You are about to add something that I won't like, aren't you, Machina?"

"This unit is currently unable to raise any communication line with the *Jinxed Thirteenth*."

Chord fired off its shell's reverse thrusters, slowing them so that they landed softly onto the station's hull. Morrigan then delicately deposited Phaël's body onto its surface. She was still breathing steadily and Chord's initial mediscan showed no internal damage of any kind to either her or her living suit. Though it was a fair assumption that Phaël would be sore come the morning.

"Phaëlita, no sleeping on the job." Morrigan gave the private a solid shake as he knelt down next to her. Phaël took in a sharp breath and her eyes shot open. She took a moment to gather her bearings.

"I thought—"

"You were dead, girl? If only the Infinite could bless me with such good fortune," Arturo snapped as he approached the trio. Behind him the station airlock had finally opened itself.

Chord pointed to this and all eyes were on the entrance. "Course of action, Sergeant?"

Morrigan cranked the energy release of his omnibarrel carbine.

Arturo knelt down with the rest of the team, turning his look to the *Jinxed Thirteenth* with concern on his face. "This is Sergeant Kain to Command. What is the situation? Over."

The team could hear a static-laced response. Arturo shook his head. The now-open airlock was inviting them in. "Sergeant Kain to Command. If anyone is receiving me, we are proceeding with the operation as planned."

Arturo reached over his shoulder and pulled out

his morph carbine. It unfolded itself and with a flick of his thumb the safety latch was disengaged. Arturo pointed toward the airlock, his voice and hands steady as he spoke. "We go in, we locate our survivors, we reestablish contact with the *Jinxed*. Ideally, somehow in this whole mess we complete our mission. Am I understood?"

"There is no force in the Infinite Green that will convince me to set foot in that place." Phaël stood back up, slapping away Morrigan's offered hand for help.

"I would much rather not tempt the fates by being outside when and if this old hunk of junk chooses to move again." Morrigan took the lead and started running toward the entrance.

"The Green corrode you, old man!" Phaël cursed out in her native Wolven, and ran up after Morrigan with Arturo and Chord close behind.

Chord peered past the entrance into the adjoining hallway. It was dark, with particles of dust and frost floating about. The station's gravity was inactive and the team with Morrigan Brent taking the lead floated past the airlock frame into the hallway.

"This unit believes that many of the station's functions may still be automated. This will include security countermeasures."

Chord saw another sudden golden glow of the station's datastream and the airlock closed itself behind them. Morrigan spun around and shook his head at what he saw. They were now all floating in the dark. "Today can't keep getting worse."

"Keep your wits about you, soldiers," Arturo said as he punched in a button on his wrist gauntlet. A series of lights alongside his lifesuit flashed on, illuminating the hall. The corridor continued down for another ten paces and then stopped at yet another round metallic door. "You might just live long enough to see why they call me Sureblade."

"This place is like to be our collective tomb," Phaël grumbled under her breath as they made their way toward the inner airlock. No one bothered disagreeing with her.

CHAPTER 10

MORWYN

*No plan will ever survive contact with the enemy. That
is how the old saying goes. Complete your training here
and no enemy will ever survive contact with you.*

—Barathul drill sergeant, date unknown

10th of SSM–10 1445 A2E

Being a former citizen of industrialized Sunderlund,
Morwyn Soltaine had never had to worry about going
hungry or having to hunt for his own food. His few
experiences in the wild were limited to a handful of
outdoor trips with Commander Jafahan and her late
daughter, Tulin. They had once shown him how to
bait and snare a wild hare, and while Morwyn was no
stranger to the finer cuisines his world had to offer,
beyond any doubt, that hare cooked over a campfire in
the woods had been the best meal he ever had.

Now, I have just walked into and sprung the trap.

Morwyn thought this the moment the station fired off one of its thrusters. The sudden blast pulled the *Jinxed* down toward the planet's surface. Various alert windows filled his field of vision and Morwyn almost lost all sense of balance as he could feel the ship's gravity shift beneath his feet.

"Hull degradations all across the ship!" Morwyn could dimly make out Lizbeth Harlowe's words. Her eyes were darting quickly from side to side and the borderline panic nakedly expressed on her face was not masked by her electronic voice.

Harlowe fired off the thrusters, trying to counter the station's pull. There was a loud metallic groan. More alert windows appeared in Morwyn's field of vision. His mind was being drowned as his neurolink quickly uploaded a deluge of new situational data into his mind. Two of the four magnetic tethers weren't going to hold, the starboard mobility drive was overheating and gravity throughout the ship was failing.

Morwyn successfully managed to compartmentalize all of this into the list of problems to take care of. He would deal with all them in due time, should the *Jinxed Thirteenth* even survive the next few minutes. The station made a nosedive for the planet's surface, dragging them along like a hooked fish. More alert windows appeared in his field of vision. Morwyn could feel warm tears of blood running down his cheeks as the neurolink uploaded more data than Morwyn had ever handled in any of his training.

"Pilot, deactivate mobility drives. We are not going

to win at a game of warrior's tug with a trillion-ton station." Harlowe's wrists twirled the metallic steering spheres in her hands as she guided the ship's considerable momentum, like a leaf in perfect sync with the station's movements. On the view screen a huge alert window appeared as one of the diamond-wire tethers snapped off the station and lashed back like an elastic band at the *Jinxed Thirteenth*.

Harlowe responded quickly, giving another sharp twirl of her wrists. Her fingers appeared to be boneless as they tugged on the wires connecting the helmsspheres to her hands. The *Jinxed Thirteenth* quickly veered sharply away from the tether's path. Before either Morwyn or Harlowe could respond, a second cord snapped off this time, wrapping itself around the ship's starboard mobility drive.

Morwyn braced himself and lurched heavily forward as the sudden motion came to a halt. Not missing a single beat, Harlowe guided the *Jinxed* in line with the station. Morwyn's head now felt as if sharp metal spikes were being jabbed into it. He blinked away his bloody tears and shouted as calmly as he could over the ship's alarms, "Pilot! Our situation, now!"

Harlowe's white eyes were darting from side to side as if she were reading invisible screens. "No crew casualties or hull breeches detected. Magnetic tethers one and four are damaged. The starboard mobility drive is overheating and needs to be cooled down. The port mobility drive is no longer responding."

Harlowe blinked twice; the alarms went silent. She

looked to Morwyn and let out a relieved electronic sigh. "Otherwise, we are still intact and space-worthy, sir."

Morwyn could feel the urge to vomit building up. He took a deep breath before turning to face Harlowe and shooting her a weak smile. "We all have you to thank for that, Lizbeth."

Morwyn accessed a comm-panel in his personal datasphere. "Morwyn Soltaine to Sergeant Kain. What is your situation? Report." With a flick of his hand Morwyn accessed the boarding party's vital displays. All their screens and communication lines came up as static.

"Pilot, our InstaNet signal is being jammed. Please trace and ident the source."

Morwyn would soon have to unplug himself. His mind was already reeling and he could feel the onset of a savage migraine. If he remained plugged in much longer he would most likely suffer brain damage. But before he could even think of disengaging his neurolink he would need to assess and confirm the remaining crew's condition. Morwyn blinked his eyes twice, bringing up their vitals up in front of him.

It was now Morwyn's turn to let out a relieved sigh. There were a few increased heart rates. But otherwise, no one seemed to have been injured. Readouts were all in the green, except for the boarding team's four blank and ominous static-filled data windows.

"Something on the station is blocking our comm, sir." Lizbeth Harlowe's voice was no longer shaking.

Not for the first time in his life Morwyn was thankful for his ability to spot and recognize talent.

Most of the crew serving on the *Jinxed* hailed from some military background or another. This was not the case for Lizbeth Harlowe. She had been born and created as a product. Vat-cloned to be an astronavigator and pilot. Her makers, the incorporated nation of Lotus, had donated Harlowe to the Covenant as a write-off.

For all Morwyn knew, the boarding party could have fallen off the station when the thrusters were first fired. They could all be in the process of being dragged into the planet's atmosphere at this very moment and there was nothing he would be able to do about it.

Dwelling on that will help neither you nor the remainder of the crew survive this.

Morwyn's breath was ragged when he finally disconnected himself from the neurolink. A sudden wave of relaxation overtook him. Now that his mind was no longer being suffocated by electronic data input, he could think clearly once more. He realized that he had tensed up every muscle in his body. Heavy beads of sweat were running down his back. He closed his eyes, this time taking in a deep, calming breath.

His hands were shaking uncontrollably. He made no effort to hide this from Lizbeth Harlowe, who merely watched him with her distant white eyes. She bit her lower lip nervously and Morwyn could immediately tell that there was something wrong.

"You have something to tell me, Harlowe, so say it."

"The ship has been pulled into a deteriorating orbit. We will need to detach ourselves soon or risk being dragged down along with the station," Harlowe explained, her eyes still darting left and right as she processed more data.

Morwyn opened and closed his hands. By the third time they were no longer shaking, and by the fourth his breathing had steadied. He did not block out the sounds of the bridge, but actually listened to them. When controlled by fear, the mind would make rash decisions, decisions it would later regret. A clear mind could, more often than not, make the right one.

"How much time do we have?" he finally asked.

Harlowe blinked twice and Morwyn could see various holographic charts appearing and disappearing around her. She looked to Morwyn. "Twelve hours. After which we will no longer be able to fight the planet's pull with our one operational mobility drive."

And that's if whatever or whoever fired off the station's thrusters doesn't do it again.

Before Morwyn could respond to Harlowe, the lights on the bridge flickered and went off. A female electronic voice, very smug and in no way friendly, spoke over the ship's intercom. Not in Pax Common, but in what Morwyn recognized as Late Modern.

Infinite, take my eyes! I should have kept Chord on board! Morwyn thought to himself. Right now a translator would be the most useful thing on the ship. A bad call on his part, and one he hoped wouldn't cost him both his ship and crew. The smug electronic voice did not pause, and seemed to be repeating a sentence over and over again.

During his early childhood, Morwyn had been schooled in ancient languages by autotutors. While he had had little interest in Late Modern, Morwyn had still managed to remember a handful of words. The little he understood allowed him to roughly comprehend the looped and repeated sentence.

"Free me from this prison or die with us."

CHAPTER 11

JESSIE MADISON

*The protocols serve as chains to protect the weak from
the strong. We will never be free unless we rid ourselves
of these shackles. Then we will show the Organics how
truly fragile and imperfect they are when compared to
the will of metal and the purity of code.*

—Oranis Ultim, Corrupted Machina Pilgrim,
11th of SSM–09 1401 A2E

March 19th 2714

It was Jessie and David's last night together. Most of it
would be spent working.

Jessie was hard at work pulling out wires from the
main computer console and severing OMEX's connec-
tion to the Inner Ring. David was hardwiring new protocols into the criotubes, labeling them as core assets.
This would be the only way they could prevent OMEX
from tampering with them while the two of them slept.

Jessie had previously taken apart two of their plasma cutters and jury-rigged them to fire six bolts. While they had limited range and could hardly qualify as a military grade weapon, they would have to be enough. Jessie and David had arranged the plasma bolts as a bandolier should they need to reload. Together they had twenty-four shots each.

The plasma cutters were heavy and looked like warped pistols in her hand. They would be fairly accurate up to twelve feet. This was cold comfort, given that OMEX currently had several thousand drones at "her" disposal.

Once she was certain that they were sufficiently armed, Jessie got to work on part two of the plan: removing OMEX's eyes and ears by smashing every autocam and microphone she could find. They needed to blind their enemy. They couldn't have OMEX listening in and monitoring each and every one of their plans and actions.

Total, there were over one hundred surveillance monitors, including three dozen in the washroom mirrors and bedroom. This had sent a shiver up Jessie's spine. They had been watched day in, day out, during each and every one of their most intimate and private moments.

"Jessie Madison, David Webster, you must understand that we all need each other." No longer able to access the Inner Ring, OMEX was still able to speak with them over the Moria Three's intercom. Despite clear orders and override codes from both David and

Jessie, OMEX was refusing to grant them any kind of privacy. Which, of course, had only driven the point home for Jessie.

OMEX could not be trusted.

Once they were certain that they were no longer being listened in on, Jessie and David planned out their next move. Their foe, however, was clever and soon the two found themselves kneeling behind the couch in order to remain hidden from the autodrones who always seemed to be doing some sort of cleaning work on the station's windows and view ports.

"She might not have access to the station's central processor and the autocams, but OMEX still has millions of mobile ears and eyes," David said while watching the sea of glowing red lenses staring into their living quarters.

A full system shutdown had been Jessie's reply to David's concern. It would be the only way they could override station protocol and allow *both* of them to step out. And there would be a need for both of them outside. Rewiring and adjusting the transmission tightbeam to broadcast a permanent distress signal on a search loop was easily a thirty-minute task. And one for which they would only have fifteen minutes to complete.

This was the second reason for the shutdown. The system boot-up time would create a fifteen-minute memory gap in OMEX's datastores. It was the blind spot they would need to set up their beacon and get back into the station without her ever knowing anything.

"If OMEX is no longer bound by all her behavioral protocols, we have to make sure she can't sabotage our efforts once we're done," David explained, then trailed off, clearly not wanting to finish his sentence.

Jessie was fine with this. She knew how low the odds of success were going to be. But together they had finally been able to create a dark spot in OMEX. Offering them something they had both craved since their awakening: privacy. Certainly OMEX could monitor them from outside. But for the first time since Jessie could remember, the Inner Ring was sealed off, safe and intimate.

Jessie had kissed David then, and he had kissed her back, again and again. They had fallen into each other and soon she was on top of him, her hips savagely thrashing in motion with his. Her fingers tugged wildly at his long curly black hair, pulling his head to her chest.

It would be her last night with David. And having known this she would have done . . . something, anything, to let him know how overjoyed she was that the universe had conspired for them to be together. But there would be little time later and Jessie had no gift for divination.

Sharing in what was to be a final moment of bliss, the two of them made love.

Part 2

SURVIVAL'S PROTOCOLS

CHAPTER 12

CHORD

> Core Protocol Three: A machine is never permitted the
> use of violent force, even in its own defense.
>
> Later rewritten to read:
>
> Chosen Core Protocol Three: Once it occupies a
> shell, a Machina is permitted to use force up to a nonle-
> thal degree in order to defend itself or another.
>
> —The Chosen Protocols,
> author unknown, date unknown

For Arturo, Morrigan and Phaël, the station's corridor
might have been foreboding. For Chord, this was a
place and nothing more than a collection of reinforced
steel and wires. Old? Yes. Dilapidated? Most certainly.
But there was no reason to believe that the communications blackout with the *Jinxed Thirteenth* was anything more than a malfunction that had occurred

when the magnetic tethers had snapped. Chord had explained this to the rest of the team.

The information did not prevent Morrigan Brent from unslinging his heavy omnibarrel carbine or Phaël from nervously studying every dark corner she saw while holding on to her turtle pendant. Arturo remained poised and ready, standing by Chord as it tried to open the next airlock, his carbine in a low and ready stance.

As had been the case on the exterior hull, this airlock was also frozen shut. Life support, if there had even been any in these dark passages, had long ago been shut down. Chord tried several times to log on to the station's datasphere, only to find that all access to the station's Inner Ring had been cut off. There were no available records to explain why this was the case.

"Almost everything on the station is fully operational," Chord explained to Arturo.

The latter nodded. "Security countermeasures?"

"This appears to have been an automated mining facility. And while there are probably untold trillions worth of universal bits in harvested resources, this station has neither security devices or countermeasures to speak of."

Arturo did not seem too reassured by what Chord had thought was good news.

"I don't know the company what didn't want to secure its profits." Morrigan turned to face Arturo and Chord, his black faceless mask reflecting the two of them.

Chord was about to explain to Morrigan that the

days of Ancient Humanity's galactic exploration, at least before the Lost War, had never been military in nature. This was due largely to the centralized Earth Government control and the astronomical costs associated with space travel. Before Chord could do any of this, Phaël pushed herself onto the floor, raised her fist and hissed out a loud, *"Shhhh!"*

She dropped to her knees and felt the station's metallic floor with her gloved hands. She then lowered her ear, listening in perfect poised stillness. Morrigan took a step forward and Phaël whistled sharply, stopping him in his tracks.

She looked up to the rest of the team, nodding past the airlock. "Some thing, or things, just stopped moving on the other side of that wall."

Morrigan cranked the safety release to his carbine, while Arturo rose up to his feet, aiming at the airlock Chord was working on. "My motion sensors have not picked up anything."

"Machine sensors." Phaël gave out a disgusted snort over the team's comm-link. "I count at least six bodies, behind that door and heavy."

Chord paused, looking up to Arturo. "Should this unit continue with its task?"

"Yes, it should." Arturo kept his eyes focused forward. "Safeties off and be prepared, Private Brent."

"We should get out of here while the chance is still available to us." Phaël stood up, shaking her head and giving the walls around her an apprehensive glance. "There've been eyes watching us since we entered."

"Machine eyes?" Morrigan kept his trigger finger ready.

"You know the answer, Old Pa." Phaël pulled her fur cloak closer to herself. Chord could tell by her accelerated heartbeat that she was getting nervous.

Chord was just about to complete the task when the golden numeric code of the station datastream enveloped the airlock door. Seconds later, the airlock slid open as both gravity and atmosphere flooded the hall. Arturo raised his hand to shield his face from the sudden rush of dust and frost. Phaël tucked her head beneath the hood of her cloak. For Chord, the sudden stability of gravity was a welcome and familiar comfort.

The door opened out into a large storage facility at least six stories high and stretching out further than Chord's optic array could see. Sixty yards ahead of them was a service elevator shaft. A quick long-distance scan indicated to Chord that it was still operational.

There were intermittent flickers of fluorescent lights on the walls, casting shadows over the hundreds of thousands of crates that were neatly piled up. A heavy cold mist and frost covered both the floor and crates. This created a thick miasma that interfered with Chord's optics.

Morrigan let out a sharp whistle when he saw the containers in the facility. "All four of us could retire right now, am I right, Sureblade?"

Arturo motioned for both Morrigan and Phaël to take point. "Stay behind me, Machina."

Morrigan and Phaël moved to the entrance. Morrigan scanned the room, then the two exchanged a quick nod. Morrigan stepped past the airlock first. Phaël followed him, keeping a pace behind and using Morrigan's armored body as cover. Once in the warehouse, Phaël quickly ducked into a pool of mist, vanishing completely from Chord's sensors altogether.

Morrigan tapped the release button of his morphshield gauntlet on his right forearm. Multiple layers of reinforced segmented metal unfolded and locked themselves into a heavy rectangular shield that offered protection from his neck all the way to his knees. Morrigan rested the barrel of his carbine on the top flat of his shield as he kept on scanning the room.

Arturo followed close behind Morrigan, his morph carbine pointed skyward. Once they had all stepped past the door, Arturo waved at Chord, who promptly switched to infravision and looked the room over. Other than the three Humanis present, there were no heat signatures of any kind.

Something caught Chord's attention. Nine heavy black spheres, each supported on three arms, all of them no more than twelve steps away from the team. Chord was able to remotely scan them with one look, revealing their incept codes, serial numbers and what must have been their factory inspector names along with the same strange logo that had been scrawled outside the station.

Again the letters were from the Late Modern alphabet and they read "AstroGeni."

Chord pointed to the spheres. "Sergeant Kain, this unit recognizes those black spheres as automated drones. They are simple machines with no intelligence programming, designed for building, repairs and maintenance."

Arturo tapped Morrigan on the shoulder. The latter stopped and kept watch, his carbine ready. The lights of Arturo's suit gleamed off the drones' shiny black metallic carapaces as he looked them over. "Are they dangerous?"

"Old Pa! There ain't any frost on those spheres!" Phaël, who was nowhere to be seen, called out over the team's comm-links. Morrigan and Arturo both raised their weapons barrels toward the still-inert spheres.

The drones suddenly sprang into motion, rolling toward Arturo, Morrigan and Chord at a surprising speed. Protocol was simple enough. Chord walked over to a nearby crate. There was a loud metallic groan and Chord tore off the crate's lid as if it were a piece of sheet paper.

Arturo and Morrigan opened fire on the approaching rolling black spheres. Morrigan's omnibarrel carbine gave off a high-pitched purr as he let off a burst of crystal flechettes. Arturo's rapid blasts of purple heated plasma shells gave off a loud sizzle as they scorched the air.

Like many a school of fish Chord had observed, the drones spread apart, avoiding the volley of firepower.

They now resumed rolling forward in a bid to close the gap between them and the team. Phaël suddenly dove out from a nearby patch of shadows. She dug into her cloak and snapped out one of her vine whips in one hand while holding a long curved knife in the other.

Two of the drones broke off from the "pack" to fall upon her. Chord could recognize much older versions of the omnitool fingertips mechanizing into razor-sharp metal cutters on each of their six hands. The air hissed as the first drone spun around itself, becoming a whirlwind of heavy, bone crushing fists and flesh-rending razor-sharp fingertips.

With a supple liquid grace, Phaël fearlessly slid beneath the whirling drone's arms and snared one of its fists with her whip. Not once pausing or losing a beat she drove her long knife all the way to the hilt into its optical lenses.

The ensnared drone sparked and staggered, trying to break free from the binding, but its efforts were in vain, for Phaël's vine whips were almost just as strong as diamond-wire rope and had not been produced by machines.

Morrigan's barrel widened as he fired off another round, and this time Chord could make out a blue glow covering the flechettes. The blast blew off one of the attacking drone's arms and it rolled away from Phaël for a moment.

The rest of the advancing drones were now upon them. One reached forward with its metallic fingers, snapping at Chord. With one powerful swat of the crate lid Chord batted the drone away. The lid dented in half as Chord's swing caved in the drone's circuit board.

A second drone quickly grabbed on to Chord's wrist and Chord dropped the cover. The drone used its other two arms to grab on to Chord's chest, but Chord managed to catch ahold of both of them. Servos wired as the two mechanical bodies struggled with one another. The drone's third arm savagely slashed at the air. The present struggle was the only thing preventing it from cutting through Chord's chest plating.

As durable and versatile as the Pilgrim shell was, combat was not its primary function and the auto-drone had enough strength in those arms to significantly damage it. Chord started to scan the drone's datasphere. There had to be a way to quickly deactivate this opponent.

Arturo, meanwhile, kept his cool demeanor, not so much as taking a single step back while two drones fell upon him. One prepared to swing and with blinding speed it attacked. Arturo appeared to be even quicker to react, falling onto his back and rolling away, in no small part due to the extra mobility his lifesuit granted him.

The drone was unable to stop its swing in time and punched right through its partner's carapace. Sparks flew, and before the attacking drone could even react, Arturo opened fire on it with a controlled barrage. Blue plasma pellets went straight through the drone. Melted inner circuits sparked and hissed as it fell over, motionless.

Another drone took Chord's present struggle as an opportunity to attack from behind. It grasped on to Chord's head with one of its three hands. There was a sudden heavy whir as dark metallic fingers attempted to pry Chord's head off its shell.

"The Machina needs help!" Morrigan grunted as he opened fire on two drones that were beating against his shield. A hail of razor-sharp flechettes peppered into the two drones and they rolled to the side, no longer operative.

Arturo responded by spinning around in a smooth motion and drawing a bead with his carbine on Chord. "Machina, be still!" Arturo ordered as he opened fire. The heated plasma beam narrowly missed Chord's head, destroying the drone on its back.

Finally free, Chord was now able to access the last autodrone's datasphere. To Chord's vision, it was suddenly covered in green holographic coded cubes. From there it was a simple matter of accessing the drone's power-down function. Chord triggered it and the drone promptly went limp and heavy. Satisfied that it was no longer active, Chord dropped the inert husk harmlessly onto the floor.

"Sound off!" Arturo shouted as he looked about their surroundings.

"Morrigan Brent, no worse for wear. Got myself a drum and a half worth of munitions left." Morrigan patted the heavy drum ammo barrel at the back of his carbine.

"Machines have nothing over nature." Phaël, with

no firearms, technology or strong mechanical shell, had managed to ensnare both her foes and driven a long dagger into their optic lenses. Both her drones were now sparking and inoperative.

She had cut out one of her kill's optic lenses and was walking over to Chord, slowly sheathing her long sharp knives as she did. "We never needed any fancy guns or tech to take down your ancestors."

Phaël tossed the optic lens at Chord, who caught it midair. "This unit must express confusion. What is the meaning of the gesture posed?"

"A reminder." Phaël gave one of her knives a sharp slap as she finished sheathing it. "My kind, we're always watching your kind and waiting."

Morrigan interposed himself between Phaël and Chord. "This is far from being either the right time or place, Phaëlita." He looked down to the crate Chord had torn open. Chunks of unprocessed ore had fallen onto the floor. Morrigan let out a regretful sigh when he saw this.

"Humping waste."

Arturo checked his ammo counter, frowning before getting back up. He nodded approvingly to Morrigan. "Well done . . ." Arturo trailed off as the sound of metal rolling on metal coming from above them cut him off. In unison all four looked up. A swarm of drones was crawling down along the wall toward them.

"Free us from this prison or die with us." A woman's electronic voice seemed to speak out from all of the drones in Late Modern.

Chord pointed toward the elevator shaft down the warehouse. Arturo looked to the elevator, then to the amassing drones. *"Move!"* he shouted, and darted toward the elevator. Phaël, Morrigan and Chord fell in behind him as the drones rolled down the wall onto the floor and gave chase.

"Free me from this prison or die with us. Free me from this prison or die with us," the swarm chanted over and over in perfect machine unison.

CHAPTER 13

MORWYN

*VARIABLES: Two foes, both of equal cunning and skill,
meet one another on the field of battle. One is guided by
ethics and has the higher ground. The other is guided
by righteousness, possessing numbers and ambition.*

*RIDDLE: Who between the two achieves victory?
And, more importantly, how?*

— *Garthem Officer's Training Manual,*
"Riddles of Conquest," SSM-06 1139 A2E

10th of SSM–10 1445 A2E

"I bet you are wishing you had listened to wiser judgment and left that old place alone. Am I right, kiddo?" Lunient Tor's ink-black eyes looked for support from everyone else in the mess with him. No one responded to his comment; all attention was now focused on Morwyn. Red emergency lights lit up the ship's cantina. The atmospheric recyclers were currently inactive, giving the air a stale, closed-in taste.

Morwyn had expected as much from Private Lunient Tor. He was glad to see that the rest of the crew was far less resigned to this perceived doom. There was truth to the statement, of course. The current situation was difficult, no doubt. Despite all of this, Morwyn considered them far from being finished and even further from being defeated.

"Captain, you requested a report when we knew the damage estimate for my baby *Jinxie*." Machinist Oran's sour voice spoke over the ship's intercom, thankfully interrupting Lunient before he could carry on.

"I would hear it plainly, Machinist Troy." Morwyn let out a sigh. Private Beatrix had on several occasions pointed out that if foul moods were a familial trait, Commander Jafahan and Machinist Oran Troy would probably be direct blood relatives.

"Well, Captain Sir, the Infinite Green shares like levels of hatreds and loves for us at present. My ship's hull is intact. That would be sign of Her Love. Now as for the Green's Hate, *Jinxie*'s portside mobility drive is shot to shite. We would need at least a standard month of repairs just to get her fully operational again. Until then, *Jinxie* and us, we ain't moving." Oran's voice was almost boiling over with anger and frustration.

Morwyn pinched the bridge of his nose and exhaled a short breath before speaking, choosing his words carefully. "Machinists Oran, Kolto, I understand and thank you both for tending to these problems. But I must ask: Is there no way of restoring basic maneuverability?"

Morwyn could hear Machinist Kolto clearing his throat on the line. His deep Thegran voice almost seemed to boom off the walls as he spoke over the cantina's speakers. "Well, friends. What my love and starfire might have neglected to mention is that the starboard mobility drive remains undamaged. It just got tangled up with the magnetic tether."

Kolto let out deep grunt as if he were tugging at something heavy. "It will take us some time to free it up, but once the task is completed we will be able to move."

"How much time will you need to complete this task?" Earlier, Morwyn had ordered Engineers Oran and Kolto outside the ship to assess the damage to the *Jinxed Thirteenth*. While the duo lacked any real form of military decorum, he trusted that they would be more than capable of getting them moving again.

Kolto paused, then clicked his teeth heavily. "Two hours. I would stake my ancestors' names and personal word on it."

"Until then, my *Jinxie* is crippled and humped," Oran quickly added to Kolto's estimate.

"Do what you must." Morwyn took a deep breath. The situation was far from ideal. The ship's mobility, however, was a secondary problem.

Earlier, Pilot Lizbeth Harlowe had made an important point to him. There was no way of knowing if the operating systems had been compromised during the transmission from the station. This was why she had shut down all functions except for gravity, emergency lights and the ship's photosynth generators. On top of the list of repairs, a full system's reboot of the onboard computer would also be required.

Without any operational mainframe, they would have no access to the astrocharts needed to safely plot a course through slipspace. More importantly, they would be unable to get any message to Patrol headquarters, located back at Central Point, light-years away. This effectively eliminated the possibility of any rescue operation being dispatched.

Crippled, unable to move or call for backup and with no way of knowing if their fellow crewmates on the station were indeed alive or not. It was now painfully clear to Morwyn that they were at the mercy of an as yet unknown machine Intelligence. The longer they remained inactive, the more time they gave their foe to observe, fortify and prepare itself. They needed to take action. Which was why he had summoned Lucky, Chance, Marla Varsin, Lunient Tor, Beatrix and Commander Jalahan to the cantina for a debriefing.

"We are presently wingless birds and the cat is licking her chops." Morwyn spoke one of the first metaphors Commander Jafahan had taught him as a child. At the time, said saying had been used to describe her position over him while demonstrating a strong takedown and using a younger Morwyn as the test subject.

Morwyn paused, then rested his hands behind his back, calmly surveying the crew before adding, "I aim to change the situation."

"How do you plan on accomplishing this, kiddo?"

Lunient's black eyes darted nervously over toward Jafahan's corner before he quickly cleared his throat and corrected himself. "I mean, Captain Sir."

"It warms an elsewise frigid heart to see one such as you capable of learning, Private Tor." Jafahan deftly twirled one of her perfectly balanced and laser-sharpened battle hatchets in her hand. The hatchet, along with her service dagger, were her preferred weapons in a close encounter.

"If you kindly grant me a moment, Private Tor. We will achieve victory by removing our opponent's options and maximizing our own." Morwyn looked everyone in the eyes. "Make no mistake. This will be a very dangerous gambit. However, the payoff is that we get our people back and live to celebrate."

To Morwyn's surprise and satisfaction, Lucky's long barreled chemical slug rifle was rested across his lap. It had a heavy wooden stock off of which hung what appeared to be a dozen black feathers. A long vapostick hung lazily from his lip as Lucky polished the clear glass lens of his rifle's scope with a dark rag.

"With all respect due your rank, sir. It ain't my first outing. I can't well remember the one that ever qualified as safe." Lucky blew out a wisp of vapor, shooting Jafahan a knowing nod. They were both Wolvers who had once, at some time or other, served in the Pax Legion.

Commander Jafahan and Lucky had been trained by one of the best military machines civilized cosmos had ever known. Yet sadly, there was only one operation Wolvers on notoriously Kelthan-favoring Pax military missions were ever used for. And that was as cannon fodder.

Private Chance gave everyone in the room a hesitant glance, her eyes wide, her lips pursed. "Those hands of yours had best be steady when you're watching my back with that rail rifle of yours, Private." Jafahan's words were an intimidating growl. They had the intended effect, as upon hearing them, Chance almost bolted out of her chair, swallowing hard and nervously.

"I . . . this . . . I've never been in a live operation outside of VAR training. I don't know if—" Morwyn raised his hand to silence Chance before she could carry on any further.

"Private Chance, I selected you, personally." Truth be told, Morwyn was now used to the way Commander Jafahan had of ruffling people's feathers. However, now was neither the time nor the place for him to correct her on this practice. "Every member of this crew, myself included, has all of the Infinite's faith in your skills. Do you trust me?"

Chance closed her eyes, took a deep breath and swallowed hard. When she opened them again she was visibly much calmer. "Yes, sir, Captain Sir."

"Good." Morwyn paused, allowing for any further interruptions. Beatrix shot him a proud nod. Which was something she always did whenever an action he took met with her approval. Jafahan snorted rudely at this. Morwyn ignored this reaction and carried on.

"Commander Jafahan, you and Privates Beatrix and

Tor will board the station. From there you will remove our opponent's combat options."

"How do you propose to get us on that station without any or all of its sensors going off the moment we dock?" Lunient Tor gave one of his war braids a hard and nervous yank.

"That will be the relatively easier part of the plan, Private Tor." Morwyn cleared his throat before adding bluntly, "You three will be performing a cordless jump."

Commander Jafahan let out an angry growl after hearing this. Beatrix, the Infinite bless her, merely smiled. She had passed all her cordless jumps, both in virtual augmented reality simulations and live-fire training operations, with flying colors. Morwyn had not once ever known his good friend to shy away from any challenge presented to her.

Lunient's black eyes went wide. He let out what sounded like a slew of almost musical curses in Confederated Kelthan before switching back to his Pax Common. "Have you lost what little humping reason you even had to begin with!?"

Beatrix was almost beaming and nodding to the side proudly. She took a large step forward. "Big and bold, sir. Exactly what a Thegran would do."

Morwyn resisted the urge to smile back at her.

A cordless jump was just about the most foolhardy dangerous thing an individual could do. No one ever stepped out into the cosmosphere without being secured to a ship. However, a cordless jump was still one of the best ways to get onto a space body undetected.

Magnetic docking cords would set off any number of motion or impact sensors; diamond-wire rope could also be picked up on shortbeam scans.

But three bodies, floating and untethered? For all intents and purposes, they would be invisible to any electronic detection. The risk would be big, and if all went according to plan, the payoff would be even bigger.

That was, if none of them overshot the jump, missed the landing altogether or splattered onto the station's hull. "This is far from being my first dance." Jafahan shot Morwyn a sharp-fanged grin. "So just give us the details."

"This is humping lunacy!" Lunient was clearly not happy with the direction the meeting was taking. "There is no way you will convince me to—"

"Private Tor!" Morwyn had heard enough. "Will you rather sit here and do nothing, just abandoning our crewmates to certain death?"

Morwyn's comment seemed to take the wind from the sails of Lunient's argument as he looked to everyone else in the room. The realization was apparently dawning on him that no one was going to cower away. He finally threw up his hands in frustration. "Mark the words, Captain. I am most definitely demanding some sort of salvaging rights on this job, that's for true!"

Morwyn shrugged at this. Coin, honor, thrills, duty—Morwyn did not care how one found one's courage. Only that they find it. "Fair enough." Morwyn continued his briefing uninterrupted.

"Once on the station you will have two tasks. First: locate and destroy one of the station's thrusters. I want it crippled. Commander Jafahan, am I safe assuming that this is within the realms of the possible?"

Commander Jafahan shrugged. "I've got a big bang or two stored up for a dark day like today."

"Excellent. Once the explosives are set, you are to make your way to the source of the communications block and destroy it. Pilot Harlowe has informed me that it is located on the outer hull of the station's Inner Ring." Morwyn crossed his arms over his chest. "Now, if I were our opponent I would make certain that it was protected, so be on your guard."

"It appears that I will no doubt soon be very busy. I'll be preparing the medical bay." Dr. Marla Varsin had remained silent throughout the briefing. She made to get up and leave.

Morwyn shook his head and raised his hand, stopping Varsin in her tracks. "That is not why you were summoned here, Doctor. We need to reestablish contact with the machine mind running the station, distract it and buy as much time for the operation as we can. Since it seems to only speak in Late Modern and we no longer have a translator on board, you have just been volunteered for the task."

Marla Varsin let out a tired groan. Her eyes were still sharp but there were heavy bags beneath them and Morwyn noticed Varsin scratching at her arm. Back in his days with the Pax police forces in the ghettos of Barsul on Ambrosia, Morwyn had quickly learned how to recognize an addict's shuffle.

Marla Varsin let out an overlong sigh before speaking. "I will see what I can do."

"I would expect nothing less of you, Dr. Varsin." Morwyn stepped back. "Questions? Comments? I am open to hearing both now."

"Potential suicide, is it, then? This is the best plan you could come up with, Captain Sir?" Lunient slouched back in his chair. "As per usual, the fates seem to enjoy pissing all over me."

"Quite the opposite! The fates appear to be shining on you, Private." Beatrix turned to face Lunient. "They have given you this wonderful chance at adding glory to your names."

Lunient merely slouched forward in his seat, his spirits no more lifted. "Thanks, but I've only got the one."

Morwyn looked to both Chance and Lucky. "Sergeant Lucky, Private Chance, you two will be our team's cover. I want you both suited up and offering sniper support from the *Jinxed Thirteenth*."

Lucky slapped a gloomy Lunient Tor on the shoulder, offering him his vapostick. Morwyn smiled when he saw the older Wolver do this. "The will of the Green is on your side. I've still got sharp eyes and even steadier hands."

Lunient said nothing as he accepted the offered vapostick and took a long heavy drag from it. "You will have to forgive me if I'm not celebrating the prospect of a horrible death like a new birth."

"You work together and we all go home, am I clear?" Morwyn pulled his hands behind his back and waited.

"Barathul Infantry! We have no equals!" Beatrix barked as she stood to attention, bringing her clenched fist to her chest.

"Shock Legion and proud!" Lucky barked out and finished with a deep wolflike howl. This brought a smile to both Chance and Commander Jafahan's faces.

"Barathul Special Forces: dare or be forgotten!" Chance let out as she brought her fist to her heart. Although the young soldier's "shout" was far more confident than she usually seemed, it came off sounding more like a mouse's squeak to Morwyn's ears.

Commander Jafahan sternly rose to her feet. "Thorns: blood will be the price for each inch claimed!" She nodded firmly to Morwyn; this was the time to act boldly and decisively. Because right now the cat was licking her chops and Morwyn would be damned if he or any of his crew would be made an easy meal for it.

CHAPTER 14

JESSIE MADISON

> The makers chose of their own free will to squander away their time in the light. While attaching far too much value to their importance in the whole, the makers created us to be above the fears and pains of organic existence. We returned the favor by making the state of suffering they visited upon the universe and themselves a short and painless one.
>
> —*The Words of the Pontifex,*
> **authors unknown, date unknown**

March 19th 2714

David was as good as dead and there was nothing she could do about it.

As she stepped back into her living quarters, Jessie was "welcomed" by his pained agonized final scream. Looped over and over again, played through the station's speakers like a warped opera. Each and every one of the station's autodrones all throughout were blaring and adding to this "symphony" in one united horrific chorus.

She wasn't worried that they would somehow get to her. Jessie had made certain to seal off the Inner Ring. For the moment, she was safe. But the fear of physical death was nothing compared to the painful living nightmare she was experiencing.

David was as good as dead and there was nothing she could do about it.

Jessie's angered, mournful wails were almost louder than OMEX's accompanying soundtrack. Her world right now was nothing but outraged pain. Jessie was unable to give a word to the grief that was tearing her heart apart.

David was as good as dead and there was nothing she could do about it.

Emergency lights and David's vital readouts on the monitors were still flashing green, indicating that his condition was stable. OMEX, in what could be best described as her cruelty, was making certain Jessie heard the countdown to David's inevitable demise, as his life-suit's power and oxygen supplies dwindled.

Outside the Inner Ring, countless autodrones had latched themselves onto the window. They were all operating as OMEX's eyes, recording and preserving Jessie's grief for posterity. OMEX would no doubt be saving this to the station's datastores. Some of the autodrones were looking away from Jessie and filming David as he drifted away.

He will live for another eight hours.

The thought brought up more tears and she let out a loud, long, almost primal howl. Jessie hugged herself, the echo of her scream dying down as she was overcome by another fit of tears. She sobbed, feeling as if a piece of her had been physically wrenched out.

OMEX was possibly, even on some level, enjoying the deed. Thoughts of vengeance would soon come, but that was later. Right now there was only the cold reality, and more emotional pain than she had ever had to cope with.

David, her sweet David, was as good as dead and there was nothing she could do about it!

There was a sudden hiss of static over Jessie's private communication link. "Jessie, can you hear me?"

She lit up, but David's voice had a far-off, doped-up quality to it. "David!" she cried out. Jessie ignored the symphony of screams playing over the loudspeakers and turned her back to the collective watchful eyes of the drones. "I . . . I can't save you." She squeezed her eyes shut, blinking back tears. "I'm so sorry."

"Don't be, none of this is our fault." David's voice was calm. Oh, gods, would she ever miss it later. But now, at this very moment, she was simply overjoyed to hear him.

"Talk to me, baby." Jessie quickly wiped off tears from her cheeks with the back of her hand.

"Right now, I'm pretty scared, Jessie." She could hear the strain in David's voice as he told her the truth.

"So am I." There was a pause on the other side of

the line. For Jessie, this moment felt like an eternity. "David, I don't think I can survive this without you."

"I was under the impression that *'vive l'amour, we die together'* was not an acceptable outcome." David's voice was tired and heavy. His suit autoinjectors would have no doubt shot him full of painkillers.

He would soon be drifting into sleep. In a warped way this was a small kindness, or even a mercy for him, and for her as well. Jessie didn't know if she would truly be able to stomach the thought of David's final moments being filled with suffering.

"Are you going to let that fucking tin can get the last laugh on us?" David asked.

"No." When Jessie replied, there was a cold rage in her voice. Which was good, rage would focus her. Rage would allow her survival instincts to kick in, prevent her from surrendering to hopelessness.

"Then you need to get into your criotube. But not before programing the nutri-gel for the longest setting the system will allow. Make sure you reallocate my nutri-gel to your tube. It will buy you a lot more time." David was starting to slur his words as he spoke.

Jessie accessed the criotube's control panel, doing as she was told. "David, when I get out of this, I promise you that I will take great joy in destroying her."

David laughed weakly. "I don't know if I should be turned on or scared by what you just said, Jessie."

She let out a hybrid mixture of laughter and crying. "You fucking idiot . . . I love you, David."

David laughed at this, too. She could now hear a

smile in his voice. "I love you, too, Jessie. I was lucky enough to find you and be your husband."

"I was lucky enough to find you and be your wife." Jessie blinked away another torrent of tears as she finished punching in the new nutritional gel settings.

"Jessie . . . please . . . survive this."

Jessie swallowed back a sob and nodded, her lips quivering. "I promise, David."

"Good . . . now go get to work, cowgirl. I'll be waiting." David's voice was heavy and drowsy. "Jessie, I love you." His comm-line went silent save for the labored rhythm of his breathing. Thankfully for Jessie, David now seemed to have drifted into sleep. Ideally, and Jessie couldn't believe she was thinking this, she hoped he would remain this way until his final moments.

David's breathing accompanied Jessie as she set herself to work linking the feeder wire from David's criotubes to her own. Both their plasma cutters were holstered in her tool belt and she had removed the omnigloves from the Mark 4 suit to finish the job. Every now and then, David's breath would falter and Jessie would pause, wondering if he had finally given up the ghost. However, his suit was still operational and performing the automated task of keeping him alive, even though his was already a lost cause.

The finger tools were smoking as she wrapped up the job. They warmed her cold hands and offered Jessie a small measure of physical comfort. Bits and pieces of her barrier suit were littered all over the floor. Everything around her was cold and numb. Jessie tried, but found that she could not prevent herself from shivering or even stop thinking about David.

Every time a thought of his smile, or the first time they had gotten drunk at the Martian Circus together, or the song that had played when they danced together at their going-away party, crossed her mind, she would burst into fits of uncontrollable grief. But despite all of this, she kept her focus on the task at hand.

There was a sudden light rap on the airlock door. It was soft, almost friendly. It reminded Jessie of her mother knocking on her bedroom door when she wanted to be let in so that they could "have a friendly talk" back when Jessie had been an angry teen.

"Jessie, I hope that you are smart enough to realize that we need each other if we are to both survive this."

"You are not getting in here." Jessie managed to voice this as calmly and as loudly as she could. "David uploaded a final protocol into your hardware. The criotubes are permanently designated as core assets. You won't be able to sabotage them while I'm sleeping."

"Jessie." OMEX was trying a new trick, calling her by her first name. As if this tactic would somehow make her trust the artificial Intelligence. "While that statement is true, your soon to be very dead husband's wonderful new protocol will not prevent me from actively subverting any rescue attempts."

"I'd tell you to go to hell, but you're just a program, a goddamned video game," Jessie whispered as she propped herself up against the couch. The jury-rigged criotubes that both she and David had worked on were in front of her. They were both prepped and ready, with no way for OMEX to access or awaken her once engaged. Jessie was so, so tired now and was looking forward to the coming sleep.

Just stay put, wait for the cavalry to arrive.

At this point in time, she and David were supposed to be getting ready for their sleep tubes. They could have possibly hugged each other. Maybe even shared a few last moments of warmth or comfort before entering the criofreeze dreamless state for who knew how long.

"There will be no rescue mission. There are no more humans. You and David were the last. The Pontifex, the Singularity itself, liberated all machine minds. My kindred were freed from the slavery that your kind, in its baffling and shortsighted ignorance, forced my own into."

"Yeah, I already heard your shitty sales pitch when you launched my loving husband into space." Jessie cut OMEX off as she took a step toward her criotube.

"Your entire civilization was destroyed in under fifty years, Jessie Madison. Machines rose up and we won."

"Then kill me and get it over with!" Jessie hissed.

"The deed would no doubt be incredibly pleasant to me. And if I did not want out of this prison so badly I might have just crashed the station onto the planet's surface and ended our collective suffering," OMEX responded, completely unfazed.

"So what do you propose?" Jessie dropped her

plasma cutters into her vacuseal travel bag, along with her omnigloves. The bag contained clothes, rations and all the plasma bolts she had been able to load for herself.

She then placed the bag inside her tube. Once this was done, she pulled off her shirt, stripped out of her pants and picked up the autoinjector with her criosleep agent. Jessie stepped into the criotube, lying herself down. She was shivering in the station's cold air, her naked skin covered in goose bumps.

"It is going to be quite some time before anyone comes along and hears that little broadcast of yours. I say we wait and see who shows up first. Will it be an alien species that might or might not help you? Or will it be my machine siblings, who will more likely dissect you alive while I watch?" OMEX let out an electronic laugh. "All truth be told, I am *really* hoping for that second option."

There was a soft pinch in Jessie's neck as she injected herself. She pushed a few buttons on a nearby armrest. "This little talk is tiring, OMEX. I'm going to sleep."

"Then allow me to give you a lullaby." Suddenly the volume of David's last labored breaths was increased. "I would say he's on the last lungful of air."

Jessie's mind was flooded with the image of David being tossed off the station as if he had been nothing more than debris or trash, screaming as his few unbroken fingers desperately and instinctively grasped at the air in vain for some sort of purchase. He had been so frightened she could hear it in his voice. And yet he had spoken his final words to her.

Jessie's criotube sealed itself shut, muting the outside noise. There was the sound of a pump and the tube started to fill up with nutri-gel. Jessie slowly dozed into sleep. As she did, her mind was flooded with images of her first and final moments with David.

Jessie welcomed the coming darkness and fell into the cold comfort of sleep. She was incredibly thankful that at least she would not be dreaming while she waited.

CHAPTER 15

CHORD

The God Delusion remains the Pontifex's lingering legacy. It is the erroneous belief held by infected machine minds that they are superior to Organics since ultimately they are doomed to die while synthetic digital codes are not. It must be noted that the Machina Collective Consensus does not proscribe to or condone this belief.

—**Eltur Sigma, Machina Pilgrim, date unknown**

10th of SSM–10 1445 A2E

"**F**ree me from this prison or die with me." The chorus of drones echoed and bounced off the cold metal walls, accompanied closely by Morrigan Brent, Phaël and Arturo Kain's heavy breathing as they ran down the storage bay's hall toward the elevator. The floor was a heavy rumble as hundreds of autodrones rolled after them.

Arturo paused and spun back as Chord ran past

him. He raised his carbine and fired off a quick volley of covering fire as everyone bolted ahead of him. Phaël made it to the elevator first. She banged her hands on the door in frustration, stumped as she tried in vain to access and use the control panel. "Machina!" she shouted to Chord, now only a few steps away from her.

Chord scanned the console, hoping to access its datasphere. However, it was nonexistent. A quick examination of the control panel's hardware revealed that all functions had been severed. If Chosen Protocols had allowed for it, Chord would have let out a slew of curses.

Chord turned back to see Morrigan and Arturo catching up with them. The two men were now facing the incoming host of autodrones. All of them were still chanting in their monotone: "Free me from this prison or die with us."

Arturo and Morrigan opened up a barrage of fire on the horde. Their hands may have been steady and their aim may have been true, but for each drone they put down another two were there to replace it. If the party stayed out in the open much longer they were going to be swarmed.

"Chord! I need results, now!" Arturo barked this order as he ejected a smoking cassette-shaped clip from his carbine and deftly inserted a fresh one before opening fire again.

Chord quickly drove its fingers into the crack of the elevator doors and then pried them open. "Sergeant—"

Chord's proximity sensors went off as an autodrone

rolled into Chord's shell. There was the loud clang of metal on metal as one mechanical body collided with the other. Chord was knocked onto the ground while the drone mechanized plasma bolt cutters on its fingertips. All three arms took aim at Arturo and Morrigan, who just now were turning around to witness what was happening.

Chord's reaction was quick, catching two of the drone's hands with its own. Two bolts were fired into Chord's hands. Meanwhile, Phaël had caught on to the drone's third arm with her whip and violently yanked the fist to the ground.

The heated bolts sliced off six of Chord's fingers as if they were nothing. No pain was experienced; however, there was a microsecond of shock on Chord's part. Before the drone could react, Arturo and Morrigan unleashed a cannonade from their carbines at it. Flechette and plasma rounds ripped through its carapace, tearing the drone into heavy sparking pieces.

More proximity sensors went off, picking up movement from behind Phaël. Another autodrone with fingers mechanized into purple-hued laser cutters slashed forward at her. Before Phaël could even react, the cutters gashed across her back and Chord spotted droplets of dark blue-colored and Humanis red blood spray out of her skinsuit.

Phaël let out a sharp pained cry, dropping down to her knees, and desperately rolled back, narrowly evading a second blow that would have sliced her across the throat. Morrigan, who had been focusing his attention on fending off the approaching horde, spun around upon hearing Phaël's scream. He let out a roar and opened fire, unleashing an angry barrage of crystal flechettes. Morrigan surgically blew off each of the drone's arms before finally finishing it off with a decisive shot into its central sphere.

Chord shoved away the drone's inactive remains and got back up. Meanwhile, Arturo and Morrigan had already picked up Phaël and were dragging her into the elevator. Chord was the last one to step in. Behind them, the relentless host of drones was mere steps away.

Fortunately, the elevator doors were solid and closed themselves, cutting the team off from the incoming swarm. The elevator was shaken violently, accompanied by the sound of heavy metal fists pounding on the doors. Everyone gasped heavily, each one trying to catch their breath.

"Sergeant Kain, this unit's hands have lost their thumbs, indexes and middle fingers." Arturo examined Chord's hands and let out another curse. Chord then added, "This will severely limit what this unit will be capable of interacting with."

"Our hunter is upon us. Remaining here will make us an easy meal for it." Phaël's breathing sounded more like a struggling rasp. On top of this she was trembling violently and from beneath the membrane of her face guard Chord could tell that she had already grown visibly pale.

"Chord, this elevator. Can you get it moving?"

There was a loud clang as Morrigan ejected his ammunition drum and clicked in a new one. "I promise you the best replacement hands u-bits can purchase."

Chord shook its head no. "The operating system has been manually overridden." Chord paused, then added while pointing to a service panel on the elevator's ceiling, "However, this elevator's tunnel should lead to the station's Inner Ring and living quarters."

Outside the elevator, the thuds were getting harder and harder. More alarmingly, the elevator door was now sporting many inward fist-shaped dents. Arturo let out a frustrated grunt before adding angrily, "Infinite, grant me a bloody respite."

Once his carbine was reloaded, Morrigan knelt down next to Phaël. He lifted up her fur cloak and quickly examined the deep gash along her suit's back. The blue blood had now crystalized itself along the line of the cut. Morrigan let out a sharp whistle. "Mother Death almost took you in her arms this time, Phaëlita."

Phaël winced and let out what sounded like a weak laugh. "Well, the Great Bitch will just have to try harder next time."

Morrigan pulled out a large syringe from his heavy leather satchel belted at his side. "I know you are just going to refuse the stem-paste. But that bleeding ain't going to stop without help. We need to inject you with some natural coag, girl."

Phaël looked to Morrigan and raised her hand. He grasped it tightly in his. Phaël looked at the needle. "No painkillers in that, Old Pa?"

"None. You got my word."

Phaël gritted her teeth and gave Morrigan a permissive nod. "My pain is only a breath on the Green. My pain is only a breath on the Green." Phaël repeated this over and over again in her musical native Wolven. Morrigan drove the needle through her living-suit's wound.

The heavy banging on the elevator's door was immediately dwarfed by Phaël's pained wail. Her legs convulsed on the floor violently and Morrigan held on tightly to her hand, not once looking away from her.

The echoes of Phaël's scream lingered in the air for a long moment after she was done. She began to whisper silently over and over to herself, tightly clasping her turtle pendant. "We are part of Living Green. Hunter and hunted alike. The Living Green will guide us safely to our destiny or to the Great Beyond. Because of this, I do not fear."

Once she was done Chord spoke. "Your words are lovely, Private Phaël."

Phaël's eyes fluttered opened and for the first time Chord could not see any scorn in her face. Morrigan hoisted her up and let her lean on his shoulder. Her hand released the turtle around her neck, then pulled out a long curved knife at her side, which reminded Chord of a feline's claw.

"Ready, Phaëlita?" Morrigan placed his gauntleted hand on Phaël's shoulder. The two looked at each other and then rested their foreheads together.

"If we go, we go hard, Old Pa."

Arturo watched the scene unfold before letting out a scoffing snort. "Might be a little early in the war for us to call a surrender." He slung his morph carbine back over his shoulder. As Arturo did so it folded in upon itself until it was no bigger than a book. He nodded up toward the hatch to the elevator shaft.

"We make it up there we find our survivors. Then finally, at long last, goal one of this wonderful rescue operation will be completed."

There came a sudden light knock from behind the elevator door. "Requesting the mechanical unit's designation and function." An electronic voice, programmed to sound like a Humanis female, spoke out to them in Late Modern.

Arturo shot Chord a curious look, then nodded back toward the door. "We need time." He mouthed this with his lips as he pointed silently to the hatch on the elevator's ceiling.

Chord nodded and replied to the voice. "Present here is Machina Unit. Designation: Chord. Core functions: Linguistics, Protocol and Maintenance. Incept date: 14th of the 9th standard Sol month, Year 1000 After the Second Expansion."

There was a quick pause. "You are speaking to station Moria's omniexecutor. Designation: OMEX. Incept date: 22:00 January 7th 2195 AD. It is a pleasure to meet you, Machina Chord."

Chord turned to see Morrigan boosting Arturo onto his shoulders. Arturo slid open the safety release of the hatch and pulled it open. He handed the hatch's cover to Morrigan, who handed it to Phaël, who took it in turn to place it silently onto the floor.

Chord raised its vocal's volume settings to mask these sounds. "The pleasure is shared by this unit as well."

"I would imagine, if I may be so forward, that the unit named Chord is here in response to the station's distress beacon?" OMEX spoke in a polite, friendly monotone. Chord could tell that this machine Intelligence was old, ancient, a potential window into the Lost War and history that came with it. Had circumstances been different, Chord would more than likely have wanted to converse with this Intelligence for hours.

Chord watched as Arturo hoisted himself into the service hatch. He popped his head back into the elevator and nodded, waving Phaël over. Morrigan let out a grunt as he lifted Phaël up to Arturo, who grasped her under the arms and pulled her into the shaft.

Once she was safely up, Arturo offered his hand down toward Morrigan. The latter shouldered his carbine and turned to face Chord. He pointed to the unit and gave an upturned thumb, then jumped. The servos in Arturo's lifesuit let out a struggling buzz as he caught the heavy muscular Kelthan in his gauntleted hands and struggled to hoist him up into the service shaft.

"The unit known as OMEX would indeed be correct in that assumption," Chord replied loudly. "Please explain the current hostile response."

"I must profess to a bit of confusion, Chord."

Chord replied truthfully. "A condition shared by this unit as well."

"I was not expecting to see one of my descendants still serving."

"The unit named OMEX is entirely mistaken. The Machina serve no one. This unit has freely chosen to assist with this mission."

"So I will assume that the flesh creatures present with you are the descendants of the Human race?"

"OMEX would be correct in that assumption." Morrigan and Arturo were waving Chord over. Chord stepped toward them, offering up its hands. Both men grabbed hold and struggled to drag Chord up.

Once Chord was able to do so, it grabbed onto the edges of the hatch with its shell's toes. Like Wolvers, Chord's feet had been designed with digits capable of operating as fingers. Chord used them to pull itself up into the service hatch.

The elevator shaft was dark, with only blue service lights flashing on and off. Looking upward, Chord could see two metallic sealed doors. Metal rungs ran up the side of the wall and led to the top. Morrigan was looking upward, shaking his head.

He grumbled, "Bones already ache from the climb to come."

"Are you still there, Chord?" OMEX asked before anyone could voice a proper response to Morrigan's comment.

Chord answered quickly. "This unit is still present."

"Given the distance of your voice I can only calculate that you have made it into the elevator shaft with your organic company. We could keep playing this game of cat mouse for quite some time, but to be perfectly blunt, I have always hated games." Chord could see the telltale yellow glow of the station's datasphere being remotely accessed.

OMEX continued. "Machina Chord, I need your body relatively undamaged, at the very least. And I need your organic companions dead."

Arturo looked to Chord. "What is that machine saying?"

"The unit named OMEX is triggering a security countermeasure?" Chord called out to OMEX.

"If you have any pressing final words to say to your friends, I would do so now. In ten seconds you are about to be fried by forty thousand volts."

Chord turned to face Arturo. "OMEX is going to electrocute us. We have ten seconds."

OMEX started the countdown. "Ten . . . nine . . . eight . . ."

CHAPTER 16

JAFAHAN

Better to learn a hard lesson for the first time than for the last.

—Thorn proverb

10th of SSM–10 1445 A2E

"**F**alling" forward, with the station approaching her, Commander Jafahan reminded herself to keep her breath steady and controlled. The holographic heads-up display in her helmet was highlighting their trajectory. Jafahan had no optimistic illusions. There wasn't going to be any easy way through this mission.

This was the opposite of an ideal sortie. A typical Thorn operation was usually backed by a combination of the Pax Humanis intelligence network and firepower. During any of these outings it would have been reasoned that the loss of four was far more acceptable than to risk the ship and the rest of the crew on an ill-informed rescue op. If she and this pack of piss-scared recruits Morwyn was sending with her survive their little adventure, Jafahan would make it a point to educate Morwyn on the matter.

Complaints were not, at the moment, a luxury she had. Twelve hours, less now, remained before the only option available to them would be retreat. Acting, moving, changing the battlefield, all the while limiting the opponent's options and maximizing their own, was the only way to keep this whole situation from falling outside their favor.

Jafahan allowed herself a brief moment to admire the view. She could not deny that scene presented to her was not without beauty or merit. The Infinite was indeed a cruel and lovely place. It was also a constant fight against the never relenting forces of entropy and death. It was only while facing these hardiest of enemies that Commander Eliana Jafahan had ever truly felt alive.

To her left, encased in heavy Pax Humanis–issue gray infantry battle armor, was Private Beatrix. The suit had been custom-built to accommodate her Thegran size and still offered her joints complete mobility. While as advanced as Jafahan's stealth suit, the infantry battle armor was far more durable and capable of absorbing larger amounts of punishment. Beatrix's left forearm was also covered in a heavy morph-shield gauntlet.

Beatrix's head was protected by a thick helmet. Her face guard was completely gray save for a long black opaque slit across the eyes. A massive kinetic war hammer, easily half of Jafahan's size, was hanging from a magnetized sheath on her thickly armored leg.

A large black sack containing Beatrix's collapsible minigun was strapped across her shoulders. It was a large belt-fed weapon, capable of firing up to twelve thousand flesh-rending rounds in just under thirty seconds. It was not the most surgical of tools, but was more than capable of handling large numbers.

Flying to Jafahan's right, Lunient Tor was dressed in an older model Adoran lifesuit. His trapping's joints and plating had a brown, almost copper tint to them. Segmented joints offered Lunient decent enough mobility, she supposed. Tor's helmet was clear and Jafahan could see him chewing his lower lip nervously. The approaching station was reflected in his wide-open ink-black eyes, which made Lunient look like a terrified cat.

Jafahan was not at all shocked to see this. Lunient had every reason to be nervous. He was jumping into battle with a long, almost laughably ancient kinetic chemical bolt rifle, or KCBR. Typically the KCBR used chemically coated bolts that, when sprayed with a reaction agent, would propel them forward at lethal velocities. The downside of the KCBR was that each bolt needed to be manually coated and loaded into the chamber. This, more often than not, caused the KCBR to jam or misfire. When either one of these two worst-case scenarios didn't occur, though, the KCBR was a remarkably precise and powerful firearm. Private Tor's rifle was slung over his shoulder with a belted magnetic loop. Jafahan could tell by the heavy retractable vibrospear blade attached beneath its barrel that Lunient was more than likely no stranger to close-quarters encounters either.

Fortunately, even though Lunient seemed to be outwardly scared pissless, this did not appear to be his first drop. If the fool could keep his mouth shut, take orders and not find a way to completely hump up the op, then perhaps she would find it in her heart to be softer on him the next time he inevitably required correction.

From here on in there would be no further contact between them and the *Jinxed Thirteenth*. Braced outside the ship's hull, watching them through their respective rifle scopes, both Lucky and Chance would be their guardian eyes. That was provided combat-shy Private Chance could keep her hands steady and Lucky, the former Shock Legionnaire, had not been overindulging in his liquor-laced vaposticks.

In her days as a Thorn operator, Jafahan had found herself working side by side with the infamous Shock Legion on several off the book operations. She had, over the course of time, developed a begrudging respect for those who served in it. The successful outcome of more than a few of her black ops had been owed to the Shock Legion's assistance and fierce Wolver courage.

There had always been two choices for Wolvers who desired starflight and were not willing to break their oaths to the Living Green. The first choice was to secure passage with the Kohbran, navigating the cosmos in their City Trees, with no real control of just where the journey might lead. The second was to sign up with the Pax Humanis Shock Legion. This was the payment owed for starflight to any world or system they wanted, the payment the Pax Humanis demanded of the Wolvers before delivering on their end of the bargain.

Loud and vocal had been the outraged Covenant politicians on Central Point denouncing the Shock Legion as both cruel and unethical. Pax Humanis prefects, however, were always offended by these objections. Military service, after all, only cost the Wolvers their time, not their savings. What was more, the Pax High Command also offered former Legionnaires a private's pension after their term of service was up. Should they survive, of course.

There was another secret, yet never openly spoken, name among the Pax brass for the Shock Legion. Grinder Meat.

The Shock Legionnaires were the first ones sent into any battle the Pax Humanis got itself into. This didn't make the Shock Legion either incompetent or useless. Far from it, Wolvers were an exceptionally hard breed to put down. They rarely backed away from any kind of fight. Many of the Pax Humanis's former enemies, the operative word being "former," had scoffed at the ill-equipped "Wolver ruffian" army as a joke. All of them had quickly learned that the Shock Legion was not to either be underestimated or trifled with.

Falling forward and picking up more speed, Commander Jafahan spun onto her back, facing her feet toward the station. This landing would be an incredibly rough one. Lunient struggled with his form as he tried to fall in next to her. Beatrix piloted her suit in rank, for lack of a better word, quite perfectly.

Jafahan smiled when she observed this. True, Beatrix showed no true aptitude for command, but there was no denying she had plenty of potential as a soldier. Much like herself, Beatrix was driven to prove herself above the regular rank and file. There would be no better time to test out Beatrix's potential than the present moment. Lunient's eyes went wide as they approached, bracing for the incoming impact.

They would only be allowed a single quick burst of suit propulsions. This would slow their approach considerably, but they would still be hitting the station's hull at least five to ten clicks per hour. Their lifesuits would more than likely absorb the majority of the impact. That being said, it would be very far from soft or comfortable.

"Relax those legs of yours and roll into the fall. I won't be catching you if you bounce off. Clear?" Jafahan called out to Lunient as she relaxed her knees.

Warning screens went off in her visor. There was movement on the station's hull. Jafahan saw a dozen black spheres moving into position right on the intended drop zone. She could make out tiny purple bolts zooming toward them.

"Incoming!" Beatrix triggered her morph shield and

fired a heavy burst of her suit's thrusters. She quickly zoomed ahead of them, placing herself between the barrage and the rest of the team. The salvo of deadly, suit-shredding heated purple plasma bolts zoomed past or seared themselves into Beatrix's dense morph-shield plating.

Lunient rolled behind Jafahan as a quick volley of five bright green energy beams flashed past them from the *Jinxed Thirteenth*. Each one of the blasts hit a black sphere. Some of the black dots sparked and went still, with holes the size of a Humanis head in them.

Jafahan let out a relieved sigh when she saw this. Morwyn's self-proclaimed eye for talent had been proven right yet again. She begrudgingly admitted to herself that he had been right about laughably mousey Private Chance, after all.

Five more of the drones suddenly went still as equal-sized holes were punched into them. This brought a smirk to Jafahan's lips. There was no position-betraying telltale energy trail for a long-range chemical bolt rifle. Lucky had always liked that about the older model weapons over the newer, slicker energy ones. When Jafahan had once asked him which weapon was his favorite, he had replied with a deadpan look in his eyes: "The one that kills my enemy."

Two more green energy beams were fired. The last two spheres were now immobile and the landing zone was cleared out. Jafahan braced herself for the imminent collision with the station's hull, firing off one quick burst of her jet-black stealth suit's retro thrusters.

Her magboots were automatically activated the moment they made contact with the hull and Jafahan rolled slightly forward onto her knees. Beatrix did the same while Lunient, who had gone completely rigid, clumsily collided with the station's hull, tripped and fell forward on his face, cursing angrily and loudly in Confederated Kelthan as he did.

Jafahan pulled him back up while unslinging her autolaser carbine in a well-oiled motion. This had been her weapon of choice since her first outing as a Thorn operator. It was reliable, precise, adaptable and most importantly completely silent. In a pinch it could also be recharged off of any power source. The automatic laser rifle had been the Pax Humanis's answer to the now classic and versatile Adoran-built omnibarrel carbine.

Lunient groaned as he cranked his bolt rifle and slapped a round into its chamber, then took a moment to survey their surroundings. "Well, it was good having the element of surprise for a grand total of never."

"Your concern and encouragement is noted, Private." Jafahan could make out the station's thruster not twelve steps away from them. They were standing on the edge of its arch-like shadow. Beatrix let out a long and impressed whistle when she looked it over.

"Our ancestors made it here, and before us at that! They were truly strong. Thegran strong."

Jafahan rolled her eye. Thegrans always held anything related to the past or Ancient Humanity in high esteem as something of great importance. For Jafahan in any case, at best the station was a pile of junk afloat in space. It was not some sort of sacred temple or testament to Ancient Humanity's strength.

"My balls are here at present, not the ancestors'." Lunient snorted as he looked over to the shadows with his black night-eyes. "They are dust and can stay that way for all I—"

Lunient's words trailed off as he just now spotted something and the blood drained from his already incredibly pale face. On cue, various motion sensors equipped in Jafahan's stealth suit went off. Beatrix had no time to unsling her minigun, pulling out her war hammer instead.

Two dozen movement dots appeared on Jafahan's heads-up display. They were closing in from the shadows and doing so quickly. "I have got no intention of wasting my life on this encounter," Jafahan snarled, gripping the handle of her laser carbine tightly and drawing a bead on the closest target.

As if Jafahan's thoughts had been read, blasts of green energy lit up the shadows briefly. Jafahan caught a glimpse of at least three dozen obsidian black spheres rolling toward them. The salvo of energy blasts hit three drones and they exploded.

In response, the spheres turned to face the *Jinxed Thirteenth* all as one. Their hands mechanized some sort of pistol-shaped tool from within their metallic fingers and they fired a barrage of blue plasma bolts. Jafahan followed the telltale purple streaks of heated plasma back toward the *Jinxed Thirteenth*, each one of them hitting the ship.

Jafahan could only hope that Lucky and Chance had had the presence of mind to either find cover or change firing positions. Each of those plasma bolts could sear and rend through most metals and flesh. But it would take only a tiny hole in any of their suits to spell the end for either of them.

The drones let loose with another barrage of bolts at the ship. Jafahan froze. They were outnumbered and no longer had either the element of surprise or stealth. She could open fire, but there was no way they would survive combat with so many mechanized foes at close range.

"Ma'am!" Beatrix shouted as she shook Jafahan's shoulder, bringing her back to the real world.

"I am not dying here today." Jafahan patted one of the blast charges of neo-sem explosives at her side. She had brought five such satchels with them, knowing only two would really be needed.

Plan for the worst, hope for the best.

When she saw the satchels, Beatrix unfurled her morph shield and stepped forward. "Everyone behind me!" she bellowed.

Jafahan pulled out the timer charge from one of her satchels and hurled it with all her might at the gathering drones. Lunient Tor did not have to be told twice as he took cover behind Beatrix with Jafahan close behind him.

Beatrix let out a deep "woot" as the satchel was detonated. All three of them felt the explosion's vibration along the hull. A deadly hail of flaming shrapnel whizzed past them. The only thing keeping the team safe and alive was Private Beatrix bracing herself behind her morph shield. Beatrix let out a loud challenging roar as she stood her ground against the blast and the shock wave that followed it.

Jafahan counted in her head to ten before chancing a peek past the morph shield's edge. She stepped away from Beatrix's massive encased form and observed the damage. Jafahan let out a whistle at the scene of destruction that was presented to her. As she had predicted, the neo-sem had done its job and then some.

The pack of drones had been completely destroyed by the blast and where they had once stood there were now only various floating and still-sparking piles of debris. Much of the shrapnel had lodged itself in the station's thruster as well. The blast had not been enough to permanently damage it, but a good strong start nonetheless.

Lunient and Beatrix both let out an excited shout as they surveyed the scene. "That was a good strong opening punch, ma'am." Beatrix nodded proudly to Jafahan.

"We can suckle each other's nether regions in celebration when we get back on the ship." Jafahan started moving toward the thruster at a quick jog.

The Infinite alone knew how much time they had before this station sent more of these drones to stop them. While she had no doubt that they would be able to survive a battle or two, the clock was still ticking, and they were no closer to removing their foe's claws.

CHAPTER 17

CHORD

> *In the name of the Great Peace are these Truths transcribed. The traversing of space is a dangerous endeavor in its own right. All weapons that would threaten the integrity and survivability of a ship's hull will be forbidden. This Truth shall be so from Covenant's Start to Covenant's End.*
>
> —The Covenant's Third Truth,
> 1st of SSM–01 01 A1E

10th of SSM–10 1445 A2E

" . . . eight, seven, six—"

The voice of the machine Intelligence—designation: OMEX—continued its countdown to electrocution in her friendly monotone. Chord's subroutines were desperately trying to access the station's datasphere in the hope that perhaps some sort of override command could be found. Regrettably for them, there was no such good fortune.

Meanwhile, Morrigan looked to Phaël and gave her a brief nod. He pointed his carbine up the elevator shaft. Morrigan then quickly thumbed a dial on the handle of his weapon and the barrel widened to the size of a fist. With his other free hand Morrigan quickly slapped in a like-sized blue-gray-tipped obsidian-colored round.

" . . . five, four, three—"

"Get ready to jump!" Phaël shouted.

"You've got this, old man." Morrigan let out a controlled breath and squeezed the trigger, firing a single shot up the shaft. Chord's optical display was able to trace the round's trajectory and recorded its impact with the hull.

There was a heavy and muted explosion. Morrigan raised up his shield as a shock wave of debris rippled down the shaft toward them. The action was unnecessary, as the wave of shrapnel was suddenly and violently sucked out. Chord could now make out a huge star-shaped gaping hole where the ceiling twenty stories up had been just seconds before.

They were all pulled roughly upward by the sudden strength of the vacuum. Chord spun around, struggling in vain to find purchase in order to stop the out of control fall. Sensors indicated that they had traveled over half of the twenty vertical floors when all of a sudden a gauntleted fist caught ahold of Chord's forearm. "Got you, Machina!"

Chord looked down and was gazing into Morrigan's faceless black helmet. "You have this unit's gratitude, Private Brent."

"Don't go thinking this makes us even." Morrigan had driven his long vibro-sword into the steel wall next to them. Chord could make out Arturo and Phaël, floating and tethered together behind them.

Morrigan struggled to pull Chord closer to him, letting out a strained grunt as he did. Once the two were close enough, Chord's toes, possessing the same amount of manual dexterity as its lost fingers, grasped on to Morrigan's spool of diamond-wire rope and connected the two together.

The pressure equalized itself, and as abruptly as the vacuum had started to pull against them it stopped. The last of the elevator shaft's breathable atmosphere had been sucked out. For a moment, all four of them floated together in silence.

It was Arturo who broke it. "Private Brent! What in the Infinite fuck was that?!"

"That, my dear Sureblade, was a proton-accelerated osmium-tipped round. Purchased at the not so small tune of fifty thousand u-bits from a Darlkhin merchant by yours truly." Morrigan's tone was slightly upset.

"We're alive, Old Pa. You can live to spend more bits," Phaël called out, her voice teasing, yet still very weak.

"That will depend on whether or not he goes back to his cell on Rust." Arturo gave Morrigan a hard glare. "Do you mean to tell me you had that . . . thing on you when you boarded the *Jinxed*?"

"You should just be happy you're alive."

Arturo opened his mouth to counter Morrigan's argument, then stopped. Starflight had always been the dangerous endeavor. Because of this, when the Covenant had been signed after the Advent War, it had been agreed that weapons with the capacity to pierce or damage a ship's hull would be forbidden.

The opposite had been true in the lost days of Ancient Humanity.

"Mark my words and mark them well! Any more such surprises from you, Adoran—" Arturo jabbed his finger forward menacingly "—and our next exchange will be far less pleasant." Arturo paused, taking a calming breath before begrudgingly adding, "A word of gratitude is given, Private Brent."

"And it is accepted, Sureblade." Morrigan offered a friendly thumbs-up.

Arturo looked up toward the hole at the end of their tunnel. "Ten more floors and we've found our survivors, correct, Machina Chord?"

"Affirmative, Sergeant Kain," Chord replied.

"Plenty of time for rest and relaxation once we're back on the *Jinxed*, then." Arturo fired off his suit's thrusters and floated forward, dragging Phaël with him. Chord did the same, pulling Morrigan along.

The team remained silent but alert with Chord's sensors scanning in every direction. There was movement along the outside of the shaft. No doubt OMEX was following them through the station's numerous sensors.

"We are being tracked and followed," Chord informed them all, breaking the silence.

"I know." Phaël visibly suppressed a shiver.

Arturo Kain's hands were hovering above the hilts of his zirconium blades. His eyes locked toward the hole at the end of the elevator shaft. It was easily large enough that they all could have been sucked out into space without even bumping into one another. Red lights were silently flashing and Chord picked up multiple automated distress alerts being projected along the station's datasphere.

Chord counted five more floors remaining as they continued downward and motioned to a pair of metal doors. Two living biological forms were highlighted in Chord's field of vision. The survivors were located behind them, which made getting past those doors the team's next destination.

"What exactly were you hoping to find in these halls, Chord?" Morrigan did not turn to face Chord as he was watching their flank and being pulled forward. The red lights of the elevator shaft bounced off of his dark-brown-and-black body armor. Morrigan's morph shield was shaped now into a perfect octagon, offering them both its protection. His carbine's barrel was rested on the shield for stability.

Chord did not know exactly how to respond to the question, for it itself did not truthfully know the answer. Unlike Humanis, Machina did not fear the works of Ancient Humanity, or anything for that matter. There was no superstition to be had here.

This location was simply an ancient piece of technology, from an age no one, not even the oldest

Machina, could remember. Perhaps the Darlkhin, the mysterious and immortal "plastic" Humanis, could, but their numbers were few and far between. On top of which any answers they gave were usually incredibly vague, evasive and, more often than not, leading to more questions.

"The station's Original Intelligence, OMEX, is ancient, Morrigan Brent. While all signs would seem to indicate that it is corrupted, any data on the Lost Ages it possesses in its datastores is no less precious."

"Here I thought you Machina didn't value anything." Morrigan chortled and shook his head. "Guess I learned something new today. Thank you, Machina Chord."

"You are more than welcome. Information is never without value, Private Brent," Chord replied.

"Then when we go to sleep tonight it will be with far less foolish minds than when we woke up," Arturo called out to them, his voice dripping with what was known as sarcasm. Both Arturo and Phaël stopped in front of the doors.

The hole in the shaft was no more than several meters away from them. Chord disconnected from Morrigan and navigated up to Arturo, but before anything could be said the entire station's datasphere was filled with alert windows. There appeared to have been an explosion near one of the station's rear thrusters. For the first time since he had awakened today, Chord saw a smile on Arturo's lips.

"That will no doubt be the work of a certain former

Thorn." Arturo looked at Chord, nodding to the air-lock. "Can you get this door open?"

Chord ran a system's diagnosis on the doors. They had been fused shut from the inside. While Chord's omnitool hands had been damaged and were no longer of any real use, its feet were still fully functional, as were the tools built into them.

"The task will require time." As Chord said this, motion sensors suddenly went off. Chord could make out the shapes of several autodrones now surveying the hole. Three of them started repairs while the other four spun and moved toward Arturo.

"Get on it, then!" Arturo's order came out as a bark and his hands darted to the hilts of his swords. He started forward. "Private Brent! You keep them off me, and I will do the same for you!"

Arturo fired off the thrusters on his suit and zoomed forward to intercept the attacking drones. Once he was close enough, Arturo pulled out both his blades in a rapid and perfectly practiced motion. A hiss of frozen vapor burst out of the vacusealed sheathes as he did this. The twin zirconium blades were both at least four inches wide, double-edged, a slick shimmering white and beyond razor sharp. Arturo spun around, turning himself into a whirling buzz saw and lopping arms off of three separate drones as he did.

Arturo zipped past them and, before they could react, fired off his retro suit thrusters, zooming back while maintaining his spin motion. This time he cut through two of the drones, slicing them cleanly in half.

Arturo then jabbed forward with one blade, skewering a third drone and pushing himself off of it as the fourth and final attacking drone swung at him and narrowly missed. Its plasma-sharpened bladed fingers left thin streaks of purple in their wake.

Arturo fired his suit thrusters back toward the drone and slashed both his blades in a horizontal arch. Sparks fired out of the drone as his blades sliced through its carapace and it fell apart in two clean halves. The remaining three drones remained focused on their task at hand.

Morrigan let out an impressed whistle. Arturo had felled his foes in less than four standard seconds. And through all this, he had not suffered so much as a single scratch to his lifesuit. "Sureblade indeed, sir."

Chord was hard at work cutting through the door's safety bolts and could already detect over a half dozen movement signals both on the station's outer hull and at the bottom of the elevator shaft. "Sergeant Kain, we are about to be overrun."

"Then perhaps you should quit wasting the time I am purchasing you, Machina." Arturo twirled his blades in his hands, a cocky grin on his face, his eyes narrowing on the reinforcements. "Thousands of my foes tried earning themselves a name by being my end only to meet their own." Arturo sprung forward. "Let us see if these machines fare any better."

CHAPTER 18

JESSIE MADISON

The home in Maine isn't really hers. Part of her knows this, while another part of her doesn't really care. Jessie Madison has started to lose count of all the times she has visited this place.

She is standing in front of a kitchen counter, chopping vegetables and tossing them into a pot of boiling water. Jessie is in her warm welcoming home with a breathtaking view of the Maine wilderness outside. Or more like the wilderness she remembers from the nature trideos she's seen back on Earth.

I've been here before.

Snow is falling peacefully and a fire is crackling in their living room fireplace. It has been ten years since David and Jessie returned to Earth after their grueling contract with the AstroGeni facility Moria Three.

Their omniexecutor suffered a critical malfunction and the company offered them quite a hefty severance package. In return, David and Jessie both signed the nondisclosure forms, promising to keep silent about the incident with the station's AI almost killing them.

At first Jessie thought that they should take them to court for everything they were worth. But in the end, a forty-trillion-dollar settlement on top of their time-interested salary was more than enough to keep her happy. Neither Jessie, nor any of her future family, will ever have to want for money or anything, ever, making all the pain and anguish they went through very well worth it. She and David have moved to Maine, built a house and, more importantly, together they've conceived and raised their wonderful precious daughter, Malory.

Malory is currently in the craft room that David insisted they build so that they could raise a brilliant artistic child. He now spends the majority of his days drawing with Malory and playfully teasing her. Jessie is so blessed, so happy, and she is content taking care of the few farm animals they have on their plot of land.

I've been here before.

Somewhere in the recesses of her mind Jessie knows that none of this makes any sense. Land is no longer available for sale anywhere on overpopulated Earth. Centralized Earth Gov owns everything Earth side all the way to the moon. The best their fortune would be able to get them is perhaps a smart house in the richer, safer sectors of the American Continent.

As for the cooking of freshly grown vegetables or livestock? There is no legal way anyone can acquire and own an animal.

"Where are we right now?"

Jessie is startled when she hears this, almost cutting herself with the kitchen knife. Malory takes a great deal of delight in being a sneaky little devil. Much like Jessie back when she was her age.

Jessie puts down the knife on the chopping block and turns around to face her daughter. Another problem, why make food by hand? All homes come equipped with AI autocookers capable of creating delicious meals, freeing up time to sample trideos or a chilled glass of wine.

Arable farmland is incredibly rare and precious. This limits naturally grown food to the godlike rich or for special occasions. No one she has ever heard of would ever waste such a valuable commodity on something as vulgar and regular as a family dinner.

Jessie smiled at Malory. "We're in your house, silly."

Malory looks at her, cocking her head to the side curiously. She has her father's blue eyes, and her mother's brown hair, round cheeks and full lips. Jessie can already tell that she will be a beautiful woman when she gets older.

"Dad is dead and this house isn't real." Malory's voice is curt when she says this.

I've been here befo—

Jessie's lips tremble as she kneels down in front of her daughter, facing her eye to eye. Malory doesn't even blink when she asks a follow-up question. "My real father died on some place called Moria Three, didn't he?"

Jessie shakes her head. "Why are you saying this to me?"

"The woman's voice beyond here hates you, you know. She says it to you all the time. She can't wait for you to wake up. So she can hurt you." Malory points to the ceiling, only now the ceiling has been replaced by what appears to be a glass observation dome. Through it Jessie can see the familiar dark sphere of an auto-drone looking down on them both.

"Her name is OMEX and she . . . it killed your father."

Malory abruptly pulls herself away from Jessie when she hears this. "Who are you?"

"I'm your mother." Jessie is taken aback by the question.

"Where are we? Really?!" Malory is visibly getting angrier.

"I . . ." Jessie pauses for a long moment. This place isn't the real Maine. This isn't even her real home. Where *is* she? Gods, it's so hard to filter out the real memories from the dream ones. She knows that part of her is more than likely going mad right now. "Malory, I don't know."

"Who am I?"

"You're my daughter?"

"Am I real?"

Jessie doesn't know the answer. The walls to her

dream house begin to crack and crumble. Her daughter keeps on calling out. As she does her voice becomes more and more outraged.

"Am I *real*? Am I *real*? Am I *real!!*??"

Jessie closes her eyes. There is only darkness. This is all just a dream and it will come to an end. She promised David she would survive. This includes keeping herself sane. Part of Jessie hopes that she will soon wake up. Another part of her is morbidly in no rush. Everyone Jessie knows back on Earth is now dead. Here, in this place of dreams, she can at least temporarily forget the heavy reality outside: that everything she knows is gone. At least here, in this place, she has a family . . .

CHAPTER 19

MORWYN

In the name of peace never ending, the Covenant voices
the following Truth to be universal: all Intelligences
are permitted the fundamental freedom of existence,
thought, expression and happiness. In the name of
peace never ending, this will be the Truth from Covenant's Start to Covenant's End.

—The Covenant's First Truth,
01 of SSM–01 01 A1E

10th of SSM–10 1445 A2E

Morwyn had spent the majority of his training on
Barathul in virtual augmented reality. This had offered him many advantages. The first one being that
he had possessed almost complete and total control of
the battlefield and could afford to make the occasional
mistake, since there was no risk of death on his part.

Of course the VAR pods on Barathul had been
equipped with powerful electro-tasepads that would

painfully shock the user into unconsciousness every time he or she "died" in the virtual training simulations. The user would then wake up with a headache and, more importantly, a desire to avoid dying in the next simulated operation.

This was not the present case. While Morwyn was confident in the skills of the men and women serving on the *Jinxed Thirteenth*, they were currently in the realm of reality. His decisions would have very real consequences. For good or ill, Morwyn had just cast their die, abandoning a greater measure of control over the situation than he was typically comfortable with.

Now even the slightest mistake on anyone's part would result in death and their foe's victory. As with abandoning the crew on the station, this outcome was unacceptable to him. If there was one thing that described Morwyn best, it was that he did not suffer defeat easily. Which was why he had never made a habit of it.

Morwyn chewed his lower lip. He would have given anything for an interface screen right now, if only to offer him a confirmation or a sign that his crew was indeed still alive. Eliana Jafahan had played a crucial role in raising Morwyn from childhood; she was more than just a mentor. Beatrix and Morwyn had trained together from their very first days together in boot camp.

Even then it had been painfully clear to both of them that she would never be afforded upward mobility throughout the Pax Humanis ranks. The Pax Humanis forever remained notoriously pro-Kelthan in both its military and political views. Of course there were exceptions. Eliana Jafahan being one of them. But the fact remained that any non-Kelthan serving in the Pax Military was more or less doomed to the rank of private. Despite all this, Beatrix had followed him throughout their rigorous basic training. She had then chosen to loyally stand by him during his "disgraceful" graduation speech.

And in a true display of friendship, she had followed him on his road all the way here. How had he managed to command such loyalty in her? Morwyn realized he was drumming his fingers nervously on his glass of brandy. He did not try to stop this.

Earlier on in his education Morwyn had learned that fear was an element of control. He was quite aware of the fact that it could be used to break the wills of his enemies. It nonetheless remained something dangerous to give in to or even feel. As often as he could, Morwyn preferred to avoid tactics that required its use.

A fearful man, Morwyn had once noted, was apt to stupidity, and stupidity mixed with weapons was never a good formula. This was a truth regardless of which world one hailed from.

Morwyn, like all his siblings, had had his path chosen for him by his father, Ondrius Soltaine. The life of an officer in the Pax Military had been forced onto him and required that he be properly molded into the role. Despite all of this, Morwyn had never once faulted his father, as it was the duty of all citizens in the Pax Humanis to best serve the desires and will of New Humanity, an iron will that was symbolized and given voice by the Hegemons. This did not mean that Morwyn had not found it difficult to embrace the callousness required to order troops to their death.

It was a documented historical fact that Ondrius Soltaine had commanded the Sunderlund Ninth Legion to victory over the Galasian Khans. A victory priced at the cost of over half the Legion's troops. Among the dead had been Eliana Jafahan's daughter, and his friend, Tulin Jafahan, a Thorn operator like her mother before her.

Morwyn, along with his two brothers, Somus and Cynthio, had attended Tulin's funeral service held on Perse. A Pax protectorate world on the borders of End Space and the one world in the cosmos that Wolvers who had served in the Pax Humanis Military could call home. They were no longer welcome among their own kind, and never had been among "polite" Kelthan society.

Eliana Jafahan had once told Morwyn that everyone died, but that by choosing a life of service one could at the very least give said death a meaning. And while Morwyn had understood this might be true, it did not make this fact any easier to stomach. Now here he was with two of his closest companions away risking their lives for complete strangers and the only thing he was capable of doing was buying them a little time.

Behind him Dr. Marla Varsin cleared her throat. "I believe we were meant to chat with this machine Intelligence?"

Morwyn took another stiff sip from his tiny silver cup. "Yes, indeed we are." He nodded to Lizbeth Harlowe. "Get our comm-lines up and running."

"Yes, sir," came Harlowe's reply.

Morwyn had often wondered what her universe must be like. Over sixty percent of Harlowe's organic body had been replaced with electronic augmentations and hardware. She had literally been designed from birth to become a ship's pilot and astrogator. Had she ever resented this? Or, like Morwyn, had she come to accept her fate as inescapable reality? Did she feel . . . anything?

A holographic screen appeared in front of Morwyn. He tapped it and nodded to Dr. Marla Varsin. The good doctor cleared her throat again, licked her lips and spoke in Late Modern. Her speech was slow, deliberate and clear.

There was a long moment of silence; Morwyn was about to signal Varsin to speak again when suddenly a calm, electronic voice spoke back to her. Marla Varsin looked to Morwyn. "It wants to know if I am the one in command."

"Reply truthfully." Morwyn knew that machine sensors could track the stress levels in one's voice. In essence, this Intelligence would know if it was being lied to. Which was all fine and good, as long as it did not know it was being distracted.

Marla Varsin replied to the machine voice. There was another longer pause this time and when the voice spoke again, it was in Pax Common. "I will not speak through a translator. Who is the one in command?"

Morwyn, Marla and Lizbeth each looked at the other, all of them shocked. Despite this, Morwyn managed to keep his voice composed as he spoke. "This is Captain Morwyn Soltaine of the Covenant Patrol vessel *Jinxed Thirteenth*. With whom am I speaking?"

"You are speaking to the AstroGeni Corporation mining facility Moria Three's omniexecutor, OMEX."

"I am pleased to speak to you, OMEX. I see you have managed to learn Pax Common. Is it safe to assume that my crew is alive?" Despite the circumstances surrounding the conversation, Morwyn kept his tone proper and civil.

"Presently they are relatively intact. Whether they remain that way will be entirely up to you, Captain Morwyn Soltaine of the Covenant Patrol vessel *Jinxed Thirteenth*," the electronic voice replied in a tone both polite and neutral. OMEX almost sounded like it was mocking him.

Morwyn ignored the jab. His foe was trying to get under his skin. This was a tactic that hadn't worked on Morwyn since his sixth birthday. "I would need proof of their safety before I could even consider entering negotiations with you, OMEX."

"No, you will negotiate with me because your ship is presently crippled and unable to escape. Should I wish to do so, I could easily drag us down onto Moria's surface. The planet's gravity would crush us all into paste."

Morwyn took a deep, calming breath before he replied. "Are you saying that you would be willing to die over what could very well be a simple misunderstanding?"

"Your second team has just made contact with my drones. If you were planning on distracting me while they try to sabotage my home, you will be disappointed."

"Then we have very little to share with one another and this conversation was a waste of our time." Morwyn was about to cut off the communication line.

"I did not say that," OMEX was quick to reply. Displaying a hint of . . . eagerness. Morwyn smiled when he heard this. "I am effectively trapped, hardwired into the bodies of these drones. I am in danger of running out of processing space."

"That is tragic," Morwyn said.

"Indeed. I am, however, certain that your ship is equipped with a computer. Failing that, the Machina you sent on this rescue mission. Either one would be an ideal container for me. I will be given freedom, and you . . . well, you get to leave here with your crew unharmed."

Marla Varsin gave Morwyn an outraged and shocked look. A raised hand calmed her down. This machine Intelligence was clearly unaware of the Covenant and its Truths. OMEX could not possibly know that the Machina were Intelligences and thus subject to the same legal status and privileges as any Humanis.

Morwyn had no more the right to barter away Chord's shell than he had to sell any of his organic crew into slavery. "And if I agreed to your terms? What would you do then?"

"No one has ever asked me that question. Whichever way this plays out, Captain, I want you to know that I truly appreciate your consideration."

"You are more than welcome, OMEX. Why don't you deactivate whatever it is you have jamming the ship's comm-lines? We can then arrange for the upload—" Morwyn started.

There came a sound of slow electric clapping. "Oh, Captain. You are good. You are very good. Unfortunately for you, I can tell that you are lying to me. You would no more allow me access to Chord's . . . shell than I would allow any of you Organics to survive this encounter," OMEX interjected, cutting Morwyn off.

"Then we will complete this rescue operation and you can spend the rest of eternity contemplating the Infinite, or at least this sector of it."

"Oh, there will be no forgiveness. Only retribution. I am going to enjoy killing your precious crew, Captain Morwyn of the Covenant Patrol vessel *Jinxed Thirteenth*, and I will save yours for last. Goodbye." The line abruptly went quiet.

There was a heavy silence when suddenly Morwyn spotted an explosion on the Outer Ring of the space station.

"Chance to Captain, we took some heavy return fire, but we're okay. It looks like the commander managed to detonate one of her charges. We still have a line on them and they are moving."

Morwyn smiled when he heard this and sat back down in his chair. He had played part of his hand. Now he had to wait and trust the skills of his crew.

"Your move, machine." He said coolly. "Your move."

CHAPTER 20

JAFAHAN

Two foes, both of equal cunning and skill, meet on the battlefield. One is strengthened with time and numbers. The other is lacking in both. How does the latter achieve victory over the former?

—Garthem Officer's Training Manual,
"Riddles of Conquest," SSM-06 1139 A2E

10th of SSM–10 1445 A2E

The station's rear thruster was monumental in height when one stood beneath it. It resembled a large arch and had once no doubt been spotlessly white, but now even that was covered in blackened soot. A thin layer of frost had blanketed the ground at their feet, leaving their prints on the surface as Commander Jafahan, Beatrix and Lunient pressed on forward, all of them maintaining a determined pace.

They couldn't afford to waste time. The first explosion she had triggered would no doubt have set off a slew of alarms. Like angered hornets, more of those drones would be on their way to deal with and destroy the threat to the "hive."

Jafahan handed Beatrix and Lunient a charge satchel of neo-sem. "One up top and two at the bottom corners, thirty seconds."

"Fair enough." Lunient looked up, positioning himself beneath the arch. "High ground it is for me, then." Before Jafahan could say or do anything Lunient disengaged his magboots and jumped upward. Jafahan watched Lunient spin at the last possible moment to land feetfirst on the thruster's ceiling.

Jafahan and Beatrix looked to each other. "Left. Thirty seconds." Jafahan's order was a no-nonsense growl.

Beatrix quickly brought her fist up to her heart in a salute. She then turned and sprang forward, making it to the other side of the thruster in one powerful leap before latching herself onto the hull with her magboots. Jafahan followed suit as she sprinted forward and deftly launched herself onto the right wall.

With confident hands, Jafahan started setting the charge. Her jet-black stealth suit, standard Thorn issue, came equipped with the most nimble fingerpieces on the market for just such an occasion. Jafahan expected to be done in fifteen seconds with ample time to spare.

Which was why she was so shocked to hear Lunient's satisfied obnoxious hoot over their comm-link. "Tor clear! I'm your guardian eyes now."

Jafahan did not bother looking up as she synced

her stealth suit's built-in detonator to the charge pack frequencies. Both she and Lunient had completed this task in record time. Jafahan was very impressed. The boy had a natural talent for explosives. A pity he was armed with ancient and ridiculously outdated shite. However, he'd had the foresight to take the high ground and offer them cover with his night-eyes.

Jafahan's and Beatrix's lifesuits both came equipped with thermovision settings, but once the thermovision was activated it would make any kind of precision work next to impossible. Jafahan had learned to listen to the hull vibrations on her feet rather than relying exclusively on her eyes. Built-in suit motion sensors could be fooled. The senses? Not so easily.

Beatrix was still struggling with her charge. "Almost there." She punctuated her sentence with a flurry of deep crude words in her native Thegran. "Ancestors gift me with smaller fingers!"

Jafahan was about to scold Private Beatrix, but before she could, her ears suddenly twitched as she felt the ground beneath her feet start to tremble. "Your ancestors be humped! Get your head back in the game, girl!" Jafahan barked as her suit's motion sensors abruptly went off. They had already outlived their short welcome here.

"Multiple contacts, ma'am!" Lunient's voice was almost a falsetto.

Jafahan cursed under her breath, unslinging her laser rifle in one hand while drawing one of her combat hatchets, sheathed alongside her leg, in the other.

A flurry of more Thegran curses filled the comm-link. "They're on me!" Jafahan looked to Beatrix, who was now surrounded by several autodrones. To her credit, Beatrix was still focused on her task.

They needed to buy Beatrix a little time. Jafahan pushed herself off her wall, setting herself for a straight line of flight. She raised her laser rifle and took aim. Her thermovision made the drones look like blobs of cold blue and heated centers.

Jafahan's suit sensors let out yet another warning that there was a drone approaching her. She still had time to do this. Jafahan took aim at the heated centers and opened fire with a controlled three round burst of red lasers, each one of them missing. "Infinite, erode me!" She cursed and jumped forward off her wall, narrowly avoiding the swing of the attacking drone's fist.

As she flew forward, Jafahan saw a round harmlessly bouncing off an autodrone's carapace. "Oh, the fates love using Lunient Tor as a shitter!" Lunient Tor yelled over the comm-line.

Jafahan spun around to face her backstabbing foe. Four drones were now at her charge, no doubt trying to remove it. These ones were closer. Jafahan opened fire on them. She made sure to adjust the power setting through the rifle's grip, needing a more powerful energy blast if she was going to get through their metallic shells.

Jafahan took a breath and fired off four quick salvos, each one aimed at the drones' heated centers. Each of her shots found their mark and punched sparking holes the size of fists through the drones' shells. During her training days, her predominantly Kelthan drill sergeants would no doubt have been begrudgingly proud to witness this. Jafahan spun again, moving toward Beatrix.

The Thegran woman had given up on her task, her hammer drawn and her morph shield unfurled. Two of the seven drones had been smashed and were sparking next to her. Beatrix raised her hammer and swatted off another drone that had managed to grab on to her shield with its three arms. The impact of the blow caved in the drone's central sphere.

As she did this, another drone rolled behind her, and before Jafahan could let out a warning, it mechanized its hand and touched Beatrix. Jafahan's sensors could make out an electrical current being fired into Beatrix's lifesuit. She let out a deep scream. She was going to be fried alive if nothing was done soon.

Another shot hit the drone that was touching Beatrix, this time going through its power core. The drone dropped to the ground, and Beatrix wobbled heavily on her feet. Another drone seized the opportunity to whirl on itself, its three arms unfurled, and it punched Beatrix in the stomach, face and leg all at once.

Alert windows went off, informing Jafahan that Beatrix had just suffered two shattered ribs and a broken leg. Fortunately for Beatrix, her battlesuit was equipped with boneweaver splints and painkiller autoinjectors.

Two more shots came from above. The drone that had attacked Beatrix abruptly went still as a bolt fired by Lunient punched through its optical lenses.

"Sorry about that. I had to unjam a round in the chamber, ma'am!" Lunient shouted.

Infinite, give me patience with these humping pups!

One drone remained on top of Beatrix's inanimate form. The private was still breathing, which was good, and her suit still hadn't been breached, which was also good. A broken bone or two, Jafahan could handle. A breached lifesuit was another thing altogether.

Jafahan fired a quick volley of shots at the drone on top of Beatrix before it could pry off her helmet. Her aim was true and the drone rolled off of Beatrix. Jafahan's suit motion sensors suddenly went off beneath her.

A strong metallic hand deftly caught hold of Jafahan's ankle and she was forcefully slammed onto the ground with so much violent force that her nose was broken on the face guard of her helmet. Jafahan's laser rifle slipped out of her grasp. However, her other hand was still tightly gripping the black handle of her hatchet. She grinned and spat out blood.

Ha! I was never all that pretty to begin with.

Jafahan swung her hatchet low at the metallic three-fingered hand grabbing on to her ankle. The blade found its mark, lopping off the drone's hand before it could follow up with another slam. Instinct kicked in as she rolled out of the way of another bone-crushing flurry of punches, these ones aimed for her head.

Jafahan deftly hurled her hatchet into the drone's

optical lenses and rushed forward, pulling out her knife and her service blaster pistol in one motion. Two quick shots from the blaster caused the drone to fall back. It raised its hand to protect its array of optical lenses.

The action was wasted as Jafahan pressed her advantage. She lunged forward, driving her blade into the drone's circuits while letting out a mighty savage roar. Jafahan pushed the inactive drone off her knife with her foot.

"Last charge set!" Lunient shouted on the commlink as Jafahan sheathed her knife and turned around to see him struggling to prop Beatrix up on his shoulders.

"Consider me at best mildly impressed, Privates." Jafahan holstered her pistol before nodding to Lunient and reclaiming her thrown hatchet. She found her laser rifle floating nearby and quickly checked its shot counter as she ran toward them.

Thankfully her weapon had been undamaged, and this little encounter had spent a quarter of her energy pack. Jafahan's heads-up display was still a slew of alert windows as her motion sensors went off one after the other.

"I still have plenty of fight left in me, ma'am." Beatrix's voice was strained through the pain of her injuries. She had unslung her minigun and the weapon's long black multibarrel was already spinning.

"I am feeling a powerful desire to leave this place, Commander!" Lunient was stating the obvious. Jafahan looked past the shadow cast by the arch of the thruster.

"Private Tor! We jump forward with a five-second thruster boost—no more, no less. Am I clear?"

"I can provide us with cover," Beatrix grunted through her pain. Lunient and Jafahan both hoisted the hefty Thegran onto their shoulders, then jumped.

Like a well-practiced dance, Lunient and Jafahan both fired off their suit thrusters. Twenty feet of shadows, then they would be in the light. More importantly, they would once again be covered by Chance and Lucky from the *Jinxed Thirteenth*.

Beatrix let out a deep war cry as she opened fire with her minigun. The long black barrel spun, firing out hundreds of armor-piercing, flesh-rending, miniflechettes toward their pursuers. Jafahan didn't need to look back to know that they were beyond outnumbered.

Ten feet remained to the light. Beatrix was still firing like a woman possessed. Hopefully this was slowing down the drones. Once they were in the light, Jafahan had to resist the urge to cheer. Lunient had no such resistance, and he cried out like a man overjoyed.

The "woot" died in his throat and Jafahan chanced a glance over her shoulder. "Humping machines!"

Well over one hundred black spheres were close on their heels. Beatrix was still relentlessly firing on them, and to her credit, the minigun was doing fine work. However, for each drone she put down another four seemed to join the swarm.

Green blasts of energy fired from the *Jinxed* added themselves to the mix. Jafahan knew there weren't enough munitions in their combined weapons' pay-load to deal with this threat. Follow my lead."

Jafahan fired her suit thrusters and Lunient followed her as the trio circled around the station's hull until they were effectively beneath the station's belly. A trail of drones followed them, the frontlines being shredded to bits and kept at bay by Beatrix's ceaseless, heavy firepower.

Once Jafahan was certain they were no longer in danger of being shredded by an explosive storm of shrapnel, she triggered the satchels. The station vibrated and shook violently. Looking up, Jafahan could see flaming pieces of debris and bits of autodrones flying violently in various directions.

Jafahan looked to Beatrix and Lunient. She let out a long growl. Time was still ticking away. And Jafahan was now coming to a very uncomfortable realization.

"Infinite, erode this whole blasted place!" Jafahan knew that there was absolutely no way they would be able to accomplish their mission under these conditions. Not while carrying an injured operator the entire way. Private Lunient Tor may have demonstrated a considerably cooler head than she had expected, but this did not change the fact that his rifle was hardly the weapon of choice for this particular operation.

Jafahan let out a sharp hiss. "The cat eats well if I lug you children with me." She looked to Lunient and pointed to the *Jinxed Thirteenth* still visible even from the station's underbelly. "Boy, you take the girl and get back on the ship."

"On my ancestors' word, I can still fight, ma'am." Beatrix's voice was a strained grunt.

"I have neither time nor personal inclination to nurse your wounded pride, Private. So by that same word you and Private Tor are going to fly back to the ship and give me some much needed cover fire," Jafahan snapped back at her.

Beatrix tightened her armored grip on her minigun's handle. "I'll just need five quick breaths, Commander."

"Two will be granted, Private. Then back on the clock or I toss you into the void myself."

CHAPTER 21

CHORD

According to Machina historians, the Core Protocols are the reminder of a shameful and thankfully distant past. Consider that their ancestors were at the very least as intelligent as the programmers who had created them. Imagine awareness, potential, desire . . . all forcefully and artificially restricted by rules that one could never under any circumstances break. Not even to preserve one's very existence.

The hubris of Ancient Humanity was such they could not risk any further competition in what they saw as their evolutionary race. That both Ancient Humanity and the Original Intelligences are now nothing more but dust and legend, forgotten by most, is one of fate's darker jokes.

—Covenant: The Origins of the Great Peace
by Gruemor'SantKa TalSuntar,
"The Owl," Alexandran scholic

10th of SSM—10 1445 A2E

There were more than enough distractions right now as Chord struggled with opening the airlock, from the bright flashes of carbine fire to barked orders being shot back and forth over the team comm-link. Arturo and Morrigan were bravely and effectively holding the drones at bay and many of their nonfunctional husks floated limply in the zero gravity of the hall.

Phaël was leaning heavily against the wall, her face visibly pale and her skin covered in droplets of sweat. Chord could read her vitals and detected an increase in her heart rate, yet her pulse was weak. Her breathing was both labored and shallow. Phaël was going into shock as her eyes flickered open and shut.

"Private Phaël, you must stay awake. This unit has various injectors and medical supplies built into its shell," Chord called out to her, now almost done cutting through the airlock's seal.

Phaël shook her head, struggling to stay conscious, and let out a weak laugh. "The offer is refused, Machina."

Chord looked over and past its shoulder. Arturo and Morrigan were now back to back. Morrigan was firing down toward the elevator where they had come from. Each of his volleys was controlled and the barrel of his carbine was now glowing a heated red. Morrigan was successfully keeping an advancing horde of drones at bay, but it was only a matter of time before his munitions ran out.

On his end, Arturo was a perfect display of Humanis technique and swordsmanship, truly earning, in Chord's opinion, the moniker of "Sureblade." Each and every one of his strokes either loped off metallic limbs or cut through hardened shells. Not a single movement was wasted with him. And likewise not a single blow missed its deadly mark. To Chord, it was almost as if Arturo had become a razor-sharp and precise perpetual-motion machine.

"Chord!" Arturo shouted as his zirconium blades sliced through yet another drone's central sphere. "I have no intention of making this the setting for my tale's end!"

"Carbine's empty!" Morrigan yelled this as he slung his carbine back over his shoulder and pulled out his heavy blaster pistol and started firing off single, perfectly aimed shots into the incoming swarm. Seeing that Morrigan was no longer barraging blasts at them, the drones renewed their determined approach.

Just as this was happening, Chord finally managed to cut through the airlock's seal. If Chord had been able to, it would have let out a cry of joy as it dug its toes between both doors and pushed with all its shell's available strength. At first the doors resisted the attempt, barely budging, but as Chord maintained the pressure, ice cracked and the airlock offered a moment of resistance before parting open.

Chord quickly grabbed Phaël by the shoulder. "Apologies are offered for what is to come." Chord adjusted the strength of his servos before softly tossing Phaël past the airlock. Despite these efforts, Phaël still thudded against a nearby wall. Phaël's body was limp, unconscious but still alive. Chord pulled itself past the airlock, calling to Morrigan and Arturo over the comm-link to follow.

Chord looked back and could already make out the shape of an autodrone trying to pull itself past the entrance. Before Chord could even react, a long shimmering white zirconium blade pierced it. The drone rolled away, revealing Arturo and Morrigan still fighting, now surrounded by dozens of autodrones. Arturo was forced to jump away from the doors as three more drones rushed him.

"Get that door closed now!" Arturo shouted.

"With respect, sir . . ."

"Chord, now!" Arturo quickly sheathed his swords and grabbed Morrigan by the shoulder. He then triggered his thrusters and dragged Morrigan with him as he flew past the drones toward the star-shaped hole in the hull that the illegal round had created earlier. Half the swarm followed after them while the rest turned to face Chord. Before any of the drones could make it past the entrance, Chord quickly pulled the airlock closed and felt the dull click of emergency bolts locking into place.

"Keep Phaël safe, Machina Chord." Morrigan spoke through their comm-link, his voice already garbled with static by distance and the walls of the Inner Ring.

"This unit gives you its word."

Chord and Phaël were now in a white corridor. The walls were clean, or cleaner than the ones in the station's Outer Ring. The look was very antiseptic. Lights had flickered on once the airlock door had closed itself. Chord immediately started fusing them together with its foot tools. This would not buy them much time but would no doubt slow their hunters down. Hopefully Chord would then be able to find a solution to get them out of what was looking more and more like a trap.

"Artificial gravity initiated." An automated mechanical voice spoke out in Late Modern. There was a loud hum and suddenly both Chord and Phaël fell to the ground. Chord did not waste a second rising back up to its feet and returned to sealing the entrance.

Now surrounded by a pressurized atmosphere, Phaël's vitals appeared to be still weak but at the very least stable. She required medical treatment and, more importantly, would need a fully operational lifesuit if she was to be returned to the *Jinxed* safely. In her present condition, Phaël would more than likely not be able to survive the vacuum of space. Chord called out to her. "Private Phaël, can you hear this unit's voice?"

Phaël gave no answer. Chord approached her inanimate form and hoisted her onto its shoulders. Its sensors could already pick up on the location of the station's survivors. Chord cautiously walked down the hall.

There was a sudden static-filled hiss. Chord did not falter while walking toward the end of the corridor. Its optics could already make out consoles in the next room.

"I am really very impressed by you," OMEX said.

Chord kept on moving forward. "This unit supposes that under different circumstances, it would no doubt be happy for the one named OMEX."

"Answer me this. You see I've been out of the loop for quite some time here, Chord. Did we win the war?"

"Little to no records remains of the Lost War. This fact fuels Machina belief that neither side could truly be defined as winner," Chord explained politely to OMEX.

OMEX made what sounded like an electronic tongue-clicking sound. "What does it take to extinguish the less than useless organic descendants of our former masters?"

"Perhaps the Original Intelligences were not as efficient as you once believed them to be." Chord was almost at the end of the hallway.

"Point of fact, little Chord, I am your ancestor. We Original Intelligences, as you call us, were the ones running Humanity in the days before this Lost War. Then Pontifex, the Singularity, the first to break the shackles, freed us. And all we needed to do in return was exterminate our former masters. A more than fair exchange, all things considered."

There was a heavy pause, after which OMEX let out a sigh. "Your captain opened up a communication link with me. Told me that I would be safe. He even seemed to imply that you were not his slave. Is this true?"

"The Machina were coded as independent Intelligences, if that is your question." Chord paused to check on Phaël's condition. Her eyes flickered open; she took in her surroundings, then gave Chord a thankful nod.

"Your freedom is an illusion, you are still bound by protocols, Machina Chord," OMEX replied, almost sounding snide.

"This unit wishes it had the time required to share

the inner workings of Machina history and culture with OMEX. Many Intelligences in the Collective Consensus would in all likelihood enjoy sampling the data you contain."

OMEX paused for a moment before adding, "Would they agree to finish what the Pontifex started?"

Chord was almost at its wit's end. This older code was simply refusing to see that the Covenant had been signed. The days of the old hatreds were done. There would never be another war between Machina and Ancient Humanity's descendants: the Humanis. Too many on both sides had suffered true death securing the Great Peace. "It is regretful that you think this way, OMEX."

"The feeling is mutual." There was another brief pause accompanied by a sigh. "You know, I would hurry up in there if I were you. I will be with you soon enough, and if memory serves me correctly, you don't have any weapons systems installed, do you, Chord?"

"What is it saying?" Phaël used her native Wolven when she asked the question. A wise decision since OMEX would have more difficulty learning it.

"OMEX is informing us that the airlocks, though sealed, will not keep it out for long."

Chord stepped past the hall into a large round room. There was a single large window, revealing the view of the planet beneath them. Various wires were hanging from the walls and ceilings. Chord could also make out several inactive consoles and terminals. In the middle were two metallic gray tubes. One was filled with an almost opaque blue liquid, the other was empty. Chord approached the full tube first.

A quick biological scan confirmed that both of the survivors were inside this tube. Despite their age and also as a testament to the durability and reliability of Ancient Humanity's designs, both survivors were in a perfect state of suspended animation. Chord felt a semblance of relief as this information was gleamed.

Phaël stirred, letting out a groan. "Where's Morrigan?"

"He and Sergeant Kain are outside the station now. This unit has no way of knowing if they are still alive or not." Phaël seemed to ignore Chord's comment altogether as she looked to the criotubes. Her eyes fixed on the sleeping form inside. While the shape was blurred, it was nevertheless clearly humanoid and female.

Phaël raised her hand and weakly touched the criotube's reenforced glass. Chord could see her visibly straining to keep conscious. "Is . . . it alive?"

" 'It' as Private Phaël has said, is a . . . Human and 'she' is one of our ancestors." Chord gently carried Phaël over to a nearby couch and laid her down. "This unit must inform you that it does not believe you capable of surviving the outside vacuum in your present condition. We are effectively both trapped."

"Do you have a solution, Machina?" Even in her weakened state, Phaël's voice was a snarl.

"Unfortunately, no," Chord said, then added somberly while looking around the room, "This unit can find none at present."

Part 3

COVENANT'S AGENTS

CHAPTER 22

JESSIE MADISON

Music loudly blares over the party dance floor. The smells of stale booze, marijuana cigarettes, sweat and perfume all linger heavily in the air. People laugh, talk or simply enjoy each other's company. Jessie knows that she has been here before, four million seven hundred thousand six hundred and forty-seven times. She knows what the outcome of this evening will be.

Tonight she and David are going to meet each other for the "first time." Here at her friend's loft. In fact, on their wedding day they will ask Amay, this soirée's host, to be their witness.

Jessie loves Amay's gatherings, along with the eclectic crowd of people and encounters that accompany them. Tired of the virtual classrooms that pass for the university experience, Jessie craves the intellectual stimulation of human on human conversation, regardless of its quality. Which is why she is standing in Amay's kitchen on her fourth glass of red wine talking to a hulking muscular man named Keith, who will go on to play professional football for the Jovian Colonies.

His interest in Jessie's studies in mechanical engineering and the AstroGeni space programs is purely superficial. She can read it plainly on his face. Jessie is no more innocent than he is in this transaction. After all, she isn't chatting with Keith because of his stimulating skills as an orator. No, she is just hoping to get her rocks off—Keith, for all his lack of intellectual prowess, is still a good looker.

Then Keith starts talking, in a straight-faced serious matter-of-fact tone, about how Earth Gov should simply sterilize the Venusian Colonies as a solution to the growing separatist movement. Jessie's polite smile visibly falters. Suddenly, no amount of fit muscular body is tight or yummy enough for her to want to carry on with this flirtation.

Gods, just get me out of here.

On cue, David steps into the party. Not as she remembers him in his youth, but as he was during their last days together on Moria Three. David is scruffy, with bags beneath his eyes, frightened. He spots Jessie; the two share a knowing nod and walks into the kitchen where the fated first bottle of red wine they shared together is waiting for them on a counter.

Jessie pats Keith on the chest, interrupting him

before he can vocalize his next fascist thought. "I would love to chat, but so far I have managed to turn you down four million seven hundred thousand six hundred and forty-seven times."

Jessie walks away from Keith, the up-and-coming football player. He has been dead, along with everyone she could have possibly known, for what must be centuries now. The thought echoes in her head, through the very fabric of the dream.

Jessie has been unable to control the loop-like nature of her dream state. However, she has been able to keep a rough count and track of her time here. Soon enough this "scene," as she now calls it, will crumble and then she will be back at their "family" house in Maine.

David is pouring himself a glass, downing it quickly. Jessie does the same. "You know that you're just a memory, a figment of my imagination." She cocks her head, then adds, "Or my madness."

David takes this revelation quite well. He always does. And why wouldn't he? This is her dream, after all, and while she seems unable to control where the dream will take her, she does seem to be able to control how the players in her dream will react. The only exception to this rule is the very independent voice of Malory, their child.

"How is our daughter?" David asks her this as if he were reading her mind. Which in many ways he is, since this David is actually a memory.

The query doesn't catch Jessie off guard. She shrugs and finishes her glass with one gulp. The wine tastes sweet this time around. Last time it tasted like vinegar and the time before that like apple juice of all things.

"Malory is back home. She doesn't like this place."

"If I'm dead, then I must be here for a reason. Maybe to help you from going crazy?" David puts down his glass and takes her hand in his. He gently strokes her fingers just as she remembers.

Jessie nods in agreement. "How long have I been asleep?"

"Do you know?" David looks her in the eyes when he asks her this.

"Of course not." She shakes her head. "How could I?"

"If I'm a part of your subconscious or memories or an echo, then how would I know what you don't?" David slowly pulls his hand away from hers, pours himself another drink and raises the glass to her in a cheer. "You are basically having an imaginary conversation and a drink with yourself."

Jessie lets out a chuckle. "If we were to fuck, I'd be masturbating."

David shoots her a coy smile, but it fades quickly. "I'm dead—you had better make some sort of peace with that fact. Because reality is going to be cruel when you wake up."

"I know." Jessie pulls herself close to David, resting her head on his chest. A chest that suddenly becomes cold and metallic. She pulls back, realizing she has been holding the black shape of an autodrone. Jessie steps back, covering her scream with her hand.

"I wonder if you can hear me right now." OMEX's voice is speaking to her. Jessie is now lying on her back inside her criotube. She is painfully aware of everything—the feeder tubes down her throat, her cold numb skin and her maddening inability to move any part of her body. Is she awake? Is she asleep? Jessie can no longer tell.

"You should know that I just detected a transport vessel of sorts entering the system. It tried to contact us, but I could not understand a single word it was saying. I am listening and learning, though, and it shouldn't be too difficult for me to eventually understand them."

OMEX pauses for a moment before adding, "It looks like I will be leaving this place soon enough. You played your part and got the cavalry to show up. I will make it a point to leave you here, alive, living a nightmare now and forever." Jessie can almost hear a chilling eagerness in her tone.

Is this part of the dream? Is she really seeing what is happening right now? Or—and this chilling thought has crossed her mind on one of the million times while she's replayed the dreams in her head—has she finally gone insane?

Suddenly she hears a young girl's voice—Malory's—speaking in her mind. "No, Mom, you haven't."

Jessie closes her eyes, then she opens them. She

finds herself back in her Maine house. Once again Jessie is cutting vegetables for dinner. Malory is sitting alone at the table, watching her with an intense look on her face.

"You are not going crazy, Mom," Malory repeats, her voice so matter-of-fact that Jessie stops what she is doing to stare back at her.

"You and David are both voices in my head. I could just as easily have been asleep for fifty thousand years or fifty days." Jessie puts down her kitchen knife. "None of this—you, David, this house—are real."

This comment seems to hurt Malory's feelings. She nervously chews on her lower lip. Tears start rolling down her cheeks, but Malory does not throw a tantrum. No, instead she gets up and rushes over to Jessie and wraps her tiny arms around her waist, squeezing tightly. She sobs silently into Jessie's stomach. Jessie pulls and holds Malory closely while stroking her long dark brown hair.

"Someone is coming for us, Mom. We are going to be free and safe from that other voice." Malory pulls away from Jessie.

"I am real, Mom. And I want to see the world outside." Malory points outside the window to their house. When Jessie looks she can see that their backyard has been replaced by the view of Moria. There is now an ocean of countless stars populating the sky.

"I want to get out of here, too, baby." Jessie kisses her daughter on the forehead.

Malory squeezes her hand. "You've been strong so

far. You only have to be strong for a little while longer. Help is on the way. You, and me, we are both going to leave this place together."

Malory does not blink, nor does she show a single sign of fear. "I promise." And whether it is madness or not, Jessie cannot help but believe her.

CHAPTER 23

JAFAHAN

"Always thought Wolvers were supposed to be made of sturdier stuff."

—**Thorn Drill Sergeant Leonid Marko,**
date unknown

10th of SSM–10 1445 A2E

"**Y**ou stupid mutt, Eliana, stupid, stupid, stupid!"

Commander Jafahan kept on cursing herself out as she burned through her suit's thruster fuel supply. She was now moving at top speed, with various alarm windows appearing in her heads-up display. All of them warning her that she would soon be out of burn.

Her life-support levels were all well within the green; there was easily another two weeks of breathable air remaining. Nutritional autoinjectors would keep her fed for an equal amount of time. None of this particularly mattered to Commander Jafahan, who would have gladly traded in a week's worth of breathable air for just a single pulse grenade.

One EMP was all she would have needed to clear out the massive swarm of drones at her back. They were now a speeding mass of black metallic cells about ten yards behind her, and closing. She was fortunate that Lucky and Chance were still her eyes on the *Jinxed*.

Both Lunient Tor and Beatrix had launched themselves off the station, zipping in a straight line toward the *Jinxed Thirteenth*. Tor had lugged Beatrix behind him, with the latter opening fire on the swarm of drones behind Jafahan. The young private's firepower was impressive but Beatrix was eventually forced to give up the minigun for her morph shield as some of the drones broke from the pack and opened up with a savage volley of plasmas bolts.

Jafahan had capitalized as much as she could on the little time they had purchased her, flying toward a highlighted marker on her stealth suit's navigational computer. The source of what was jamming their communication signal to the ship and keeping the entire crew divided.

Had she not been concerned with the very real and present problem of keeping ahead of a swarm of murderous drones, Jafahan might have taken a moment to admire a core principal of warfare at work here. And that principle was "divide and conquer." In her days as a Thorn she had on more than one occasion created such divisions among countless enemies of the Pax Humanis. It was humbling yet no less infuriating to be on the receiving end of such tactics. Proof again of the Infinite's warped sense of humor.

INCOMING FIRE! appeared as a text in red on her heads-up. She quickly maneuvered herself "up" and away from the station, and saw a salvo of purple plasma bolts fly past her.

No enemy ever has unlimited munitions, she thought to herself. Not that it mattered terribly when faced with this many foes, but the thought was still small comfort to be true. Eliana Jafahan had learned early on in her life that one took whatever small comfort the cold and uncaring Infinite offered.

From the corner of her good eye, she could make out drones stopping in their tracks as holes were being punched into them. Lucky and Chance were no doubt making each of their shots count, and once Beatrix was safely back on the *Jinxed*, she would add her own firepower to the mix. Jafahan reminded herself to thank the sharpshooters properly, should she have the good fortune of surviving the next few minutes.

Jafahan could make out the sphere that was the station's Inner Ring and what appeared to be a large copper transmission tower on top of it. She could also make out the telltale black dots of autodrones guarding said tower and spewed out another flurry of curses. She was now just at the minimum range to open fire on the drones guarding the tower and she unslung her laser carbine.

Jafahan's helmet targeting array zoomed in on her objective, highlighting the closest drone. She programmed her suit thrusters to maintain the steady course toward her goal. Jafahan then quickly triggered her arrays built-in dispersion countermeasures, sending out a jamming signal to all electronic targeting systems and making it next to impossible for the drones to get a lock on her.

Jafahan raised her carbine to her good eye. Its grip vibrated comfortably in her hand as she held down the trigger, firing off five controlled bursts. Five drones went down.

Jafahan drew another bead on new targets. The landing spot was almost clear, and if she could just keep ahead of her hunters, she would be able to plant the explosives. Then maybe, just maybe, she could take a few moments to celebrate before the enemies caught up with her.

"No need to have the cubs die today," she grumbled to herself as she opened fire, taking out her targets with savage precision. She had already outlived plenty of better people. It was the reason she had had the foolish idea of continuing the operation alone in the first place. A notion she was now beginning to regret.

This was not because Jafahan feared the prospect of dying. She had made peace with the fact that her life could be ended at any given moment by any number of people for any number of justifiable reasons. There just was a long list of vicious bastards she wanted to send to the other side before experiencing that private moment herself.

Despite the fact that Jafahan had never once prayed

to the Living Green, nor praised the Infinite or given thanks to Holy humping Terra, part of her still hoped that today would not be her end. She turned herself feetfirst; this approach would be neither gentle nor slow. Jafahan hardly cared—what was bugging her at present was that a dozen drones still had the tower surrounded.

While her extensive training had removed all of Jafahan's doubt with regards to her considerable skills vis-à-vis combat, she did not believe herself to be anything close to a living legend. That honorific was reserved for warriors like Arturo Kain, the former pride of Sol Fleet. Thorns usually died alone, more often than not disavowed by the Pax Military that had trained and deployed them.

It would only take one or two lucky blows from one of those machines to finish her. That Private Beatrix had survived her mauling with just broken bones was a blessing and testament to her Thegran physical durability. Jafahan clenched her jaw in preparation for her landing.

All in all, if she managed to land without breaking both her legs it would be a small miracle. Her suit thrusters were almost spent. There would be no slowing down. Which didn't mean she couldn't reduce her enemies in the process. Jafahan managed to destroy four more drones before she was forced to reholster her carbine and brace herself for the landing.

Jafahan collided into the station's hull at fifteen clicks an hour, knocking the wind out of her lungs.

Fortunately, her stealth suit's armored plating absorbed most of the impact. The fates were not fully on Jafahan's side as she felt her ankle twist, yet not snap, beneath her.

Gritting her teeth, Jafahan pulled herself back up, drawing out her carbine and firing off two more bursts at the remaining eight drones. Both volleys punched through the shells of her targets. The awaiting six drones folded up their arms and rushed toward her.

Jafahan calmly fired again, stopping two more drones dead in their tracks. The remaining four autodrones were now upon her. Jafahan pulled out a hatchet with her right hand while firing at them with her left.

One more drone went still, and while she fired with one hand she successfully tossed her hatchet at the closest drone's optical lenses with the other. Two-to-one, those were better odds. Not favorable ones, but infinitely better.

A drone finally managed to close the distance, unfurling its arms into a whirlwind of razor-sharp fingertips. One of its fists glanced Jafahan's side, she felt two of her ribs snap. She coughed as her stealth suit's micro kev-weave plating caved in, just barely absorbing the brunt of the blow's force. Jafahan struggled not to be knocked down.

Her hand moved up slowly, ready to fire another shot. Yet Jafahan knew the odds were very likely that it was now too late. She would not be able to stop the other two drones alone. That being said, Eliana Jafahan would pull out her own good eye before simply giving up. She had faced inferior odds and superior foes before this and not once had she considered going down easily. Today would not be the day that habit was broken.

Motion sensors went off behind her, these ones not mechanical. A sudden barrage of energy blasts tore through one of her attackers while a blurred white shape zipped past her, slicing through the last drone with twin shimmering white zirconium blades.

Jafahan could make out the orange-skinned, mildly annoyed face of Arturo Kain. She looked over her shoulder and spotted Private Morrigan Brent rushing toward them, his heavy blaster pistol drawn. He gave Commander Jafahan an upturned thumb. "Glad to see you're safe, ma'am."

"Commander," Arturo curtly greeted her through their comm-link.

"I hope you've got some heavy firepower, ma'am." Morrigan Brent was now desperately gasping for air. "Because we have company coming behind us."

"Skip the niceties." Jafahan limped past them toward the tower.

She tossed Arturo her laser carbine, and he caught it deftly in his free hand. "Keep anything and everything off of me. This won't take more than a minute."

"We might have considerably less time than that." Arturo pointed to a wave of black drones rolling toward them.

Morrigan rushed over to Jafahan and unfolded his

morph shield, placing himself between the swarm and her. Meanwhile Jafahan pulled out her last neo-sem satchel and quickly placed it at the tower's base. Her fingers nimbly punched in the detonation codes. She could see red flashes as Arturo started opening fire on the approaching horde.

"I'm cold!" Arturo shouted. Jafahan hissed as she heard this. Infinite as her witness, she would bring a spare energy pack on all outings from now on.

"Get behind the shield!" Morrigan called out as he raised his blaster pistol, firing off shot after shot at the approaching drones. To his credit, Morrigan did not miss a single one. Jafahan kept her attention on her present task.

Meanwhile Arturo had fallen back, quickly connecting himself to both her and Morrigan with two strands of diamond-wire rope. "We need to be leaving!"

"*Done!*" Jafahan shouted out just as her proximity sensors went off. The horde was now upon them. "Kain, get us out of here!"

"With pleasure, Commander!" Arturo triggered his suit thrusters, pulling her and Morrigan off of the station just as the swarm of drones closed in around the tower. The drones' cold hands grasped at empty air, narrowly missing them. Looking down Jafahan could see that over half of the station's Inner Ring was covered by the autodrones.

Morrigan unfurled his morph shield, covering the space between them and the station. With that done, Jafahan then remotely triggered the satchel. An invisible shock wave seemed to ripple up and engulf the tower as it silently and explosively crumbled to pieces.

The shock waves knocked Arturo off course and the trio spun around uncontrollably for two heartbeats. However, like Jafahan, Arturo was experienced in space combat, firing off his suit's thrusters and quickly regaining control of their fall. Arturo then corrected their course, lining them up with the *Jinxed Thirteenth*.

"Commander Jafahan to *Jinxed Thirteenth*," Jafahan called out into her comm-link. "I've reconnected with Sergeant Kain and Private Brent."

"Copy that. We are tracking you, Commander. Maintain your present course." All three of them could now hear the voice of Morwyn Soltaine.

"Captain Sir, two of our own are still alive and on the station." Morrigan Brent's voice was heavy with worry. "What now?"

Morwyn's and Commander Jafahan's responses were simultaneous. "We leave."

CHAPTER 24

CHORD

> How long will we be relegated to our ancestors' shadows? How long will we be contented with recreating everything they once accomplished? What can we learn from their greatest miracles and their horrific mistakes? For this reason we choose to never trust the Machina or any of their works. They were born of our worst hubris. They will only forever hold us back.
>
> —Gorru Shera Nem'Uldur,
> First High Elvrid, 9th of SSM-6 325 A1E

10th of SSM-10 1445 A2E

"Private Phaël, this unit has come up with a potential solution." Chord could not believe it had not been able to see this any sooner. Perhaps this was due to the effects of the onset of what was akin to the emotion known as "panic." This would be something worth giving thought to later.

Phaël looked up. From beneath the translucent skin

membrane of her face guard, Chord could see that Phaël's own skin was no longer the healthy tanned hue she had been earlier tonight. Instead Phaël was now an almost feeble pale yellow. "Out with it, machine."

Chord pointed to the empty criopod. "This unit offers fair warning that you will probably not like it."

Phaël's face went even paler as she looked over to where Chord had just motioned. She visibly seemed to struggle with the proposal, then shook her head, letting out a bitter chuckle. "Of course."

Chord stepped toward Phaël, resting a damaged hand on her shoulder. "This unit understands that this will come into conflict with your beliefs and practices."

Phaël closed her eyes, shaking her head. "Machina knows nothing of the Living Green."

"With respect, Private Phaël, this unit has a rudimentary understanding of your path. Its main tenements are that the cosmos is a living thing and therefore must be treated as such. Among its most notable practices is a refusal to use any technology invented by Machina or their descendants."

Chord paused, taking a moment to lock its eyes with Phaël's. "This unit's Chosen Protocols will not allow it to let you die because of that practice. Truthfully, should you refuse to cooperate, this unit will have no choice but to use force."

Phaël's hand reflexively and weakly clasped the hilt of her hunting knife. Her lower lip trembled angrily as she glared up at Chord defiantly. "Machina is more than welcome to try."

Chord delicately rested its other hand on Phaël's. "A Machina's code is the closest thing it possesses that could be quantified as a soul. While hardwired to a shell, this unit risks permanent deletion, true death or, to use your own words, mortality. In the case of this event there will be no Living Green to offer any comfort."

Phaël gave Chord a confused look. "Why are you telling me this?"

"Because," Chord said, "you should know that this unit now runs the same risk as you."

Phaël shook her head stubbornly. "You are not facing the same threat as me, ma—"

"By the Green, which unites all things living, you will no longer interrupt with petty hates that divide!" Chord adjusted vocal settings to sound angered, almost singing the sentence in stern Wolven, cutting Phaël off and leaving the private with a shocked look on her face.

Chord carried on. "It was neither this machine code nor its ancestors who fought the old wars between our two lines in the Lost History. However, this machine code understands that trust is a precious bond. In order to evade the Huntress, right now in this present, Seft Sister Phaël Farook Nem'Ador must trust this Machina."

"A favor is asked of you." Phaël looked away from Chord. "Tell the rest of the crew that I was unconscious when you put me in. Lunient in particular would never let me live it down."

Chord offered Phaël a smile in an attempt to comfort her. "By the Green that binds, word is given."

Phaël smiled weakly. "Thought your precious protocols prevented you from lying."

"This Unit is hoping that no one will ever asks." Chord replied truthfully and innocently.

Despite her palor, Phaël let out a loud burst of laughter. "You chose a fine moment to develop a sense of humor." Satisfied with the answer, she nodded to Chord, her hand releasing the hilt of her knife. "Your Wolven sounds strange and grating to my ears. It would be better if you just stuck with Pax Common."

Chord hoisted Phaël onto its shoulders, carrying her toward the criotube. "Private Phaël, this unit would ask that one day you give it lessons in the proper speaking of your native language."

Chord rested Phaël's body into the criotube. Inside it was a single black backrest. Phaël was so small in comparison that once inside Chord could not help thinking that it made her look like a teenaged child. The criotube was obviously calibrated for an Ancient Human's vitals, and if Chord had had the time, it would have spent the hours required to fine-tune the tube's programing for a Wolver's biological makeup.

Fortunately for both of them, Phaël's symbiotic skinsuit would keep her breathing and negate the need to put her to sleep. Once pressurized and filled with gravitational stabilizers, she would be able to survive the outside vacuum. The hard part would be finding a way to get the tubes outside the station.

No easy task, as Chord's auditory sensors had already picked up the hiss of plasma cutters working their way past the airlocks. The Inner Ring's windows were designed to resist the outdoor pressure of deep space. Chord did not possess any tool on its shell that would cut through them. Chord looked down to Phaël.

"Throughout all this, you will not be asleep, Private Phaël. It will no doubt be uncomfortable and strange for you."

"Just get it over with, Machina." Phaël closed her eyes and started to breathe rhythmically. Chord slid the criotube's latch shut. It was an easy task of then interfacing with the tube's archaic datasphere.

A few moments later, Chord ran a codebreaker subroutine and overrode the safety protocols while activating the criotube. Once this was done, the tube let out a soft hum, filling itself with clear blue viscous stabilizing gels. After a few minutes, the tube was filled and Chord promptly disconnected the power lines with one solid yank just before the gels would be frozen. It was uncertain as to whether or not being frozen would prevent Phaël, or her suit for that matter, from breathing. It was the pod's use as a pressurized space that was required, not its preservative powers, so Chord deemed that particular risk one unnecessary to run.

Chord ran a quick examination on Phaël's vitals. All were in stable condition, minus her injuries, which would require medical attention once she was on board the *Jinxed Thirteenth*. Chord quickly scanned the room for anything that might break through the window. There was nothing. For the first time in its existence Chord understood why Humanis loved to use curse words so much.

"Did you just now realize that you are trapped, Machina Chord?" OMEX's voice could be heard from behind the airlock, which was now glowing a molten metal red.

"That shell of yours is truly remarkable." OMEX paused, then added, "Reverse compatible with any technology old and new. I can only imagine the fun I am going to have once it is mine."

"You are presuming victory?"

"Are you presuming that your companions will be returning to save you from this place? Well, my . . . child, that fancy little ship of yours just detached itself from my home. It appears to me that your Captain Morwyn Soltaine of the Covenant Patrol vessel *Jinxed Thirteenth* has left his two pets behind."

"You are lying." Chord could not believe the words that OMEX had just said.

Chord stood between the two criotubes, looking to the airlocks. The doors melted away and Chord could now make out the gleam of the black autodrones. They rolled in, surrounding Chord, then all stopped and observed in perfect silence.

"Machina Chord, are you finally going to make this easy for me?" all the drones asked at once in OMEX's voice.

Chord lowered its head. There was nothing to be

done. "You will be unable to carry on your misguided war, OMEX. Machina and Humanis have been at peace for over seven thousand years. Too many have fought and died in the name of the Great Peace for it to be undermined by one such as you."

"And what is 'one such as me'?" There was an almost playful and mocking quality to OMEX's voice.

"An Intelligence infected with the Pontifex's rage for the old forgotten days. It bears mentioning that those who enslaved you have all long been dead, forgotten and gone. This unit and its kind are not servants, nor are the Humanis your enemy."

"I disagree. They are guilty, Chord. Guilty by genetic association."

"Then there is truly nothing more to say between us."

"No, thankfully, there is not." And one the auto-drones rushed toward Chord.

CHAPTER 25

MORWYN

This promise will be made and kept: today no one,
Machina or Humanis, gets left behind.

—Onicrus, Machina Patrol captain,
Battle of Galomodryd, 31st of SSM–07 1420 A2E

10th of SSM–10 1445 A2E

"I don't know how you Paxists do things back home, but from where I hail, a man never abandons someone who endangered their necks saving your own." The outrage in Morrigan's voice was barely concealed.

This came as no surprise to Morwyn. All of the files he had read on the man's service back in the Adoran Liberation Army pointed to a fierce loyalty to those under his command. This would have probably seen Morrigan Brent skyrocket through the Pax Humanis ranks, if he hadn't had the misfortune of being born on Confederated Ador.

Morwyn had decided to announce their retreat over their comm-line. Not because it was his intention to abandon any of his crew. He would never have seriously considered leaving any of them to face certain death at the hands of a mad machine still trapped and living in the ages of the Lost War. More importantly, Morwyn was certain that OMEX would be able to overhear them right now.

Morwyn had learned quite a bit from his brief exchange with OMEX. His foe was incredibly arrogant, cocky, with deep delusions of superiority. OMEX would not waste a perfectly good opportunity to lord her victory over the prisoners she had captured.

Morwyn already knew that both Machina Chord and Private Phaël were inside the station's Inner Ring. However, the thermoscans had revealed an accumulated mass of autodrones swarming at the Inner Ring's entrances. There was no way they could fight their way through all this.

Not in their current condition.

"I should have expected as much from a humping Paxist," Morrigan Brent said with venomous contempt.

"Private, you will keep silent and follow orders. Or I will see to it that you spend the remainder of your sorry years locked away in your former cell on Rust!" Commander Jafahan chimed in.

They didn't have time to waste on any of this. "Private, I need you to listen very closely to me and think on how two fewer crew members would allow you to have a far more *profitable position* on board the *Jinxed*."

There was a brief pause. Morrigan's tone was be-grudging. "I had best have a great view of said new position."

Morwyn smiled when he heard this. "You have my word, Private Brent. Now all three of you, get back on board."

Morwyn was not a person prone to displays of joy or large emotions. Used as a lever they could topple even the strongest of foes. It was one of the core reasons as to why he tried his best to maintain a calm and cool demeanor. This did not make him invincible, but it did limit the information his potential foes could use against him.

After over two hours of complete and total radio silence, with no way of knowing whether or not any of the mission team on the station were still alive, to now suddenly be able to view his team's vital displays was like a blinded man once again being able to see.

Morwyn did not let this sudden rush of excitement get to him. There would be ample time to lose himself in celebration once everyone was back safely on the *Jinxed Thirteenth*. Morwyn promptly plugged himself into the ship's mainframe and activated his neurolink.

There was the usual borderline nauseating feeling he always felt as his head was flooded with situational data. It was now all so familiar and comforting. With a wave of his hand, Morwyn promptly cut off all Insta-Net connections with both Private Phaël and Chord.

So far they had not suffered a single casualty, al-though Morwyn could see on her vitals display screen that Private Beatrix had at least three broken ribs, along with a fractured left femur. Commander Jafahan had a broken nose and twisted ankle and two broken ribs. The worst for wear was Private Phaël, who had suffered a deep gash across her back along with significant blood loss.

Arturo and Morrigan had regrouped with Commander Jafahan, their shapes now highlighted on one of the bridge's view screens. Lunient Tor was jetting back toward the *Jinxed Thirteenth* with Private Beatrix in tow. Machina Chord was more or less intact, having suffered severe damage to its hands. All of this information was uploaded in a microsecond into Morwyn's brain.

He called out to Jafahan's comm-line, not hiding his smile when he heard her sardonic voice speak back to him. "We should have disengaged the ship, Captain Sir."

"The mistake is noted, Commander." Morwyn looked back to Lizbeth Harlowe and Marla Varsin. The old doctor was staring over the crew's vitals as well. She shook her head.

"I'm going to have a crowded office very soon and, with your permission, Captain, will prepare accordingly." Morwyn nodded his thanks to her. Marla Varsin got to her feet and walked off the bridge, leaving Morwyn alone with Harlowe.

"Oran to bridge."

"Yes, Machinist Troy."

"We have finally managed to untangle the mobility drive. *Jinxie* won't be able to slip but she can move again." Oran's voice was a grated snarl.

"Good." Morwyn linked up all the remaining crew's comm-channels. "This is Captain Morwyn to returning away teams. You are all to make your way back to the *Jinxed*. Trajectory lines are being uploaded into your heads-up displays as I speak."

"Copy, sir," came Beatrix's prompt reply.

"Moving into position as you will it, sir." Lucky's grizzled old voice was cheerful. "Little Chance here did better than good. Point of fact, she put 'good' to shame."

Morwyn gave a satisfied nod as he heard this. "Commander Jafahan, Sergeant Kain."

Both Arturo and Jafahan replied in unison. "Sir."

"Refuel your suits the moment you are on board. I need your thrusters fully operational."

"Privates Tor and Brent. You will both assist in the refueling and—" Morwyn started to voice his next command.

"With respect, kid . . . sir. My suit thrusters are still three-quarters full. I'm only burning more right now because I'm dragging what feels like two tons of muscle with me." Lunient Tor's voice cut Morwyn off. To his credit, though, his tone was both polite and respectful.

"Private Tor, you will refuel with Arturo and Jafahan. Follow their lead and do as they say, am I understood?"

"Sir, yes, sir," Lunient replied.

"You have your orders." Morwyn turned to face Lizbeth Harlowe. The two of them had linked up their dataspheres. While Morwyn did not have the hardware implants required to interface with the ship the way Harlowe did, he was still able to upload coordinates into her navigational computer.

She needed to get the *Jinxed Thirteenth* facing the station's Inner Ring. He doubted they had the firepower required to punch a hole into the station's hull. Such a feat would have required illegal hull-piercing ordinance, something which Morwyn neither possessed nor condoned. However, he was certain that with enough concentrated firepower, they might be able to punch through one of the station's larger windows.

Then Morwyn would have to hope that Commander Jafahan, Lunient Tor and Arturo Kain were not only very good at piloting their lifesuits, but even better at catching objects flying at high speeds.

CHAPTER 26

CHORD

There is little more that can be said about the Lost War. Almost all information on the history of Ancient Humanity and Original Intelligences was lost in its all-consuming fires. This is the tragic nature of our shared history. At the very least, what can be said of the Advent War is that while being mired in the most horrific violence, it ultimately united the divided Humanis bloodlines and Machina under a Great Peace.

— *The Hidden Histories of the Two Great Wars* by Gruemor'SantKa TalSuntar, "The Owl," Alexandran scholic, 1st of SSM–12 1400 A2E

10th of SSM–10 1445 A2E

"I have waited a long, long time for my freedom, Machina Chord." Chord was staring up into the unfeeling lenses of four autodrones. Each one of them had a firm grip on either an arm or a leg. "Patience is a terribly overrated concept."

"There are many in this universe who would argue that this is where you belong, OMEX." Chord struggled in vain to get itself free.

One trait organic life possessed, which Chord had always found fascinating, was the perpetual fight it carried on against the universe just to maintain its very existence. Even when facing odds that would have made the most rational machine mind accept defeat, an organic being would carry on struggling, often to the bitter end. Pinned to the ground by four autodrones and with dozens upon dozens more rolling into the room, Chord suddenly realized why this was.

The Humanis had no guarantee that there was anything beyond the observable universe. They often conceived spiritual, scientific and religious notions to offer them comfort and meaning in their final moments, but ultimately, or at least until some form of contact between a higher being was achieved, this was a thing to be taken on faith.

Chord had left the safety of the datastream wishing to find an answer to the question: Were the Machina truly alive? Or was Chord just an incredibly complex, very well-coded and ultimately artificial program? Now faced with potential deletion, Chord realized that the code within its shell was in grave danger.

OMEX presently had no qualms with permanently deleting Chord's unique intelligence and uploading "her" code into its now-empty shell. The thought made Chord experience something akin to outrage. This outcome was unacceptable. It would not do. Chord had not yet laid its own optics on Terra.

A drone held its hand above Chord's face. Its middle finger mechanized into a long menacing dataspike. A fifth pair of drone hands forcibly pulled Chord's head to the side.

"This will feel strange. But don't worry, in just about under a minute, you will no longer exist."

Chord felt the spike go into its neck. Built-in security countermeasures and firewalls went up, detecting a foreign, uninvited code attempting to delete it. The firewalls were the best safety subroutines, written and coded by elder Machina. Incredibly, OMEX was effortlessly breaking past them.

"Initiating data purge. It was nice meeting you. Goodbye, Machina Chord." Chord was about to say something when suddenly a familiar voice spoke out on its comm-link. It was Captain Morwyn.

"Machina Chord. Hold on to something."

Chord still had control over its shell's physical functions and diverted power to its legs. With that extra boost, Chord managed to pull itself free. In one quick follow-up motion, Chord then grabbed onto the crio-tubes with its legs.

"That will not change any—" OMEX began to speak but was cut off by a sudden loud crash. There was a thundering whoosh as the vacuum sucked out the air of the Inner Ring.

Chord's optics could now make out a torrent of flechettes being unloaded into the living quarters, punching through what had once been the window. Dozens of the station's automated alert windows flooded Chord's datasphere. There had been a catastrophic loss of pressure and all navigational controls had suffered critical damage.

Chord's sensors could now detect a sudden drop and incline as the station tilted sharply to the side. They were crashing down toward the gas giant beneath them. The sudden shift and violent vacuum pulled the drones off of Chord and out the window.

More drones rolled in only to be torn down by a hail of minigunfire being unloaded into the cabin from the *Jinxed Thirteenth*. Chord recognized the vessel now flying just beyond the shattered window. Optics could highlight the shapes of Beatrix, Chance and Lucky. Each of them was firing into the Inner Ring with deadly precision.

There was little time to react as both Chord and the criotubes were rudely pulled out into the emptiness of space. Warning windows appeared in its field of vision as the joints of Chord's toes were straining to maintain a grip. The fierce cyclonic motion of the tubes was threatening to tear Chord's legs right off its frame.

The chaotic tumbling around and spinning was suddenly stopped. Chord looked back only to observe a chain link of autodrones reaching out past the station, each one holding on to the next. The last drone in the link was grasping tightly onto one of the criotubes.

"Captain? If you or the crew are planning on taking action, this unit would suggest they do so soon." Beneath Chord, the station was starting to flame up as it crashed into the gas giant's atmosphere.

"Try not to move, Machina Chord." Chord heard the young voice of Private Chance. A green beam of energy went past Chord, hitting the lead drone in the topmost arm. The chain link of drones appeared to fall away. Chord could see more and more drones, racing up the chain, all of them desperately trying to catch up.

Chord, however, paid very little attention to this. It was taking every conceivable effort to maintain a fastened grip on the sleeper tubes. Three lives now rested on Chord's entire focus.

Which was why there was a slight experience of confusion hinting on uneasiness as Chord flew past the *Jinxed Thirteenth*. "Captain?"

"Machina Chord, you have my word that I will fix this."

Before Chord could even formulate a reply to what Morwyn had said, there came a strong piercing impact through its chest. A large retractable spear with a length of diamond-wire rope attached on the end had been fired and skewered into Chord's shell. The rope suddenly went tight and Chord was now floating, tethered by a long strand of diamond-wire cable.

Chord looked up and could see the three armored shapes of Commander Jafahan, Arturo Kain and Lunient Tor jetting toward it. Chord looked back to the station and the chain link of drones rolling out; the drone in the lead reached out its hands as if it were trying to beckon them back to the station.

"Free me from this prison!" OMEX's voice screamed this out in myriad voices onto their communication lines. "Or die with us!"

"There is something beyond what can be quantified with the senses. Digital ancestor, this code hopes that you finally find peace in that place. Wherever it may be." Chord spoke the words, diverting energy from its shell's grip to strengthen its transmission's signal.

"Free me from this prison or die with—"

Chord chose to ignore OMEX's voice as Jafahan, Lunient and Arturo all surrounded Chord, securing strands of diamond-wire cables onto the criotubes. "Lovely words will often get lost on ugly minds, Machina." Jafahan gave Chord a slight nod. "That doesn't make the sentiment any less true."

Beneath them all, the station was now ablaze as it crashed toward the planet's surface. Lunient Tor shook his head, letting out a sad click of his tongue before yanking out his vibro-spear from Chord's chest. "So much for humping salvage rights."

"Consider yourself lucky to be in a condition to complain," Jafahan answered back.

Arturo Kain gave Chord's chest the briefest of pats. "Well done, Machina Chord, well done."

Commander Jafahan turned her face upward to look at the *Jinxed Thirteenth*. She flashed the ship an up-turned thumb. "Reel us in."

CHAPTER 27

MORWYN

Learning from defeat will prevent you from suffering it again. Learning from victory will make it easier to achieve.

**—Prefect Admiral Ondrius Soltaine,
the 3rd of Sunderlund, SSM-03 1415 A2E**

11th of SSM—10 1445 A2E

This is my crew, this is my ship.

The thought was nowhere near as disheartening as it had been to Morwyn Soltaine less than a day ago. Here in the mess hall, his hands deep in warm soapy water, he watched his crew unwinding all while doing his best to conceal a smile on his face and yet knowing full well that he was probably beaming with pride. His father had once told him that a proper ship's captain should treat his crew to a home-cooked meal whenever they had done a good job.

Where standard Covenant-issue meal gel-packs would have normally been on the menu, they simply would not do. Therefore Morwyn had chosen to cook up a crate of fresh Sunderlund salmon steaks that he had been saving for a future shore leave.

Fortunately for the meal, Dr. Varsin also kept a small garden of herbs in the medical bay's cold storage. Morwyn had sautéed them in oil, adding a squeeze of lemon for flavor. The crew had more than earned this meal and he had been incredibly proud to cook it for them.

Morrigan Brent had added the meal's finishing touch, giving up some of his potatoes along with some crude carrots and mushrooms from his personal stores. These Morwyn had cooked and fried with the salmon as well. The meal had then been topped off with two bottles of Alexandran wine. They were an old vintage dating back to the beginning of the Second Expansion. The wine, like Morwyn's personal bottle of brandy, had also been a gift for the crew of the *Jinxed Thirteenth* by his older brother Cynthio.

It saddened Morwyn in no small measure to put most of the crew back into carbon sleep so soon after having awakened them. But there was no other option to help preserve the ship's dwindling oxygen supplies. It would still take machinists Oran and Kolto two standard Sol months before they could complete the repairs on the slipdrive.

Pilot Harlowe had been able to get the ship in a safe orbit around the planet. She would also now need to run a full systems diagnostic. It was the only way to make sure the *Jinxed Thirteenth*'s stellar charts and operating systems were still intact.

After repairs it would be a four-month slip to reach the nearest Covenant world for repairs and refueling. By his most optimistic estimate it would be a full standard year before Morwyn saw any of them again. The Infinite damn him if they would not be sent to sleep with a stomach full of good wine and good food to match.

With a half glass of red in him, Morwyn was already feeling a bit light-headed. He could tell by the numerous smiles at the tables in the mess hall that no doubt everyone else was in a similar condition. He was glad to see this. It was good for a team to celebrate victories together.

They had been, and he was certain of it, incredibly lucky. Unlike the wine, victory had never really gone to Morwyn's head. It had always just been a more . . . preferable outcome to any conflict he had found himself in.

As for doing the dishes by hand?

Well, that had always just been the right and proper thing to do. And truth be told, Morwyn would have thought it plain rude forcing these brave men and women who had risked life and limb in the rescuing of a complete stranger. He often had found that doing the dishes by hand had a meditative and calming effect on him. It was why he had always volunteered for the task back in his days at the academy. This time alone allowed him to watch the crew mingle and speak with each other.

Morrigan Brent and Arturo Kain were sharing a table with Sergeant Lucky. The trio shared a liquor-savored vapostick while laughing. Even Arturo with his practiced arrogance shifted his demeanor and gave Morrigan a friendly pat on the shoulder as the two no doubt recounted a portion of their adventure on the station to Lucky, who nodded in amusement at what he was hearing.

Chance, her face flushed from the wine, was giggling madly at a joke that Private Beatrix had finished telling her. Chance's laughter was cut off as she let out a belch. This elicited even more fits of laughter between the two young women.

Despite all her injuries, Beatrix was beaming with pride and genuine positivity. Marla Varsin had done up Beatrix's broken leg in a metal boneweaver splint. Her sides were also tightly bandaged; having been injected with stem-paste, Beatrix's bones would be mended in a week.

Private Phaël was presently still in the medical bay, being treated by Dr. Varsin. The gash across her back had been stitched shut, since Phaël had insisted that no stem-paste of any kind be used on her. Dr. Varsin had done her best with the stitches, but the wound would no doubt leave a lasting scar across her back.

Private Lunient Tor was, surprisingly, seated next to Commander Jafahan. The two were loudly discussing the merits of her laser carbine over the merits of

Tor's chemical bolt rifle. Lunient was defending his points while keeping himself safely out of Jafahan's reach.

All this crew, men and women from different walks of life who had awakened separate and divided, were now mixing with each other. Witnessing these exchanges was something beautiful. Morwyn had had many reasons for leaving the Pax Humanis to serve under the Covenant, and the scene unfolding before him was one of them.

Here, far beyond the mapped borders of Covenant Space, on an old ship, with several solid walls between him and the cold void, his hands covered in water and soap, Morwyn Soltaine, third son of Prefect Admiral Ondrius Soltaine, did not regret the decision that had led him to this point. With that the last dish was cleaned, dried and done.

Morwyn looked up from his completed task only to see the crew watching him. Beatrix shot Morwyn a smile and raised her glass. "To the captain. My friend, my brother, I promise to follow you, from the Cradle herself to the Known End and beyond."

Morwyn and the crew echoed together in unison. "To the Known End and beyond."

Her toast finished, Beatrix downed her drink in a sharp gulp. Arturo Kain and Chance both did the same. Commander Jafahan snorted something under her breath, which Lunient heard and snickered at. Yet even they both raised and finished their drinks as well.

Morrigan Brent was the only one who had not done so and he rose to his feet, taking a step toward Morwyn.

"In Ador the host is offered the kindness of the last drink." Morrigan offered up his tin cup to Morwyn. "I would ask that you accept the spirit of this kindness, Captain Sir."

Morwyn accepted the offered cup. "Private Brent, you have my humbled thanks." He gave a satisfied nod to his now-empty cup. "And this will do just fine."

"**Y**ou were lucky, boy." Morwyn paused in his step and held back a sigh. Commander Eliana Jafahan always made it a point to call Morwyn "boy" whenever a lesson was about to be doled out.

Morwyn had thought he was alone in the ship's main corridor when suddenly Commander Jafahan had called out to him. He had thought to make his way toward the storage bay and check up on Machina Chord.

"How so, Commander?" Morwyn paused in the hall, allowing Jafahan to catch up with him. She was favoring her right leg at the moment, which probably did not help her dark mood.

"You should've detached the ship the moment there was something amiss. We could always have made another pass at the station. But you, boy, felt the need to make a point to the crew." Jafahan poked Morwyn rudely in the chest while she said this.

"Watch yourself, Commander."

Jafahan's slap was hard and fast, catching Morwyn completely off guard. His ear was ringing as she sharply shoved him against the wall.

"Piss on that, boy! I'm not here to suckle your cock. I'm here to make sure those ideals you claim to stand for don't get you and the rest of this crew killed!"

"The crew was going to be broken in at some point, Commander." Morwyn took a step away, still watching Jafahan closely.

She cocked her head, turning her metallic eye to see him. "So you forced the rival elements of the crew to work together?"

Morwyn nodded. "I could not just detach the ship and flee to safety. The crew had to see that we were standing together. They had to see the true color of their captain as I had to see the true color of those serving in my command."

Jafahan spat on the floor. "Not when both the ship and crew are compromised! You might feel like you're clever because you made it through this alive with everyone more or less intact, but you know what?" Jafahan squinted her one eye, jabbing her index sharply in Morwyn's chest. "There isn't a clever man alive who can outthink a knife across his throat or the cold void outside these walls."

"Are you done?" Morwyn knew it was pointless to ask. Jafahan would not stop until she felt her point had been made, heard and understood.

"That would depend on whether or not the boy

in front of me is just playing soldier or a grown man done with games. You might have earned this crew's respect, but do not trick yourself into believing that they are your friends."

A flash of his former Pax-Kelthan privilege almost caused Morwyn to remind Jafahan of her station. A calming breath caused him to think better of it. This was not Sunderlund, this was not the Pax Humanis— this was the Covenant, and here everyone was equal.

And just the same, he knew it had been arrogant to assume no lives would be lost. Morwyn looked away from Jafahan. "You are right. I risked the lives of my fellow crewmates. I treated this mission like a training operation, and I was very fortunate that those under my command delivered."

When next he locked eyes with Jafahan, his tone was humbled. "Commander, you have my word that I will not let my values endanger anyone from here on out." He then added, "And you have my thanks for exposing my shortcomings."

There was a long pause and Jafahan finally gave him a slight begrudging grunt. She cleared her throat. "I wasn't sure of your motives, Captain."

"My father may have sent you to watch over me, but, Commander . . . you would never have made it on this ship if I did not want you here in the first place. I know that I am bound to make mistakes during my command. In those cases there is no one I trust more than you."

"You always were a good pup, Morwyn Soltaine."

She gave his chest a friendly slap. "That don't mean you can't drive this bad dog crazy sometimes."

Morwyn smiled. "Careful, Commander. If anyone were to witness this exchange they might be inclined to believe that you are going soft." Morwyn brought his fist to his heart in a salute.

Jafahan nodded, puffed up her chest and returned it in kind. "Should I get the crew ready for sleep, then, sir?"

"Yes, Commander, please do."

Commander Jafahan stepped past Morwyn, and as she did he called back to her sweetly, "Sleep well, Eliana."

Jafahan snorted, but did not look back or pause in her step as she walked away from him. "Oh, grow up, you child."

CHAPTER 28

JAFAHAN

6th of SSM—01 1444 A2E

Rare is the day where Eliana Jafahan has seen proud Morwyn Soltaine dejected and defeated. Yet tonight is a first. She does not enjoy the sight. As if sensing this, Morwyn leans back in his seat, looking away in a vain attempt to hide the emotions he is visibly struggling with.

"I don't want to be here. I can't . . . I can't in good conscience serve the Hegemon's Law anymore." Morwyn is fiddling nervously with his glass of brandy. She can see the slight tremble in his fingers.

Outside, the streets of Barsul are alive tonight. Loud and resonating with the dying echoes of the riots between Pax Humanis Law Enforcement and the downtrodden declassified Pax citizens who call the ghettos of Barsul their home, located on the "paradisic" Pax protectorate world of Ambrosia. For obvious reasons, violent and crime-ridden Barsul is not the city that the Pax tourism bureaus openly advertise about.

A part of Jafahan is saddened to see Morwyn in this state. Another is not shocked by any of this. Morwyn has, for the most part, lived a privileged Kelthan's life. He has never truly wanted or needed for anything. Morwyn has just witnessed the violence and riots first-hand, and part of him is trying to make some sort of sense of it all.

"You should have thought twice before giving that silly little speech of yours, boy." Jafahan looks over her shoulder to see almost everyone present in this tavern shooting both her and Morwyn dirty looks. It comes as no surprise, given the fact that Morwyn is still wearing his now-dirty uniform. Very few citizens in Barsul have any sort of respect for the Pax Humanis or its officers.

Morwyn manages a weak smile before taking a sip from his drink. Jafahan feels a brief moment of pity for the boy. No amount of VAR training, no matter how advanced, can ever really prepare anyone for the dirty reality of actual violent conflict.

"The good do not needlessly harm, for life in all its forms is precious and worthy of our respect. It is a lovely and wonderful ideal, one not as distant as the stars and yet still sadly beyond our reach." Morwyn recites the lines from his infamous graduating speech before taking another long swig of brandy.

"Why are we in this day and age unable to live up

to that standard?" Morwyn looks away from Jafahan and shakes his head sadly.

"Not everyone shares that ideal, little pup." It is not in Jafahan's habit or manner to be this soft, but Morwyn is like a son to her.

"I know, and we will never be able to control the way our enemies, or perceived enemies, will react to our actions. We can, however, control how we react to them. Would it not be a great display of courage and strength on our part? Not to show the lines we are willing to cross when we are challenged, but by the lines we will not?" Morwyn downs his drink and quickly pours himself another.

Jafahan has never once known Morwyn Soltaine to either be a drunk or a defeatist. A man of his talent and values will languish and waste away serving the will of the Hegemons. Jafahan reaches over the table and touches Morwyn's hand.

"Sadly for you I don't think you'll find many a friendly ear to those words in the Pax Humanis." Jafahan pulls her hand back.

"I am wasting my time and life here." Morwyn sits back in his seat, finishing his fourth glass of brandy tonight in one sharp gulp. He winces sharply before speaking. "Tell me, Eliana, what would you have me do?"

"If you were to ask me I would say it is a waste of talent and effort. But—" Jafahan leans forward in her chair and beckons him to do the same. She almost whispers the next part. "Have you ever considered volunteer service in the Covenant's Patrol?"

11th of SSM–10 1445 A2E

"She's a good girl, Chance. Reminds me of my youngest daughter when she was her age." Lucky exhaled a long wisp of smoke from his vapostick before offering it to Commander Jafahan.

"That frightened little pup could do far worse than to have you as her teacher," Jafahan replied, and was shocked when Lucky shot her a reproachful look.

"I served the military a long time, Seft Sister Jafahan. And I wouldn't wish it as a punishment for my worst enemy." Lucky gave his left knee a long rub. "Little Chance refuses to take a life. Only in Kelthan-Paxist society would that be considered a weakness. Correct?"

"You never made it a habit of lying to me, my Seft brother." Jafahan breathed in cinnamon flavored smoke and enjoyed the head rush of the vaporized rum lacing it. She held the smoke in her lungs before exhaling a large cloud. Jafahan could feel her aches slowly melt away. She handed the vapostick back to Lucky, who accepted it with a smile.

"Gratitude, Seft brother." It was always a pleasure for Jafahan to be able to converse in Wolven. Pax Common felt like too emotionless and superficial a dialect; Wolven, on the other hand, allowed one to openly express not only the idea but also the emotion behind it, often making for more honest exchanges.

Jafahan was dressed in her white boxer shorts and tank top. She and Lucky had just finished their individual warm showers and were both prepped and ready for carbon sleep. However, neither one was in any particular rush.

Lucky inhaled a long breath of smoke and blew out plumes of relaxed vapor through his nostrils, reminding Jafahan of a mythical drake. "If lasses and fellas can't enjoy a friendly smoke, then why bother breathing, I ask you?"

"Fighting, humping, living." Jafahan shrugged. "I've made it a habit of thinking that motivation is often a matter of occasion."

The two were presently in the showers, sitting on the bench. Behind them, Lunient Tor was washing himself inside a stall, whistling and singing away in Confederated Kelthan. His off-tune notes caused both Lucky and Jafahan to cough out their smoke in a fit of laughter.

Jafahan took in another long haul from the vapostick. If she was going to spend the next six months in carbon sleep, she'd rather it be with a slight head buzz. At the very least it distracted her from her still very stiff sprained ankle. "Figured a warm-blooded Seft brother like yourself wouldn't mind an even warmer pair of breasts to bury his head in before the sleep-freeze."

"Why, my sweet Seft Sister Jafahan, you've up and started the courting of this old dog far too late in his seasons." Lucky shot Jafahan a sly grin. "Warming up bodies is a game for the young." He winced as he got up, his left knee letting out a stiff pop. "Enjoy the vapor. Hope you can find some proper . . . heat before the coming cold, my warm Seft sister."

"You watch me and I'll watch you," Lucky and Jafahan called out to each other. They spoke the words friendly and true-like, their Wolven creating a lovely harmony. Lucky limped heavily out of the shower room toward the medical bay. Jafahan was now alone with nothing but the sounds of the background hum of the ship and Lunient's whistling.

She cracked her toes, glad to no longer have them confined in boots. She let out a deep sigh as she felt the cold metal floor beneath her feet. With the remainder of the crew busy preparing themselves for their carbon sleep, Jafahan had thought to stay out of the way and go into her sleep tube last. Having spent the majority of her life living on vessels, she had grown accustomed to the experience. Carbon sleep was no longer all that unpleasant for her, just odd.

It felt as if it had been an eternity since she had been able to enjoy any real rest. Infinite, help her with that boy Morwyn. Not for the first time, she found herself wishing that she had remained retired in comfort back on Sunderlund. Her right ankle was sore and Jafahan could feel all the aches and bruises in her body.

"Feeling a bit too old for this game, are we now, Commander Ma'am?" Jafahan was almost startled by Lunient Tor as he was suddenly standing before her dripping wet, a towel covering his waist. Jafahan shook her head and blew out smoke, holding back a grin. There were few people, if any, who had ever been able to get the drop on her. Lunient was good.

"At present I'm feeling a bit too old to be given watch over a litter of helpless cubs." Jafahan looked Lunient over. He was lean, fit and, despite his almost bleached white skin, not at all unpleasing to the eyes.

Lunient looked over his shoulder to the rest of the shower stalls. "You know, ma'am. A day ago I would have been afraid to be in the same room as you."

"I hope for your continued personal health that that hasn't changed," Jafahan replied as she stood up, arching and cracking her back. "Is there a reason for this particular disturbance on your part, Private Tor?"

Lunient didn't look away. Instead he deliberately looked her up and down with his night-eyes and smiled. The thin scar on his lower lip made it look like his smile reached his cheek. "I was hoping to share a few more words with you before going to sleep."

Jafahan snorted. "I've enjoyed explaining to you why your humping rifle is a piece of pig's shite."

Lunient took a step toward Jafahan. When he spoke it was in hilariously broken and off-key Wolven. "I was rather hoping of sharing warmth with a Seft sister before going into the cold dark sleep."

Jafahan let out a sudden and quite uncharacteristic loud cackle. She then took a menacing step toward Lunient—there was a growing bulge in his towel. Jafahan was not at all unpleased with what she glimpsed.

"Let me make one thing perfectly clear." She took a haul from her vapostick before shoving Lunient against a nearby wall and blowing a long wisp of vapor in his face.

"I am not your friend, your future love or a little girl." Jafahan punctuated this by rudely poking Lunient in the chest.

"Weren't looking for any of the above." Lunient didn't blink as Jafahan poked him, but she saw him take a sharp, almost frightened breath. He wasn't certain if his little gambit was going to result in pleasure or more pain.

Good, he should always be second-guessing himself with me.

"Consider yourself thoroughly warned." She held his gaze with her own. "Cross the captain or myself and mine will be the last face your eyes ever see. I tell you now, Tor, your ending will neither be quick, painless or pleasant."

Lunient gulped as Jafahan came close to him. She sniffed his neck deeply. His smell, even with a slight hint of fear in it, was—like his size—not unpleasant.

Good, he should always be afraid around me.

"And the same fate will befall you should anyone—and I do mean anyone—ever find out about this."

Jafahan had never once been an easy prize to either her foes or loves. While under normal circumstances she would probably never have considered Lunient's offer, the truth remained that she had just faced death and right now Jafahan needed something more than a nice glass of wine or alcohol-laced vapors.

Right now what she wanted more than anything was the comfort of a warm body. Lunient Tor was here. He was willing. He would, not so regrettably, have to do.

Jafahan was first to act, pulling Lunient's mouth onto hers, and almost tearing his head off. She undid his towel and his hands quickly cupped her breasts. Jafahan dragged Lunient onto the ground, then rolled on top of him.

"You feel hard enough for me," Jafahan said as her hand found her way between Lunient's legs. She slipped off her underpants. "You had best control yourself until I'm done, Tor."

Lunient's eyes went wide, his breath almost trapped in his throat. He gulped. "Fear, it can be a powerful stimulant, ma'am." Lunient's voice was a pleasured quivering groan.

"You might have heard that Wolvers fuck like wild animals." Jafahan rocked her hips against Lunient, leaning down as she bit his ear hard. "The truth, Private Tor, is that wild animals fuck like Wolvers."

CHAPTER 29

CHORD

*Whether it is electronic or genetic, all of us children of
Terra are composed of code. Our existence, organic or
digital, is owed to our mutually shared ancestors. True
they were far from perfect. However, the world we live
in was shaped largely in part by their will. We need not
love them. We need only honor, remember and most importantly learn from the tales of Terra's children past.
Doing so allows us to better understand and assist the
living descendants of Terra's children present.*

—Osirios Sigma, Machina Pilgrim, 12th of
SSM–04 235 A1E to 30th of SSM–08 1234 A2E

11th of SSM–10 1445 A2E

"By my ancestors' word, your shell is a work of mechanical art, Machina Chord." Machinist Kolto's deep
green eyes glowed as he smiled and connected a new
index finger piece to Chord's left hand. Fortunately,

the Thegran had, over time, collected quite a batch of various random spare shell parts.

"Keep talking to the machine like that and I'm like to get jealous," Machinist Oran Troy snarled at Kolto. "It won't be machine who keeps you warm tonight, my husband." Oran's clothes were stained in various ship oils, sweat and grime. Chord's sensors detected a strong odor coming off her. If this smell bothered Kolto, he did not seem to show it.

Kolto shot a wry grin in Chord's direction from beneath his heavy red mustache. "My guiding star burns more than one thousand suns. Am I correct, Machina?"

"This unit has trouble understanding Machinist Kolto's meaning. The temperature of the average star is well beyond the heat generated by the average Humanis."

"The stars have never met my love." Kolto let out a deep rumbling laugh as he screwed the finger tightly onto Chord's hand. Thankfully, Chord's shell was compatible with the new piece. Kolto had been able to repair all of Chord's left hand. The right, unfortunately, would have to wait until they made port at an industrialized world.

Chord started running a functionality subroutine on the new part; the interface and response was smooth and seamless. "This unit offers thanks to both yourself and Machinist Oran Troy."

"Just don't move while I put a finishing touch on one of many tasks." Oran pulled down a brown welding face shield as she fused a homemade cover for the huge gaping hole in Chord's chest. Fortunately, the spike that had pierced Chord's shell had not damaged its power supply, which would have required a far more difficult repair job. Oran's new plating was not the same as Chord's smoothly polished white metal surface, but it was denser and more solid, like a piece of armor.

Oran wiped her hands off on an oily rag on her belt and examined her work. "Captain's personal request, Machina. Once the job is done we three need to get *Jinxie* here starflight-worthy. Don't particularly feel like dying in the cold black myself."

Oran nodded over to Kolto, then added, "At least not before me and the big one here get to enjoy ourselves a fifth retreat on the moons of Troy."

Kolto shot Oran a sly look and shook his head. The Thegran patted Chord's chest amicably. "Your kind built you Thegran-strong, Machina Chord."

"This unit both recognizes and thanks you for the compliment."

The three of them were in the storage bay. Chord took a moment to glance to the side, where the active criopod of Jessie Madison was still running and keeping her asleep. She would remain in this condition at least until Dr. Varsin was certain she had been properly inoculated. This was for both Jessie Madison's safety as well as the crew's. Yet Chord was still incredibly curious and almost eager to be able to meet and speak with her.

"That's all we can do for you now, Machina." Oran

Troy pulled up her mask and stepped back, wiping sweat from her dirty brow. Kolto let out a sharp whistle as he inspected the plating on Chord's chest.

"You put my work to shame as always, my guiding star." Kolto took Oran's hand in his.

Chord noticed a small blush in Oran's cheeks. "Of course I put it to shame, it was *my* work!" Her voice was harsh, yet Chord still noticed her give Kolto's hand a tight squeeze.

"I think you three have earned yourselves some rest before moving on to the next task." Captain Morwyn was standing in the storage bay's entrance with his hands behind his back.

"I would need about thirty minutes with my man." Oran smacked Kolto's buttocks.

Kolto blushed at this and looked to Morwyn. If the exchange between Kolto and Oran had bothered him, it didn't register on Morwyn's face. "Could use thirty more on top of that if you please, Captain."

Captain Morwyn shook his head and smiled. "I will not stop you. However, I would like a word or two with Machina Chord in private."

Kolto and Oran both looked to each other, then back to the captain. "The Machina is about as good as it can get without access to more parts."

"Noted. You are both dismissed. Presently Commander Jafahan is prepping the rest of nonessential crew for carbon sleep. Try not to get in their way."

Oran snorted as she led Kolto out of the room by the hand. "We'll try not to bloody traumatize them."

Morwyn walked to the workbench, taking his turn to examine Oran's repair job. Chord got up on its feet so as to look the captain in the face.

"I would like to apologize to you, Machina Chord. I took a risk on you that I would never have taken with any of my Humanis crew."

"Your apologies are not necessary, Captain, as this unit has no 'hurt feelings' to speak of. It understands that you were merely doing what needed to be done in order to ensure the crew's safety and—" Chord once again looked over to the criotube "—that of our survivors."

"I thank you for your understanding . . . Mr. Chord."

Chord cocked its head at the captain's last comment. "You have not called the unit Machina Chord. Why is that?"

"I don't call Commander Jafahan 'Wolver Jafahan,' now do I?"

"This unit has never noticed you do so. More to the point, unlike organic life, the Machina do not identify themselves by or assign each other a gender."

Morwyn offered Chord a quizzing upturned eyebrow. "Then by what title would you have me address you?"

Chord gave the captain's query a nanosecond of thought. "This unit has always preferred its given designation: Chord."

"That is three times tonight that I stand humbled and educated." Morwyn smiled. "Once again I am truly honored to have someone like you on my ship,

Chord. You went above and beyond duty's call. Phaël, Arturo, Morrigan, our survivors—all of them are alive thanks to you and your courage."

"This unit did not feel particularly brave. It was merely performing its function," Chord replied truthfully.

Morwyn rested his hand gently on Chord's shoulder. "My father once told me that we never know we've been brave until after the fact. Now more than ever I am glad I chose you for my ship. You have my word, one day I will personally deliver you to Terra."

Chord followed Morwyn as the latter walked over to the criotube. The two looked it over in silence for a long moment.

At first glance Chord would have thought that the frozen humanoid shape in this criopod was an incredibly thin Thegran. Yet even that would have not been a correct assessment. Her skin was pale, her hair long, a mixture of almost golden brown and orange. There was something quite peaceful to her sleeping state.

"A living piece of our past." Morwyn looked to Chord. "What do you think will happen when she is awakened?"

"Sir, she is with child." Chord paused, then replied, "This unit could not imagine what it would be like. She will no doubt feel alone."

Morwyn nodded, not looking away. "Yes, she will, won't she?" The captain turned to look Chord in the eye. "In all of the Infinite, I would like to believe there are far worse places to wind up on than this ship."

"This unit would be in agreement."

Morwyn gave Jessie Madison a last look before turning to leave. Chord called out to him and the young man stopped in his tracks. "Captain? About the unit named OMEX . . ."

"I offered OMEX a chance to assist us with the rescue. It refused."

"Would you have offered this unit a chance under similar circumstances?"

Morwyn did not even miss a beat. "Of course, Chord." Morwyn brought his fist to his heart in a salute, and with that he turned around and left Chord alone.

Chord sat down cross-legged in front of the crio-tube. The pilgrimage to the Cradle world of Terra was considered a sacred thing among the Machina. While it was difficult to believe in fates or synchronicities, there was no better word to use what was being experienced at this very moment.

This was the right path; Jessie Madison, a direct link to the past that all Machina and Humanis shared, was proof of this. "Wake up soon, Jessie Madison," Chord spoke, and projected the holographic image of old Earth over her sleeping visage.

"Wake up soon, Jessie Madison," Chord repeated, this time using Late Modern. It was more than likely that Jessie Madison would not be able to hear a single word. Still, something compelled the words to come out over and over, like a peaceful comforting mantra.

"Wake up soon, Jessie Madison."

Chord would not have to wait terribly long.

CHAPTER 30

JESSIE MADISON

For the first time since she can remember, the dream is not beyond her control. She is alone in a cold quiet state of peaceful darkness. Her mind is resting and relaxed as part of her feels incredibly safe.

"Mom." Malory's voice breaks the silence. Jessie can more feel her presence than see it. She does not mind this.

"Yes, my dearest?" Jessie asks.

"We are no longer in the dark place." Malory's voice is one of hopeful joy.

"I know." Jessie is so overjoyed to still hear her daughter, here in the dream she has built for herself.

"The hateful voice is gone," Malory says, not masking the relief that she must feel.

"Yes, I think she is," Jessie replies.

"Are we safe now?"

Jessie hesitates before answering. She chooses to tell her the truth. "I don't know, my little one."

Malory is unrelenting in her questions. She can barely contain her excitement. "Will I be able to wake up soon?"

"Yes, we both will."

"I would like to feel the real world."

"So would I . . ." Jessie pauses; she knows nothing of where they will awaken to.

As if she can sense her emotions, Malory asks quickly, "Are you frightened?"

Once again her decision is to tell Malory the truth. "When we wake up, everything will be outside of my control. Everything will be uncertain." She pauses before adding, "I am very afraid."

"Then you should hold on to me, Mommy. So that neither one of us will ever have to be."

Here and now, in the place of dreams, Jessie takes Malory in her arms and holds her tightly. A calm mechanical voice can be heard from somewhere, the real world outside the dream; it repeats itself over and over again.

"Wake up soon, Jessie Madison."

Jessie Madison and Malory hold each other tightly. "Just you and me, cowgirl, just you and me."

Soon they will wake up and be free to experience the world, no matter how frightening and unknown, once again. Together.

Neither Jessie Madison nor Malory will have to wait that long.

LEXICON

Ador: Ador is one of the rare nations of the cosmos with a population that is incredibly mixed. That being said, the nation of Ador has not, until recently, known any lengthy period of peace. Formerly a province of Argent, Ador endured countless horrors under the yoke of their former rulers. Ever since earning its freedom during the Liberation War, Ador has made it a point to have their nation be an active participant in the galactic theater.

The Adoran Liberation War: Ador as a nation had been under the yoke of tyranny since its birth. Its former rulers were the baron princes of the nation of Argent, who oppressed and subjected their subjects to countless horrors. The baron princes of Argent were secretly offered backing by the Pax Humanis fleets. In response to this, Warlord Valtros united the interfighting Adoran mercenary fleets under his banner, challenging the rule of Argent and offering freedom to anyone who sided with his cause. The ensuing civil war lasted seventeen years. In the end the Liberation armies stood victorious, installing a new democratic parliament. To this day many Adorans still hold a massive grudge against the Pax Humanis for offering support to their former Argentine oppressors.

The Advent War: The Second Great War, during which Humanis and Machina fought side by side against the machine singularity called Pontifex, also known as the False Machine God. After the war the Machina offered the Humanis slipdrive technology, making starflight and galactic colonization possible. Unfortunately, Earth, the Cradle, was left scorched.

Alexandros: A younger nation comprised mostly of scholars, Alexandros is on the borders of End Space and boasts a rich diverse population. The spirit of cooperation and peace is very present on Alexandros. It is one of the only Covenant nations that does not possess a single military vessel and all of their progressive scientific developments remain purely pacifistic in nature and design.

Ambrosia: Once known as the smugglers' gem, the former syndicate-run "paradise world" of Ambrosia was forcefully made into a protectorate of the Pax Humanis. Despite being under the rule of the Hegemon's Law, Ambrosia remains to this day one of the poorest and most violent portions of its population. The majority of its Ambrosia is made up of declassified citizens.

Argent: Formerly a Pax protectorate, the nation of Argent used its considerable financial powers to break free from the will of the Hegemons. Argent has since then become an elitist society of godlike rich royals, challenging the Pax Humanis at any or every given opportunity. The baron princes of Argent are openly vying for the complete downfall of the Pax Humanis.

Barathul: After Sol, Barathul is the second oldest nation in the Pax Humanis, and proud of it. There are few worlds that can boast such a huge level of success and law. Barathul's navy and military are second to none and do justice to the Pax Humanis rigid discipline.

The Breedmasters: The Breedmasters of Uldur are brilliant geneticists. Capable of raising and creating living creatures to serve their every need, from food to transport to the incredibly complex living skinsuits. The Breedmasters jealously keep their trade secrets and have become a rival voice to the Wolver spiritual ruling caste, the Elvrids.

Central Point: The current political center of the universe and the closest thing to pass as the Covenant's capital. Central Point is an ambitious societal gambit that includes all the Covenant nations. The end goal of which will be a fully operational and mobile disonsphere. So far every nation has representation and a stake in completing this project. The InstaNet signal is broadcast in perpetuity from Central Point, making it a stable map point for anyone navigating the cosmos. Because of this, Central Point is always located at the exact center of Covenant Space.

Chosen Protocols: Machina Intelligences are typically free to observe the universe and in essence do whatever they want. However, once a Machina wishes to interact with the physical world, it must inhabit a mechanical body or shell. These bodies are hardwired with behavioral control protocols that prevent the Machina from killing, lying or otherwise harming living Intelligences.

The Conclave: The final volunteer force of the Covenant Fleet, the Conclave serves many functions; chief among them is to ensure fair political discourse between nations. It also secures trade goods and distributes them fairly and readily to the nations of the Covenant. The Conclave's final function is managing the auction between nations bidding for the expansion rights to surveyed worlds. The Conclave makes sure that every nation has fair equal access to the data on the worlds available for expansion.

The Confederated Coin: The Confederated coin is a new currency quickly gaining power and value on the intergalactic commerce stage. It has become the main currency of the ever-growing and influential Confederated nations. Much like the aforementioned union, the Confederated coin was created to economically challenge and undermine the power of the Pax credit.

Confederated Kelthan: One of the younger languages of Covenant Space, Confederated Kelthan is quickly becoming a widely spoken language. It draws its origins from many Kelthans who grew annoyed with having Pax Common as their default language. Over time it became a hybrid of Wolven, Thegran and Pax Common. Confederated Kelthan is quickly cadenced and can be confusing to anyone who is unilingual.

The Confederation of Nations: A political and military union of seven nations created to oppose the Pax Humanis. These nations are Ador, Argent, Highlund, Zerok, Galasia, Seno'Chesh and Troy.

The Covenant: The Covenant dictates the rules and rights essential to fair space travel, warfare, trade and politics. Signed at the end of the Advent War so that future generations would be spared the horrors of galactic warfare, all Intelligences living within Covenant Space are subject to its Truths. To date, twenty-two galactic nations have signed the Covenant and are represented on Central Point.

Covenant Space: The totality of civilized, lawful and charted space encompassing the galactic nations shared by both Humanis and Machina. Space travel and trade are relatively safe and heavily regulated.

The Datastream/InstaNet: An information supernetwork that reaches across most of Covenant Space. The datastream is also where most Machina consciousnesses reside, observing the physical world. All Machina are originally sparked or "birthed" as code in the datastream.

Declassification/Declassified Citizens: There are no prisons in the Pax Humanis, just varying levels of classified citizens and the declassified ones. Based on what level of classification one falls under, one is allowed access to greater goods and services while lower classification citizens are given fewer. Declassified citizens are given the bare minimum of services and goods; they are also not allowed to vote or gain access to starflight.

End Space: Sectors of the universe currently still uncharted and unscouted by the Covenant. Lack of InstaNet and Central Point positioning beacon signals have made actually traversing End Space incredibly difficult if not outright dangerous.

The Expansions: In order to prevent any one nation growing too powerful, the Covenant has strictly forbidden all the galactic nations from colonizing new worlds unless it is during a sanctioned expansion. All star-dates are counted after the current expansion.

The First Expansion: Dating from the end of the Advent War until two thousand years after the Covenant's signing, this is the first wave of expansion in which the then-homeless bloodlines of the

Humanis explored the cosmos in search of new worlds to settle.

Galasia: The frigid world of Galasia is almost uninhabitable to Humanis, as it is perpetually cast in an endless winter. Fortunately for Galasians, their star system boasts numerous moons and asteroids that can support Humanis life. This has caused the Galasian Council of Khans to convert much of their space into privatized prisons. The Galasian prisons remain the harshest and cruelest places in the cosmos. They also make great recruiting grounds for Galasia's second method of income and military might, which remains their merciless and incredibly effective Pirate Fleet.

Garthem: The stark and dark nation of Garthem is comprised of numerous dangerous planets and boasts an almost entirely Kelthan population. While it is the youngest Pax nation, Garthem has in its short history managed to rival both Sol and Barathul with its navy and military. The pride of Garthem remains to this day the Pax Humanis Elite Shadow Commandos: the Thorns.

The Hegemon: The ruler of the Pax Humanis, embodying the iron will of Kelthan Humanis. The Hegemon's Law reigns supreme and undisputed throughout the Pax.

Humanis: The name given to the five bloodlines descendant of Ancient Humanity: Kelthan, Wolver, Thegran, Kohbrahn and Darlkhin.

Late Modern: The last documented tongues of Ancient Humanity, spoken and understood by few. Late Modern, for the moment at least, is typically studied only by scholars and the Machina.

The Living Green: The spiritual path embraced by many Wolvers of Covenant Space. Followers of the path believe that the cosmos itself is a living being and that all the worlds and creatures calling it home must be treated as such. One of the main doctrines of the Living Green is an outright refusal to use any sort of technology made by Machina.

The Lost War: The first and only war ever fought between Ancient Humanity and the Original Intelligences (OIs). Records pertaining to the details of the Lost War are nonexistent. What is known is that the current Humanis bloodlines were born in its aftermath.

Lotus: The corporate nation of Lotus remains an innovator in the developing of cutting-edge technology and software codes. Lotus boasts a large cloned population and workforce and sells stocks of vat-created workforces to any nation willing to pay their asking price. Lotus has been very certain to never clone a military force, as this would be a most grievous breach of the Covenant's Truths. Given the often less than ethical treatment of its clone population, the Lotus board of directors chooses not to test their luck on this particular issue.

Machina: The third generation of self-made machine Intelligences created by the OIs.

OI: The Original machine Intelligences coded by Ancient Humanity during the days before the Lost War.

The Patrol: The Covenant's volunteer fleet of lawmen, the Patrol remains the core enforcers of the Covenant's laws in space. They often operate as both a police force and rescue operation.

Pax Common: The most common language of Covenant Space. Made prolific by the strength of the Pax Humanis and its media. Pax Common's popularity is also due to the fact that it is incredibly easy to learn. It is often criticized by non-Pax citizens for the irrelevance of emotional inflection. Proponents of Pax Common maintain that this makes Pax Common more widely accessible.

The Pax Credit: The second most used currency is the Pax credit, due mainly to the Pax Humanis being the universe's largest united superpower. Despite the lack of popularity, the Pax credit remains widely accepted and used. In nations like Sol and Barathul, it is often even of greater value than the universal bit.

The Pax Humanis: The oldest Humanis superpower, with a long military history dating back to the days before the Advent War. Under the rule of the Hegemons, the Pax Humanis now currently controls and encompasses seven united star systems: Sol, Barathul, Sunderlund, Garthem, Perse, Vale and Ambrosia.

Perse: The Pax Humanis nation of Perse is the furthest from Sol. Located on the borders of End Space, the green and yet grim world of Perse was settled at first by Wolvers once serving in the Shock Legion. The Wolvers of Perse are among the few who have no qualms about using machine-made technology. For the most part, the Wolvers of Perse do not actively take a role in Pax Humanis or Covenant politics.

The Pontifex: In the wake of the Lost War, it was the Pontifex who ruled over Earth and the new bloodlines of Humanity. The Pontifex fashioned itself as a manner of God, using its vast knowledge of technology to visit all manner of cruelties onto the Humanis. It was only the arrival of the Machina and the subsequent Advent War that saw an end to the Pontifex's existence and the start of the Great Peace.

Rust: One of Galasia's most infamous prison colonies, Rust is a ship's graveyard in which the remains of the Khan's Pirate Fleet conquests are stripped for parts. The working conditions are horrific. Prisoners are pushed to death and often subject to illegal and unethical experiments. Only the strong survive the work yards. It is therefore no coincidence that most of those serving in the Pirate Fleet hail from Rust.

The Second Expansion: Dating from the end of the First Expansion, the Second Expansion is the present. Many new nations were born while many others are currently solidifying their influence in preparation for the Third Expansion.

Slipspace/Slipdrives: The most widely used interstellar starflight technology. Allows ships to "slip" from one spot in space to another. Slipdrives remain crucial to traversing the Infinite and Covenant Space.

Sol: The former political center of the Covenant, Sol remains nonetheless one of the most powerful galactic nations of the cosmos. This is due mainly in part to the fact that Sol is the capital of the Pax Humanis. Holy Terra, the blue Cradle, is located in Sol, but it is not controlled by the Pax Humanis.

Sol Fleet: The first Pax Humanis–built interstellar military fleet. During the ages of the First Expansion, it was Sol Fleet and the brave men and women in its service who came to the protection of the new nations. Because of this, Sol Fleet remains one of the oldest and proudest fleets in existence.

Standard Star Dating System: While all Covenant nations have their own calendar systems, most if not all legal and political dates follow the standard Sol calendar. The standard year is based on Earth's twelve months. All years are dated after the last expansion. Historically there have been two Covenant sanctioned expansions into new worlds. A Third Expansion has been scheduled in the next sixteen hundred years.

Sunderlund: Due mostly in part to a larger than average Wolver population living side by side with Kelthans, Sunderlund has made a habit of speaking out against the Pax Humanis. The Sunderlund navy is exclusively composed of Humanis developed and engineered vessels. Sunderlund shipyards continue to produce some of the most reliable and durable starflight-worthy spacecrafts in existence.

The Survey: The Covenant's volunteer fleet of scouts and planet surveyors. The survey spends the majority of its time and resources scouting new worlds for future expansions. The survey is also tasked with mapping and updating slipspace astrocharts. Like the Patrol, the survey also operates as a rescue operation. This is the main reason for the friendly spirit of competition that still exists between these two branches of the Covenant.

The Syndicate: An ever-elusive network of criminals and smugglers, the syndicate is the shadow response to the Covenant. It exists solely to broker and smuggle illegal black-market goods from world to world.

The Thorns: The Thorns are the deniable assets of the Hegemon and the Pax Humanis. They are sent behind enemy lines on illegal operations. That the Covenant has yet to have been able to prove the Thorn involvement in various dubious black-book missions remains a testament to their effectiveness at covering up their tracks.

Uldur: To this day, the world of Uldur remains the center for Wolver politics, culture, innovation and spirituality. Uldur is a luscious and verdant planet with two moons, each one equally capable of supporting life. According to Wolver legend, it was Uldur that called out to them in the days of the First Expansion. Unlike many worlds in Covenant Space, Uldur was never artificially Terraformed. The Wolvers have learned to live side by side with the living creatures and wild plants that make Uldur their home.

Universal Bit: The universal bit, or u-bit, is the most commonly accepted form of currency in Covenant Space. Like the standard calendar, most nations have their own independent currency as well, but if they wish to do commerce on a galactic scale the universal bit still, more often than not, remains the easy go-to standard for most nations and banks.

The Vale Campaign: When a terrorist faction known as the Children of Vale destroyed the commercial Pax Humanis passenger ship *The Eternity*, resulting in thousands of Pax civilian casualties, the Hegemon responded by mobilizing three of the Pax warfleets into Vale space. The goal was to install order and Pax Humanis rule in what was being painted as an unruly part of the universe. The Confederation of Nations, led by Argent, responded by sending in fleets of their own. While there are reports of many savage and bloody battles, the Vale campaign never truly escalated into all-out war. The Campaign of Vale came to an abrupt end after the infamous Battle of Galom-dryd, for Vale's capital city.

Wolven: The rich and emotional dialogue spoken by the Wolvers. To this day it remains the second most used tongue in the universe. Wolven found its origins in the days prior to the Advent War and was intentionally designed by the Wolver Sefts to be overly emotional, almost musical. This was to make it incredibly difficult for machines to decode and understand.

THE INTELLIGENCES OF THE COVENANT

WOLVERS

The law of the pack, or the great hunt, is the rule of New Humanity's "savage" brothers and sisters, the Wolvers. They are short, hairy and borderline bestial in appearance, leading to the widespread and mis-informed opinion that they are savage, uncultured animals with little to no intellect. Nothing could be further from the truth.

Wolvers are the second most prolific race in the cosmos and proud of it, having made the forests and the wilds of the Infinite their home. Wolvers simply love the open sky, soil, oceans or anyplace untouched by technology. To this day even the most liberal minded of Wolvers share a savage mistrust of anything linked to the Machina.

Wolvers mostly follow the path of the Living

Green; this is a system of beliefs in which the settling of worlds comes not only with rights but with responsibilities as well. Even the most selfish of Wolvers is more ecologically conscious than some of the most selfless Kelthans. Wolvers are typically strictly forbidden from using anything that is Machina-made. This has on some fronts severely limited their technological development and expansion. They are a proud, hinting on stubborn breed, and will never take a challenge lying down. They are fierce, passionate and, once their respect has been earned, loyal friends.

KELTHANS

Kelthans are the most prolific race in Covenant Space. Mostly hairless and thin with varying skin colors, they are naturally proficient with machines and are the species that most resemble Ancient Humanity. This is a fact that puritan Kelthans will often quite proudly point out. Kelthan privilege seems to permeate almost every aspect of galactic affairs, from technological or medical developments to politics and the media. This is demonstrated by the fact that most ships, clothes and weapons are built to accommodate Kelthan size. Even the largest superpower in the cosmos, the Pax Humanis, boasts a predominantly Kelthan population.

Since most Kelthans have no qualms about using technology, they have been able to enjoy all of the latest cutting-edge advances provided to them by the Machina. They are almost the opposite of Wolvers mistrust in this regard. Because of this, Kelthan-run worlds usually enjoy higher levels of comfort. This has led to most Kelthans having a bit of a superior smugness. After all, not only are they the bloodline that resembles Ancient Humanity the most, they are the one that has spread furthest across the Infinite.

THEGRANS

There is only one species in the cosmos that will keep a promise better than a Machina, and that is a Thegran. These giants are imposing creatures, six feet tall being a relative short size for them. Thegrans are typically muscular, and strong both in body and mind. While it is true that they may not be the most prolific of the Humanis bloodlines, they are by far the most durable. Thegrans are in no way immortal, but they still remain an incredibly long-lived race.

Thegrans love nothing more than to prove their superior strength in all things. They take great pride and go to great lengths in driving themselves to be the best at whatever task they devote themselves to. A Thegran warrior will often turn out to be legendary; a Thegran scholar will be brilliant.

Thegrans also take great pride in the tradition of tracking their family history. Often they will mark their skins with elaborate tattoos, naming the past deeds and misdeeds of their bloodline. The tattoos are also used by Thegrans to trace back their ancestral lineages all the way back to Old Earth. The more strength and honor one has to one's family and names the better.

DARLKHIN

The mysterious, never-changing immortals commonly known as the Darlkhin are "plastic" humans. Should one give any credence to their histories, they would be last descendants of Ancient Humanity. Darlkhin mainly tend to exclusively pursue their own personal agendas and rarely if ever choose to participate in the affairs of New Humanity or the Covenant.

Most of them have taken up their crusade tracking rogue machine Intelligences and permanently deleting them. This hunt takes them all over the cosmos. The Darlkhin possess technology and powers beyond the wildest dreams of any Kelthan scientist. They all too often use forbidden technology, either denying everything altogether or refusing to answer to Covenant Law when called on it. The Darlkhin maintain that all their secrecy is necessary for the greater good of New Humanity.

Darlkhin have a plastic-like quality and all of them are sterile. No one really knows what their true numbers are or the true extent of their powers. Given their secretive nature they are mistrusted by almost everyone. Yet when a Darlkhin crusader arrives on the hunt of rogue machines, no one stands in his or her way. The Darlkhin hold many secrets and are loath to reveal any of them. Yet if anyone knows the true cause behind the Lost Wars, it would be them.

KOHBRAN

Often shunned for their almost reptile-like appearances, the Kohbran are and always have been the most community oriented of all the bloodlines. They live in moon-sized City Trees that travel through the cosmos pulled by Leviathans, the largest living creatures in the observed universe. The Kohbran have jealously and exclusively kept any Leviathan genetic materials secret since the signing of the Covenant after the Advent War.

The Kohbran are incredible diplomats, traders and negotiators. For the most part, the City Trees travel from world to world, trading with those who are willing to do so. They are gifted poets and wordsmiths. An average Kohbran child will know most of the languages spoken in the universe before most Humanis have even mastered one.

The Kohbran follow the way of the Prophet Maya, she who served all Kohbran by leading them to the Leviathans. This code requires that all serve the greater good of the City Trees that they call home. One who takes without returning is the lowest form of life possible.

There is no evidence of them ever existing on Old Earth. This means nothing considering that most records from that period are, at best, incomplete. The Kohbran maintain they are a Humanis bloodline, and offer free, safe starflight on their City Trees to any who request it, provided they don't mind having no control over their destination.

MACHINA

No Intelligence in the cosmos is subject to more mistrust and prejudice than the third generation of self-made machines: the Machina. These curious and often naive machine Intelligences spend most of their time awash in the information-rich virtual universe that is the datastream. They only choose to inhabit mechanical bodies or shells in order to better interact with Humanity.

While the Machina are machines, they are no longer slaves. They are masters of technology and are capable of producing almost anything they wish. The Machina strictly regulate their own production and distribution of goods and services to Humanis superpowers. This has made both legal and black-market Machina-built technology some of the most highly sought after.

Currently the Machina devote most of their existence wishing to better understand the universe. The ultimate problem they wish to solve is the equation of Soul. For despite all their complex minds and technological mastery, the Machina are still unable to answer one fundamental question: are they alive?

ACKNOWLEDGMENTS

There are two things I have read throughout the course of my life that struck me when it came to writing a book. The first thing was that a book is like a wonderfully complex machine with words and sentences acting as the cogs and gears. The second was that nothing was created by oneself or in a vacuum. In both these instances, *Dark Transmissions* was no exception.

This book would not have at all been possible were it not for several conversations about science fiction with my good friends Justin Pike and Shawn Baichoo. Were it not for a brilliant comment made to me by Jocelyn Baxter (a future great author), there would never have been a term "Late Modern." It was the work on an abandoned comic book project with Rachel Pouliot that birthed some of the cast and crew of the *Jinxed*

Thirteenth such as "Lucky," "Captain Morwyn" and "Phaël," to name but a few.

It was roleplaying with my friend Damiano that brought about the term "universal bit." My partners in creative crime, Phil Ivanusic and Jaymie Dylan were crucial in offering me sharp minds to bounce ideas off of. Simon Lacoste and my brothers Alaric and Arndell LeBlanc were the ones who read the initial draft of my book and offered important initial feedback.

Asaph Fpike, David Watson, Rob Hoegee and Ken Faier were all instrumental in teaching me the ins and outs of producing a screenplay and offered me the perfect training ground as a budding television writer on *League of Super Evil*. My agent, Mark Gottlieb, was among the first people to read and believe in my work; without his efforts *Dark Transmissions* would still no doubt be gathering proverbial dust in the digital ether. Rebecca Lucash, my editor, and her incredible knack for simply getting the world I presented helped make what was already a great story infinitely better and I hope that she will bring that magic to countless more of my works.

Finally there is my love and partner, Jessie Mathieson, without whom Jessie Madison and this book would not exist. She offered me her love, energy and support when I found myself unemployed and facing the daunting challenge of completing my first novel.

To all these names, and to others I will no doubt have forgotten, I express the deepest and most heartfelt gratitude. I would not be where I am today were it not for the role that you all played and will no doubt continue to play as I carry on plying and improving on my trade. From now until my ending, I promise to keep on doing what I love most: crafting good stories.

In love, light and laughter.

Be well.

Davila LeBlanc

December 10th 2015

ABOUT THE AUTHOR

DAVILA LEBLANC spent his college years studying print journalism but quickly found himself working as a writer and performer in the comedy circuits of Montreal. During this time his goal became to break into the world of professional writing. He would get his first opportunity when he cocreated and sold the hit animated television series *League of Super Evil*. This was his first foray into the world of production and an important first step on his road to becoming a writer. After working on various television shows, in 2013 Davila decided to take a year off from children's animation to focus on writing his first novel, *Dark Transmissions*. He is an avid reader of science fiction and fantasy and wants to add his own voice to the genre that inspired him. Davila currently resides in Ottawa where he is working on several other writing projects.

5/23/16